All in Monte Carlo

Ayman

Happy Reading!
Best wishes,

Anna
x

All in Monte Carlo

A novel by
Anna Shilling

Troubador Publishing Ltd
Unit E2 Airfield Business Park
Harrison Road, Market Harborough
Leicestershire LE16 7UL
Tel: 0116 279 2299
Email: books@troubador.co.uk
Web: www.troubador.co.uk/matador

ISBN 978-1-80514-036-8

British Library Cataloguing in Publication Data.
A catalogue record for this book is available from the British Library.

Printed and bound by CPI Group (UK) Ltd, Croydon, CR0 4YY
Typeset in 10.5 Garamond Pro by Troubador Publishing Ltd, Leicester, UK

Matador is an imprint of Troubador Publishing Ltd

To love and high jinks

Contents

Prologue   ix

PART ONE   BETRAYAL
  1   Abigail   3
  2   Lucinda   14
  3   Polina   25
  4   Barbara   38
  5   Abigail   46
  6   Polina   59
  7   Lucinda   72
  8   Barbara   81
  9   Polina   94
 10   Lucinda   107
 11   Barbara   114
 12   Abigail   126

PART TWO   REVENGE

13	Lucinda	139
14	Abigail	151
15	Polina	161
16	Barbara	174
17	Abigail	185
18	Lucinda	195
19	Barbara	206
20	Polina	220
21	Lucinda	235
22	Polina	243
23	Barbara	257
24	Abigail	269

Prologue

'LIFE BEING WHAT IT IS, ONE DREAMS OF REVENGE,' SAID
Abigail.

'I'd like to castrate Leo,' said Lucinda.

'Ditto Dimitri,' said Polina.

'I want to crush Marcus,' said Barbara. 'In fact, it all sounds
good until you think about prison overalls.'

'Unless there were no jail time,' said Abigail.

All three women looked at Abigail. She began hesitantly,
thinking on her feet, her voice gaining power as the plan
took shape. What if they sought a circuitous revenge? Rather
than each seeking their own vengeance, they would settle one
another's scores. Without obvious motivation or breadcrumb
trail to the culprit, there would be little fear of detection. If
they planned things carefully, they wouldn't even have to break
the law.

With every sip of her Aberlour whisky, Barbara warmed grudgingly to the idea with one condition: they'd need to find a convincing cover story for their meetups while they plotted.

'Well, we could always set up a book club,' said Abigail.

Abigail found that the proliferation of book clubs in Monaco spoke volumes about the psychology of Monaco's desperate housewives. At the start of each book club meeting, everyone was vociferous in their efforts to clarify that there were no airheads present. But several glasses of Dom Pérignon champagne later, the desire for a drunken girls' night out trumped any desire to discuss F. Scott Fitzgerald.

'But I never read books,' said Polina.

'Then you'll fit right in,' said Abigail. 'Most Monte Carlo book club members' preferred reading is *HELLO!* magazine. At my last book club meeting, we debated which Chanel boutique had better customer service — Monaco or Gstaad. Monaco won the day with the proviso that you have a D-cup as the shop assistants presume that anyone without a boob job can't afford Chanel.'

That was the moment that this twisted tale of art fraud, murder, infidelity, and betrayal took a different turn under the innocuous guise of yet another Monte Carlo book club. It was the moment that drew together four disparate expats: a journalist, a countess, a model-cum-blogger and a billionaire businesswoman. It was the moment all four women sought redress for their collective misery. The patriarchal soul of Monaco was turned on its head. They were *all in* for revenge.

Part One

BETRAYAL

1

Abigail

ABIGAIL PEERED THROUGH THE GLASS DOOR. HANK VERT, her boss and the publisher of *Monaco Mail*, sat at his desk reading. His Ermenegildo Zegna pinstripe suit looked spray-painted onto his robust frame. On the wall behind him was *Monaco Mail's Eros* logo: a cupid fashioned from brass coins by Monaco's best-loved artist Bobby Sheen. Abigail smiled as she noticed Hank's glossy grey hair outlined by this yearning halo of money. She pressed the buzzer. He kept reading.

She let her gaze fall onto the office, blended into shades of grey from the lacquered filing cabinets to the Rococo cornice scrolls. An arched window opened onto Casino Square's manicured gardens. At the far end, an assistant adorned with a Hermès scarf was laying out the coffee tray on a glass table. She handled each silver piece slowly to ensure silence.

Abigail pressed the buzzer again. Finally, Hank looked up

and fixed his pinpoint black eyes upon Abigail, before pressing a button beneath his desk. A green light came on outside the door giving Abigail permission to enter.

'So, Boudicca, what the fuck is this on the front page?'

Hank waved a copy of this morning's *Monaco Mail* in the air with an angry flourish.

'Listen, Hank,' Abigail said, pushing her hands into her linen trouser pockets, 'I can explain.'

'You can't keep writing about murder and expect to get away with it.'

'Well, I wasn't planning to get away with murder.'

'I'm not in the mood for your sarcasm,' Hank said, striding towards the Ligne Roset sofa before grabbing his coffee cup and slugging the contents.

Abigail glanced at the newspaper waving in front of her face. The front-cover headline leered at her: *'Murder Cover-Up'*. Not her most diplomatic hour. Until Abigail had ferreted out the details, nothing had been reported in the press. Now the whole of Monaco knew about the *crime passionnel* at a local Italian restaurant: a chef had caught his girlfriend *in flagrante* with the pot washer in the larder and stabbed her to death in revenge. It turned out that the murderous chef was on the run from the Italian police with a fake Monaco ID. Dabbling in drug dealing on the side with a high-ranking government official, he had been hushed up in return for a reduced criminal sentence.

'It isn't just this article about the chef,' continued Hank, reaching to open his walnut-veneered humidor. 'In the last month alone, you've reported on a Russian prostitution ring, an armed robbery at Cartier, and a €1-million theft by the Crimson Circle charity. Anyone reading this trash would think Monaco is a dangerous hotbed of corruption. I've just had a phone call from the palace press office and they're furious about all your negative coverage of the principality. They're even threatening to take away our press passes.'

'Welcome to the North Korea of press freedom.'

'You really seem to be asking for the sack this morning.'

'Sorry,' Abigail retreated. 'I haven't had my *café serré* yet so I'm feeling crabby.'

'I'll give you daily caffeine injections if that's what it takes,' said Hank as he picked out a Cohiba Behike cigar, chewed the end off, and lit it. 'Seriously, if it weren't for the fact that I can't find anyone else around here that can pick up a pen, you'd have been given your marching orders long ago. From now on, I want nothing but positive pieces about Monaco life. Pretty pictures on social media. Charity events. Art. Sport. Beauty. You got it?'

'But...'

'No buts,' Hank cut Abigail off. 'All you think about is your precious journalistic integrity. You think you can have your cake and eat it. You think you can live in this beautiful, safe, sunny, tax-free haven while slagging off the principality whenever you feel like it. If you're not harping on about blue-collar worker salaries, you're lecturing about male bias in divorce laws. It's time you grew up, and ditched all your bleeding heart, workers' rights, women's rights bullshit. We provide entertainment, not a revolution.'

'A lot of readers have given positive feedback about the thorough editorial reporting,' said Abigail. 'We even increased our readership by 10% last month.'

'I couldn't give a damn about edi-fucking-torial reporting. Now is when your journalistic pretensions stop. If we don't turn this shit-show of a paper around from a loss-making fiasco into a commercial success, we'll be closed down in six months. Starting today, your job is to bring in sponsored features and editorial collaborations with social media influencers so we can extend our online reach.'

With every word Hank uttered, Abigail felt her journalistic ideals ebbing away. She calmed herself, looking out the window towards the casino: designed in the 1870s by Charles Garnier, the man who dreamt up the Paris Opera with its distinctive Belle-Epoque style. She loved how the Anish Kapoor Sky Mirror reflected the period architecture and its neighbouring palm trees upside down. Everything was topsy-turvy. Just like her life.

'Isn't most of that for the sales team?' said Abigail, hearing Hank tapping his fingers impatiently on his desk.

'Not if you want to keep your job.' Hank sat back at his desk chair while his fingers toyed with the guy ropes of a polished model yacht. 'From now on, it's all about the three Ms: Monegasque, monarchy and money-making. No more fucking corruption.'

'Next week we'll be launching a column called *Principality Pooches* featuring prominent local residents with their pups at their homes. I've lined you up with two interviews: the Countess de Mortcerf, Lucinda Kiddington, with her dachshund in the Millefiori and the oil billionaire Barbara Esson with her Westie at the Roccabella. And take your camera. I want some shining photos of them both with their mutts.'

•

ABIGAIL RETREATED TO THE AIRLESS, WINDOWLESS basement where everyone except Hank worked, treading carefully over the assault course of computer wires back to her plywood desk. It was piled high with back copies and dotted with post-it notes, while her paper bin overflowed with Styrofoam coffee cups. This was her home for ten hours each day. At least, she could see the funny side. On the damp-stained wall above her desk was a sign: *Claustrophobia is the fear of closed spaces. For example, I'm going to the liquor store and I'm scared that it's closed.*

'How did it go with the Terminator?' asked her copy editor Rob, an old-school journalist who survived on cheese toasties, Coca-Cola and cigarettes.

'Well, I narrowly avoided getting the sack again,' said Abigail.

'Did you ask him about my salary? It's late again.'

'I didn't get the chance. He was too busy ripping my head off. You'll be pleased to know that we're starting a dog column tomorrow.'

'I'm never quite sure where your sarcasm ends and sincerity begins,' said Rob.

'I wish I were joking.'

'What are you going to call it: *Monte Carlo Mutts?*'

'*Principality Pooches*, although I prefer your *Monte Carlo Mutts*. What do you think about a pampering-for-pooches launch party at the Hermitage with canapés for the hounds as well as their owners?'

'I can just imagine all those ladies with their handbag dogs,' said Rob. 'I don't think the Hermitage would let your scruffy mutt through the door.'

'No, my Irish wolfhound would definitely look out of place. He doesn't even have his own diamante dog collar or velvet overcoat.'

Abigail got to work on a suitably over-the-top invite. So this was it. Her career in journalism was reduced to launching a dog column for the *Monaco Mail*. She recalled the halcyon days of writing for respected broadsheets. At the *Wall Street Journal* in Brussels, she had been sent to interview the UK billionaire Keith Travis in Monte Carlo. It was the first time she stepped foot in this miniature principality, the world's second-smallest country, though the wealthiest per capita. For two hours, she listened to Travis drone on about how he was a 'working class lad who liked the simple things in life': such as Ferraris, superyachts and girls half his age.

Afterwards, she had dropped by the Italian bistro, Cantinetta Antinori, to recover over a glass of wine. There, she struck up a conversation with Hank. Compared to Travis, Hank seemed debonair. By the end of a bottle of wine, Hank had given her a job offer that was hard to refuse. Her editorship of this Monaco rag trumped the editorial salaries that she had become inured to in the UK and Belgium. It also came with a rent-free flat in Monaco. Since her arrival in Monaco just 18 months ago, she had paid off the €30,000 credit-card debt that she had built up as a single mother. She owed her solvency to Hank.

Of course, Hank hadn't started in publishing. He became a multi-millionaire dealing in artworks via a Freeport based in Luxembourg. It was an astounding ascent for a Franco-Canadian who'd spent his teens flogging watercolours of Parisian landscapes along the banks of the Seine. Over the decades, he had expanded into art dealing and developed a black book of contacts that enabled him to source works by almost any artist, modern or ancient. Never was there a man more gifted of the gab. He learnt a patter that could paper over the cracks of his patchy artistic knowledge so that only art curators would occasionally smile at his aesthetic inaccuracies. Whether an art collector was looking for a Raphael or a Rothko, Hank was the man to ask. He ranked artists in dollar signs. That said, he had a soft spot for the Impressionists. Indeed, the Monaco gossip circle rumoured that he'd procured Manet's lost *Chez Tortoni* (stolen from an American art gallery in the 1990s) for himself, and kept it locked away in a secret crypt at his Cap Ferrat villa.

Eventually, Hank moved to Monaco to be near his

increasing clientele of the principality's billionaires. Here, he developed his love for superyachts and supermodels. By the time he'd made €200 million, he came to the realisation that money alone wasn't enough to buy influence. There would always be someone with a bigger yacht and a helipad. What he needed was a publishing empire to twist the news to his own tune and provide a smokescreen against the myriad victims he'd crushed on his way to UHNW status. When he purchased *Monaco Mail*, he sacked the male editor. He wanted a female editor who he could manipulate. Ever the bad judge of women, he picked Abigail.

•

ABIGAIL OPENED HER EMAILS. SHE SNORTED WITH LAUGHTER as the first popped up:

> *I am beauty enthusiast and blogger. I co-own and write the Powder Puff blog. I have active presence on Instagram with over 100,000 followers. I am researching body washes and come across your feature: Body of stabbed Bichon Frise washes up on Larvotto Beach. Both our sites are in related niches and compliment each other. You like collaborate with me?*

It was a poorly crafted, bot-automated email. Abigail stabbed out a brief reply saying that she wasn't sure how she could collaborate with her beauty brand over a murdered dog. Her finger hovered over the send button. She pictured Hank ranting about social media. She pondered briefly about editorial integrity. Then she thought about the extortionate bills for the nursery that her daughter attended in Fontvieille. She deleted the message and wrote a different one:

Thanks so much for your email. I'd love to collaborate with you. Are you free to meet for coffee tomorrow?

•

IT WAS 5:30 P.M. ON FRIDAY AS ABIGAIL DROVE HER FIAT UNO to the nursery to pick up her three-year-old daughter. Back at her flat around the corner, Abigail spent several hours with her daughter playing, bathing, and storytelling. By the time she'd kissed her sleeping daughter's head and entrusted her to the babysitter, Abigail was already running behind schedule for Serena's 29th birthday dinner. Serena was Hank's beautiful Malaysian girlfriend. Calm and considerate: she was the antidote to Hank. Her dinner was planned as a girls-only night out, so Hank would be celebrating with a parallel boys' night.

She slung on a simple black dress from Zara. She glanced at herself in the bathroom mirror as she smoothed back her hair. She wasn't unattractive, though she sometimes felt invisible in this principality where long-blonde-haired supermodels were two-a-penny. Her pale blonde hair seemed too short, her tall figure too gangly and flat-chested, and her jaw too square to pass the elevated beauty benchmark of *Models-1-Land* as she dubbed Monaco. Her large hazel eyes were her best feature, though her prescription glasses were the antithesis of Monaco style. Still, being invisible was sometimes an advantage.

•

SHE DROVE DOWN THE JASMINE-STREWN DRIVEWAY TO THE Hôtel Métropole. It felt like a country house in the heart of the city except that this country house had a pool area designed by Karl Lagerfeld. She turned right to Yoshi, Monaco's only Michelin-starred sushi restaurant. Beneath a huge Milky-Wayshaped chandelier stood Serena. Resplendent in a high-collared purple silk dress, she fluttered like a hummingbird amongst her charm of girlfriends. Beside her, two WAGs vied for pole position: British Formula One girlfriend versus top-5-worldwide-ranked tennis wife. Abigail remained hesitantly on the outer circle.

Spotting her, Serena rushed over to greet her: with a glass of pink champagne and the stress-free smile of someone whose days revolved around yoga, spas, and looking fabulous. She introduced Abigail to her friend Beth, and then raced off to greet another arrival. Beth appeared to have had so much filler in her cheeks that she bore a passing resemblance to a chipmunk. Lost for something to say, Abigail remarked upon her gold necklace with an enormous ruby in the middle framed by a cluster of smaller rubies.

'They're Burmese rubies,' replied Beth. 'The necklace cost me €50,000. Where's your dress from?'

'It's from Zara and cost me €50.'

'Yet, I bet that my necklace is still better value than your dress. I saved about €100,000 by sourcing the rubies through a friend in the mining business.'

Beth eyed Abigail disapprovingly before continuing.

'So what do you think of Yoshi?'

'It's the first time I've dined here,' said Abigail. 'My budget doesn't normally stretch to gold-leaf sushi.'

'Fine dining isn't my thing,' said Beth. 'If I had my way, I'd be happy to survive on vitamin pills alone. So where do you live in Monaco?'

'The Memmo Center,' said Abigail. 'What about you?'

'I have a villa in Cap Ferrat, plus two next-door apartments in the Saint-André residence,' said Beth with an edge of competitive surprise that someone dressed as plainly as Abigail could afford to live in the Memmo Center.

'Why two flats?' asked Abigail.

'One flat for my boyfriend James and me, the other for my toddlers and their nanny.'

'Why would you have your kids in a different flat?'

'James doesn't want us to risk our cream carpets with the kids.'

As everyone sat down for dinner, Abigail dived to the other side of the table away from Beth. A slender blonde with a kind smile sat next to her. Abigail showed her relief with a smile that said: 'Thanks for saving me from an evil chipmunk wearing the Burmese crown jewels.'

At that moment, a suet pudding of a man from the neighbouring table barged his bulky frame between their two chairs.

'Hello,' he shouted to the slender blonde.

He didn't notice Abigail, but Abigail recognised him as Dimitri Nalimov, the online gambling billionaire. As the blonde continued in polite chatter, Abigail recalled her past encounters with him: once at a tech-industry conference, again at a charity event when he half-heartedly tried to chat her up at the bar, and lastly in the early hours of a night out at Sass Café nightclub with a blonde date upon his knee.

Finally, he turned his roly-poly hips towards Abigail.

'Sorry, I haven't introduced myself,' he said. 'I'm Dimitri.'

'Nice to meet you, Dimitri,' said Abigail. 'Almost as nice to meet you this time as the last three times that we've met during the past six months.'

'Excuse me. Got to go. I'm running late for dinner.'

With a sheepish look on his face, Dimitri rushed off.

•

THE NEXT MORNING, ABIGAIL DRAGGED HERSELF INTO THE office for 8 a.m. Rob came in a few minutes later looking even worse for wear.

'You look like you need about ten coffees,' remarked Abigail.

'While you were out with Serena, I had the pleasure of a night on the tiles with Hank at a bar around the corner,' groaned Rob. 'He was on first-name terms with every prostitute there.'

'Well, your evening sounds as bad as mine. The highlight was a hilarious run-in with that horrendous lecher Dimitri Nalimov.'

'No way,' said Rob. 'He's here right now.'

'What?'

'Sorry, I forgot to mention it. Hank added him onto the schedule yesterday at the last minute, after you'd left. He wants you to butter up Dimitri as he's our new advertiser. They're waiting for you in the boardroom right now.'

'I hate you,' said Abigail.

She skulked upstairs to the boardroom where she found Dimitri chatting with Hank.

'This is my editor Abigail Hackett,' said Hank.

'Hi, I'm Dimitri Nalimov,' said Dimitri, rising to shake her hand. 'So nice to meet you. I've heard great things about you.'

Abigail looked up to see a carefree smile on Dimitri's face. She realised with relief that he had no idea they'd crossed paths the night before. Luckily for Abigail, all blondes looked the same to Dimitri.

2

Lucinda

CHECKED HER REFLECTION IN THE FULL-LENGTH bedroom mirror. A white peasant blouse set off her mother's Yves Saint Laurent skirt with its chequered pattern of raspberry, mustard, and royal blue. Blue, Ancient Greek sandals picked out the blue rhinestones in her vintage Alexander Lauren earrings. Alexander had gifted them to her (in lieu of cash) after her first giddy fashion-week season, Spring 1992 in Paris, London and Milan. Afterwards, in his Memphis-design Monaco flat, he had reassured her: 'The future is always better than you think'.

She drifted into the kitchen. Her husband Leo, short for Leopold, Count de Mortcerf, was preparing artichokes with caper sauce. He always served them upside down — stems chopped off; outer petals splayed out — exposing the heart at the centre. Grabbing a bottle of Miraval rosé in one hand, and a Le Creuset corkscrew in the other, Lucinda edged her way to the custom-made table on the terrace. In Monaco, this 20-square-metre terrace was coveted. Anywhere else, it would have felt cramped.

Leo joined her with the artichokes. As he poured the wine, she noticed those large, athletic hands that always excited her, his tall physique bronzed from days beneath the Mediterranean sun. The sun hadn't aged him. But it was his childish enthusiasm that kept him young. How he loved to show off in the company of others, entertaining his audience with mischievous tales of the past, lit up as if he were reliving those escapades for the first time. Lucinda had heard those stories over and over. But there were no guests tonight, and Leo was sullenly silent.

Leo's phone jolted her from her reverie. She overheard George, Leo's brother, on the line then her husband's barked response:

'What do you mean she's selling the tiara? How much? €100,000? Is that all they think it is worth? *Merde!*'

Lucinda sipped her rosé, inhaling the evening's sweet scent of jasmine. Peanut, her long-haired dachshund, rested his warm body on her left foot. She watched the sun sink slowly behind the Tête de Chien.

'It doesn't look like a dog's head,' she thought, wondering where the name came from.

Soon lights would be glistening around the La Turbie village, topped by its Roman monument, Trophée d'Auguste. She never tired of this panoramic view that stretched from the French Riviera to Monte Carlo's Casino Square. Even guests at Monaco's fabled Hôtel de Paris couldn't match it.

'Bloody Isabel,' he growled as the call ended. He inhaled deeply on his cigarette.

Lucinda was happy that she was not the target of his insults for once. This was an old family feud. Leo's sister Isabel stopped speaking to their mother decades ago, and to her brothers after their mother's death. Leo said it had something to do with their inheritance.

'She's selling my mother's yellow-diamond tiara at Christie's just like she sells everything that belonged to Mama,' continued Leo. 'She's even selling the pearl earrings which once belonged to Princess Marie-Christine.'

Leo walked inside and grabbed a pack of cigarettes from the top shelf.

'I knew it.' Lucinda rolled her eyes. 'I hadn't checked that shelf.' Leo was 6'2". Those extra inches made a difference when it came to hiding things in high places.

Leo laughed. She loved when he laughed. It reminded her of better times. His laugh turned into a wheezing cough. Until she met Leo, she'd never considered herself a smoker. But smoking and drinking rosé soon became a shared habit. He still smoked five packs daily of Gauloises unfiltered cigarettes. She kept trying to persuade Leo to quit. Without success.

'I'm going to call George back,' he said.

The artichokes sat waiting on the table. Lucinda took one of Leo's cigarettes.

•

LUCINDA WOKE UP THE NEXT MORNING WITH THE SUN IN her eyes. Leo was already on his computer in his office, staring at his investment portfolio.

'The markets are going crazy. The VIX is higher than it's been in months,' he said absently, when he heard her walking past.

She noticed Leo no longer called her 'baby'.

'Have you thought about investing in cryptocurrency?' he continued, still staring at the screen. 'I've found this Bitcoin ETF — it's pretty volatile. It's going to go sky high soon.'

'Volatile. Sounds like someone I know,' she thought.

While checking on the stock market, Leo veered between celebration and vexation. She used to think his swearing in his native Belgian French was funny — like in *I Love Lucy* when Ricky would catch Lucy in one of her little schemes and swear at her in Spanish. Best not to interrupt Leo in those moods. He'd only shout at her.

She walked towards the kitchen, followed by Peanut, and started to make him a coffee.

'Don't walk away when I'm talking to you,' he hollered. 'Idiot.'

•

BY DINNERTIME, LEO HAD CALMED DOWN, AND WAS looking forward to what he did best: socialising. They were invited for dinner with Leo's college friend Frédéric and his rather boastful wife Caroline, whose apartment spanned two upper levels of the Shangri-La. It was the first time that Lucinda had been to their Monaco flat as she tried to avoid Caroline whenever she could.

Lucinda felt pretty that evening as she changed into her turquoise Etro dress that brought out her green eyes. She liked to stand out in her floaty, feminine dresses, distinct from the usual Monaco uniform of revealing Valentino mini-dresses, Louboutin high heels, Louis Vuitton scarves and Hermès bags. She had had a Goyard bag, but when she noticed everyone carrying one, and that acquaintances were carrying copies purchased in Ventimiglia market, she gave it to Teresa, her cleaner.

They strolled down to Port Hercules in silence, each lost in their thoughts. Lucinda inhaled Leo's *Eau Sauvage* fragrance, and admired his dapper, crimson shirt. At 61, he looked 15 years younger.

'You will behave, won't you, darling?' Lucinda implored.

Too late. She knew the instant the words reached his ear that she had planted a seed. An opportunity to misbehave. Leo liked mischief. It was one of the reasons she was drawn to him in the first place.

'Welcome to our Monaco abode,' said Caroline, ushering them through to drinks on the terrace that looked out over the Grand Prix starting line.

'That's quite the view,' said Lucinda, reaching for something to say.

'Isn't it, just?' said Caroline. 'Of course, it doesn't come cheap. Though the €50,000 daily rental we get during the Grand Prix certainly helps with our annual rent.'

A glass of champagne in hand, Lucinda edged away from Caroline. Spotting her two closest Monaco girlfriends, Victoria and Beth, Lucinda rushed over to say hello. Meanwhile, Leo started chatting to Beth's boyfriend: a silver fox named James.

'What do you think of my new yellow-gold and diamond Rolex?' asked Beth.

'What happened to your last Rolex?' asked Lucinda, remembering the Rolex that James purchased, at Leo's recommendation, from Grays Antique Market in London.

'That white-gold one was too bland,' said Beth. 'This sets off my tan.'

'She made James return it, and then forced him to buy a new one at three times the price at the Rolex boutique below the yacht club,' laughed Victoria.

'Did I hear my name being taken in vain?' said James, as the men joined the group.

'Vain's the word,' laughed Victoria.

'We were just talking about my new Rolex,' said Beth. 'It's all ready for the party in Chipping Norton.'

'What party in Chipping Norton?' said Lucinda.

'Oh, umm, I've been invited to this party, all expenses paid,' ventured Victoria. 'Four days of drinks, dinner and group activities.'

'I can't think of anything worse than drinking for four days non-stop,' said Lucinda.

'Lucinda Monroe Kiddington, England's best-known social butterfly, turning down a party?' joked Leo. 'It doesn't sound too bad to me.'

'Everything is taken care of,' continued Victoria. 'You just have to be invited. I managed to secure Beth and James an invite.'

'I'd prefer to stay home,' said Lucinda, a little too insistently.

'God, you can be such a bore,' said Leo.

Lucinda sipped her champagne, reflecting that Monaco girlfriends were not like girlfriends outside the beautiful bubble. Had she not been living in this city, smaller than the sports facilities of her English boarding school, she would no doubt see them less often. At that moment, it started raining.

'Ah, the rain makes me miss London,' sighed Lucinda.

'Don't be ridiculous,' said Leo, rolling his eyes. 'How can anyone miss the rain?'

'It isn't ridiculous at all. You shouldn't always put her down,' said Victoria curtly.

There was an awkward silence as Victoria walked off. Lucinda felt fortunate to have a friend fighting her corner. Two minutes later, Victoria rushed back onto the terrace.

'Lu, I need your help,' said Victoria. 'Beans has had an accident.'

Beans was Victoria's French bulldog. Lucinda was convinced the name had been a self-fulfilling prophecy as the dog broke wind constantly. She followed Victoria into the guest bedroom, where she found Beans had defecated all over the marble floor.

'Oh, shit!' said Lucinda. 'Shouldn't you have left Beans at home?'

'Shit's the word,' said Victoria.

Lucinda and Victoria giggled as they grabbed some toilet roll from the ensuite bathroom and began clearing up the mess.

'Dinner's served,' they heard Caroline calling to the assembled guests on the terrace.

Victoria and Lucinda scooped up all the remaining dog mess frantically with the toilet roll, before rushing through for dinner as if nothing had happened.

A Jackson Pollock hung above the dining table where Patrick Mavros silver candelabra mingled with jugs of mint-infused water and a bottle of Claret. The 14 guests were seated by safari-animal place cards. Lucinda saw her seat next to Frédéric, while Victoria snatched up her place card next to Leo and swapped it with that of a celebrated French interior designer.

'Not sure that lone bottle of Claret is going to stretch too far,' joked Caroline.

'Maybe Frédéric wants to keep us all sober?' laughed Lucinda. 'With so many rogues around the table, I wouldn't be surprised.'

As Frédéric poured out some wine, Lucinda said: 'I hear you thrashed Leo at tennis yesterday.'

'Did I?' replied Frédéric distractedly. 'Yes. Yes, I did.'

He changed the topic promptly to his lavish surprise plans for his forthcoming 25th wedding anniversary. Frédéric and Caroline's multi-decade marriage was a Monaco rarity.

Lucinda zoned out of Frédéric's monologue and gazed at the dinner scene. Leo listened attentively to the interior designer. Beth pouted at the unmarried heir of a billion-dollar logistics company, while he chatted towards her D-cup corset. James retaliated his girlfriend's flirtation by buttering up Victoria and making her laugh raucously.

'Victoria seems so much more confident nowadays,' thought Lucinda, as she wondered whether Victoria's dress sense had become more suggestive or whether she'd just not noticed her bosom before.

Over starters, the logistics heir started up a conversation across the table with Lucinda. It turned out that he lived in the same apartment block as she did, Le Millefiori. They gossiped about the 90s supermodel who lived in their building and who was married to a French popstar, while her ex-stepdaughter was married to an even more famous French popstar.

The main course arrived. Lucinda turned back to Leo to find him listening restlessly to Caroline boasting about her high-octane life. His wine glass was empty. Frédéric had not replenished his glass, or anyone else's for that matter.

'Darling Frédéric, have you any more of that lovely wine to go with this perfectly cooked steak?' Lucinda asked.

Finally, Frédéric fetched more bottles he didn't want to part with. After postprandial drinks out on the terrace, Lucinda and Leo bid their farewells.

'Well, Frédéric, don't just stand there. Fetch their coats,' barked Caroline. Lucinda realised that this was only the second time in the entire evening that Caroline had spoken to her husband.

•

THE NEXT MORNING, LUCINDA WAS UP EARLY TO RUN SOME errands before lunch with Victoria. With Peanut riding in the front seat, she drove her beloved white VW Beetle convertible into Beausoleil. The two-seater car was perfect for the Riviera where parking spaces were tiny.

'Small, practical and absolutely adorable,' thought Lucinda. 'Just like Peanut.'

She stopped off at Beausoleil market to buy her favourite pastel-pink ranunculi blooms ready for tomorrow's interview and photoshoot with *Monaco Mail*'s Abigail Hackett. Lucinda wanted to make sure that her flat and Peanut looked their best.

Then she sped down avenue de la Costa to drop off a skirt at the dry cleaner. On the way, she spotted Leo having coffee with a bald, short man that she recognised as a regular at Casa del Caffè.

'Leo's becoming part of the furniture there too,' Lucinda thought.

Her long, light-brown hair flowed in the wind, as she accelerated back home with the windows down, listening to *Michelle* by the Beatles. Turning right into avenue Saint Michel, she passed the non-descript Buckingham Palace apartment block, just before her own home: a 1960s residential building, optimistically named *Le Millefiori* (wildflowers). It was one of the ugliest buildings Lucinda had ever set her eyes on. Rumour had it that Aristotle Onassis, who was largely responsible for its erection, insisted it be higher than Prince Rainier's palace in the Old Town. The 37-storey, modernist concrete tower blocked out most of the sky from down below in her car. She wouldn't have wanted to live in its shadow.

She parked the car, then walked over to Piamu u Frescu, a simple, local haunt where the waitress with long braids always took care of Lucinda and Peanut. Victoria was there already. Over lunchtime salads, they exchanged dinner-party gossip from the night before.

'Sounds like Frédéric is planning a big party for their silver wedding anniversary,' said Lucinda. 'Not many couples reach that milestone in this town.'

'It's a miracle *they* have,' said Victoria. 'Before your time here, Frédéric was rumbled living a double life with a younger woman in London.'

'A double life?'

'Caroline's best friend bumped into him and his bit on the side as they walked out of a fertility clinic on Harley Street.'

'How sickening!'

'It's quite funny actually,' said Victoria. 'The best friend recognised the woman as a B-list actress from a scoop in one of the British tabloids that mentioned her IVF struggles with a mystery boyfriend.'

'Did the friend tell Caroline?'

'She did, against my advice,' said Victoria. 'And Caroline never spoke to her again.'

'I don't understand how Caroline forgave Frédéric,' mused Lucinda.

'Well, it's very Monaco,' said Victoria. 'When it's a choice between pride and poverty, the penthouse flat usually wins.'

When coffee arrived, Lucinda moved the conversation to Leo. She was happy to have a close friend to confide in.

'Leo can be such a bully,' said Lucinda.

'Well, you married him. You knew what you were getting into,' said Victoria.

'He seduced me with his naughty smile. He assured me: 'You'll find something to do."

'Well, it's not so bad here with the sun and the sea.'

'I left London: the theatre, exhibitions, my friends, and my first husband, to move to Monaco to be with him.'

'You have to read Laura May. *Journey to Healing.* It helped me. A lot,' said Victoria, forking lettuce into her mouth.

Lucinda was silent for a moment, pondering her friend's lack of empathy.

'And talking of healing, are you going to come to next week's Womb Wisdom retreat?' said Victoria.

'What?' said Lucinda.

'It's the study of the Sacred Feminine. The study of the

womb and the cervix. And the power that brings to us as women. The retreat activates your sacred sensual self.'

'Not for pussies,' giggled Lucinda.

'It's also meant to teach us not to push our men to their limits,' continued Victoria. 'But to support them as they are: a unique expression of the divine masculine. I went to last year's retreat. I really plugged in and connected with my own healing power.'

At that moment, she heard a woman at the bar counter: 'Make it a coffee to go. And snap to it. I have a meeting next door in two minutes.' She recognised the imperious tone immediately. She had never been happier to see her Scottish friend, Barbara. Escaping Victoria and her womb wisdom, Lucinda rushed over to say hello.

3

Polina

AS THE SOUTHERN FRENCH COASTLINE CAME INTO VIEW, Polina took out her makeup bag to freshen up before landing. She put on Chanel's Destiny crimson lipstick and a sweet smile. With the-end-justifies-the-means mantra in mind, she gazed adoringly at the man opposite. Rodney, or Rod as he liked to be called, sat with his balding pate, mid-life paunch, and a nose that appeared to have been bashed around on an Australian rugby field – which in fact it had. The least wealthy of her generous, gentlemen friends, he flew by private jet without bathroom facilities and on off-peak slots. That said, private is private, and he liked to pamper her to the extent that his means allowed.

As Polina watched him stab out a message on his phone, she reflected upon their weekend together in Paris with satisfaction. A suite at the smart George V, spa and shopping trips by day, and by night, Michelin-starred dining and a visit to the Crazy Horse to spoil Rod. Polina was Rod's secret indulgence, but there were no prying eyes from their Monaco set in Paris. As they strolled down rue du Faubourg Saint-Honoré, she sensed him revelling in the envious looks that she — his arm candy — afforded him. He was proud that she cost him a small fortune. In her suitcase nestled her weekend cache — a new pair of Louboutins, a Dior saddle bag, and a low-cut Hervé Leger dress — juxtaposed against a replica pistol in the compartment below. Regularly updated to outwit airport security, her special handgun was a reassuring accessory when travelling on business.

Polina stared into the middle distance and reflected on the road she'd travelled from her Belarusian roots. When she thought about her hometown Gomel, the nearest town to Chernobyl that wasn't evacuated after the nuclear disaster, she saw greyness and the absence of beauty. As she waited in those long queues for bread, meat, shoes, clothes, she was impatient for her life to begin.

A secret affair with a doctor on secondment to the local Radiation Research Centre was her ticket to liberation. The doctor told her parents that there was an opportunity for Polina to learn French as an au pair for his children. But when she arrived in Paris, aged 18, it was as his mistress in a pied-à-terre in the 6th *arrondissement*; a suitable distance from the family home in the 16th. When his controlling behaviour became too much, she spring-boarded into independence by entering the modelling world as a discreet escort for the globally wealthy and famous. Her model-escort debut came courtesy of her new Turkish friend, Leyla, who was enjoying the lifestyle already.

'Here's a little something for you, my sweet,' drawled Rod, reaching into his Louis Vuitton carry bag for an envelope stuffed with cash.

'Thank you, Rod, this is kind. You are good person,' said Polina.

Rod pushed a trophy back inside the bag, and Polina smirked. It was in the George V suite that she first saw it. As she flopped onto the chaise longue with her freshly salon-coiffed hair, she spotted the trophy with its receipt on the side table. An inscription on the cup read:

> *Best New Driver*
> *Rodney McWilliam*
> *Porsche Race*
> *Circuit des Invalides, Paris*

Noticing Polina's raised eyebrow, Rod admitted his subterfuge, with a self-congratulatory chuckle. 'I told my missus that I was competing this weekend. This is my proof.'

'Not much proof,' thought Polina, smiling to herself. 'Porsche doesn't even race in Paris.'

Rod went on to explain how he and his wife owned everything jointly: 'One of those Monaco divorces that favour the man wouldn't work for us.'

Polina made a mental note that Rod's wife must be smarter than most Monaco wives who found themselves on the receiving end of a Monaco divorce. In this patriarchal principality, there was no equitable division of assets. While ex-husbands continued to luxuriate in the marital home, their ex-wives ended up in cockroach-infested studios more often than not. Even so, Polina concluded that Rod's wife was less clever working full-time in their business while Rod swanned around.

'She knows too much about where the money is and where the bodies are buried.'

'Bodies?' said Polina.

'It's a figure of speech,' said Rod, chuckling. 'Oh God, you do make me laugh.'

'Smug bastard,' thought Polina, as she continued to look at him adoringly.

Rod could rely upon Polina's discretion. They were completely beholden to each other in that regard, particularly given her recent romantic catch.

Polina daydreamed back three months ago to the Mandarin Oriental Paris courtyard bar. There she was, sipping a skinny latte, when she spotted Dimitri Nalimov. Billionaire? Tick. He'd made it recently to the Russian billionaires' list. Single? Tick. He'd been having far too much fun partying in Saint Tropez. Looking for an heir? Tick. At just 58, he was only 30 years her senior. He checked all the boxes for the ideal husband. There was no time to waste.

'*Excusez-moi, Monsieur, vous pouvez m'aider sur le WiFi?*' she said, holding up her phone, all wide-eyed innocence and fluttering eyelashes. With typical rich-guy arrogance, Dimitri was unphased by Polina's flirtation.

He moved his portly frame across to her table to help her get online. Over chai, Polina switched to the intimacy of their mother tongue, using her beauty and 32DD assets to maximum effect. She watched him fall under her spell. Their meeting was cut short when Dimitri's driver tapped him on the shoulder.

'Look, I must go, but I have a proposition,' he said, standing up to leave.

To avoid appearing over-eager, Polina put on her nonchalant face.

'I'm having a party in Monaco next weekend,' continued Dimitri. 'Why don't you join us? Bring a girlfriend if you'd like. Let's swap details, and you can confirm later.'

Polina took Leyla to the party aboard Dimitri's superyacht, the *Bumazhnik* in Monaco port. She delighted Dimitri by bringing this additional eye candy to his event and put him in a favourable frame of mind towards her.

Ten dates and eight trysts later, and Polina was known to Dimitri's entourage as his girlfriend. To keep up appearances, she rented a roof-top apartment in Monaco's Fontvieille district. Leyla followed suit, moving herself, her two children and long-suffering Filipino housekeeper to a beachside apartment in Larvotto.

Although it was risky to see Rod while her seduction of Dimitri Nalimov progressed, Polina rationalised that her day job wouldn't pay the rent.

'Let's take a little risk and have dinner this week somewhere along the Côte d'Azur,' Rod said, bringing Polina back to the present. 'A clever-clogs friend of my wife has written a book about child-friendly restaurants in the region which is very handy.'

'But Rod, you hate kids. Why you want go to restaurant with them?'

Rod threw his head back laughing.

'Of course, I don't want to go to a restaurant full of the little buggers. That's why this book is so damn handy. It tells me where to avoid.'

•

POLINA TOOK HER MORNING DOUBLE-SHOT ESPRESSO AND stepped out onto her rooftop terrace where the sun was already giving off a scorching heat. Taking a seat in the shade of her palm tree, she consulted her phone to browse the new feedback on her blog, *Powder Puff.*

Her last post promoting a vegan-friendly, lip-gloss range had made for some ravishing photos featuring a pouting Polina sprawled across Dimitri's classic 1959 Mercedes convertible on the Grande Corniche mountainside road above Monaco. Her *Breakfast at Tiffany*'s vintage sunglasses and Hermès headscarf juxtaposed incongruously with an outrageously low-cut dress and bright-red killer heels.

Ironic! Paradoxical! Playfully delightful! read the breathless headline.

Leyla's flowery language might be over the top, but for now Polina was focussed on growing her followers. Polina had set up a bot to scan the web for beauty-related features. Any journalist writing about beauty would receive an automated 'shall we collaborate?' email. The resulting media collaborations brought thousands of new followers and tomorrow's meeting with Abigail Hackett from *Monaco Mail*. She hadn't told Leyla. Frankly, she was growing tired of Leyla crowding her space.

Polina gulped down her coffee and returned inside. She needed a good hour to prepare for her afternoon outing. She flung open the doors of all six wardrobes in search of an outfit. Today, she needed to outshine Leyla in Dimitri's eyes. Looking heavenly was pivotal to her fate.

The answer lay in her new boots. Discounted in price for the privilege of a blog mention, they were daytime sexy extremism. With their cut-out toe and heel, the high-heeled, caramel suede boots were a nod to summer. The suggestive front lacing criss-crossed up her legs to her thighs.

Next, she selected a cream body-hugging Gucci dress. Its sexiness was almost redeemed by the innocent white cuffs and high-neck collar, except for the keyhole opening revealing a glimpse of her generous cleavage. Continuing the subtle theme and to keep the focus on the boots, she selected a comfortingly expensive Hermès Birkin bag.

Polina checked her image from every angle in three full-length mirrors: a vision of caramel, cream and blonde. She calculated the cost of her outfit in rounded-up figures for simplicity.

Dress	€2,500
Boots	€1,500 (including the discount)
Birkin handbag	€20,700
Bvlgari earrings	€3,000
Rolex watch	€10,000
Harry Winston ring	€18,000
La Perla lingerie	€600

With one last tap, the calculator on her phone announced the total: €56,300. The amount made her feel valuable.

'Not my highest, but respectable for daytime,' thought Polina proudly.

•

POLINA AND LEYLA WERE USED TO TURNING HEADS, BUT when they entered a room *à deux*, the attention doubled. With Polina, a petite busty blonde, and Leyla, a tall slim brunette, they were the yin and yang of male desire as they strutted to their table, asking the maître d' to bring stools for their handbags.

'*Bonjour Mademoiselles*. May I offer still or sparkling water?' said the waiter.

'I like still water, Evian,' said Polina. 'But room temperature, not fridge, and bring small cup of ice on the side.'

'Sparkling for me,' said Leyla. 'Badoit — not San Pellegrino.'

The waiter bustled off to fulfil their drinks requests, while they perused the menu. On his return, they had their requests lined up.

'I take two small plates,' began Polina. 'The asparagus, but no egg sprinkles. Remove egg sprinkles. And I take crab avocado roll. But tell chef, no garlic and no onions. I cannot have garlic or onions.'

'There are no garlic or onions in either of those dishes, Mademoiselle,' explained the waiter.

'Sometimes it happens,' said Polina. 'You must tell him I cannot have garlic or onions. He knows me. He will remember me. Tell him Polina is here.'

'Yes, he knows you, Mademoiselle,' said the waiter.

'I take one plate,' said Leyla. '*Sole meunière*, but no tomato confit and no pine nuts. Change for pasta on side.'

'We don't have pasta as a side dish on our menu,' said the waiter.

'Anyone can make pasta,' said Leyla. 'Ask chef to make pasta.'

The waiter consulted with the kitchen and returned: 'No pasta, but perhaps a side of our famous *purée?*'

'No, too heavy for daytime,' said Leyla.

The experienced waiter smiled sympathetically.

'I am very sorry about that and I don't wish to pressure you,' continued the waiter in a servile tone. 'But, for me personally, the best choice to accompany the *sole meunière* is the *purée*. May I suggest you order the side dish of *purée* and you only take how much you want to eat?'

'Yes, alright,' she said, as she waved the waiter away from the table.

From Leyla's willingness to acquiesce to the waiter, Polina realised that she must be bursting to tell her something.

'I have news,' said Leyla. 'Sergei wants us to be official. Boyfriend and girlfriend. Not, you know, arrangement through agency, but relationship.'

'Sergei Kukushkin? He is mafia, no?' said Polina.

Leyla replied with a flick of her hair. 'I hear stories, yes. But I ask you, who makes honest money in this place? He is very protective, but he gives me generous allowance.'

'This is important,' said Polina, 'but you must be careful.

Sergei has business with my boss Marcus. Marcus is very nervous when Sergei comes to office.'

'You and me, we keep each other safe,' said Leyla. 'Listen for Marcus with Sergei at office.'

Polina nodded her agreement. They always had each other's back. They shared so much: their time in Paris, their profession, and their common goal of a Monaco-billionaire husband. Leyla divulged the details of her living arrangements with Sergei. While she lived with Sergei in his apartment, she kept her two children living at home with the housekeeper. She saw her children from time to time when Sergei was away on business. She ensured that her children received a good allowance to have fun with their friends in the safe environment of Monaco. Sergei's responsibility was simply to pay the bills for her flat, designer clothes and luxurious lifestyle.

'I think is sensible,' said Polina. 'Kids are difficult and the men don't like problems.'

Changing the subject, Leyla reached into her bag on the velvet stool and took out a copy of the *Monaco Mail*.

'Now I have the settled life with Sergei, I will get dog,' she said.

She showed Polina the new newspaper column, *Principality Pooches*, which was advertising an upcoming dog event.

Friends of Chow-Chow
Salon Excelsior, Hôtel Hermitage
6th October - 5pm
Bring your well-groomed dog to join the activities
Doggy Tinder : Tricks and Treats : Pawsome Outfit :
Meat and Greet : Pawdicures
Accompanied by drinks and canapés
Tickets €70 payable in advance
RSVP by email to Abigail attaching a photo of your dog

'I want to buy Louis Vuitton dog-carrier bag,' said Leyla. 'So I need find dog to match. You come with me to dog event?'

Although Polina would much rather help purchase the LV bag than the dog, she considered that it would be a chance to see Abigail from the *Monaco Mail* again at the dog event the day after their blog meeting. It might be an opportunity to encourage her assistance further.

'I should be at work that day.'

Polina pondered briefly how her boss Marcus Staples would react to her missing their afternoon 'meeting': code for a sundowner on the terrace of a nearby cafe. Their meetings revolved around him talking about himself and his first-world problems. His pet topics were his loathsome mother-in-law, Barbara Esson, and his failing *WeFork* restaurant chain. From Polina's perspective, it was obvious where the root of his business problem lay. After all, who would want to eat in a restaurant with such a ridiculous name?

'Okay,' said Polina. 'Boss will understand. Yes, I come to dog event.'

'Good. I register you and send details.'

Polina's day job provided both pocket money and a respectable front for her lucrative night-time employment. Her job consisted of enhancing the office décor and providing the occasional Russian translation for her boss. Marcus was an easy boss: more often found in his favourite restaurants and bars than at the office. In turn, Polina came to the office whenever it suited her.

'We must go, I meet Dimitri now,' said Polina, reaching for her bag.

Rebuffing the waiter's enquiries into dessert and coffee, they asked for the bill and split it between them in large-note cash. Cash was an occupational hazard of their non-traceable evening transactions.

Outside on the cobblestone driveway of the Hôtel Métropole, they found Dimitri's bulky frame leaning up against his Maybach. He talked loudly on his phone, oblivious to blocking the driveway. Polina positioned herself to show off her boots and bodyline to best advantage, while Leyla preened and added more lipstick in her phone mirror. On seeing the girls, Dimitri ended his phone call, threw his keys to the valet, and walked over to embrace Polina.

'Looking good,' he grinned and kissed her on the lips. 'Too bad I had to be away over the weekend. I hope you missed me.'

Leyla looked on coolly before donning a megawatt smile as Dimitri turned towards her.

'Nice to see you, Dimitri, I go shopping now,' said Leyla. 'Have fun. See you soon, Polina.' She blew a kiss to them both and walked off.

'What's up with her?' asked Dimitri, switching to their mother tongue.

'I don't know. Nothing, I think,' said Polina. 'Darling, I have an appointment at Dior to view their new collection. Maybe it's very boring for you, but I miss you so much. I would love for you to come with me.'

•

THEY AMBLED ACROSS LES JARDINS DU CASINO TOWARDS the Dior boutique with Dimitri delivering a monologue about his recent business. Deep in thought about securing Abigail's interest in her blog, Polina heard his voice as white noise, responding instinctively by nodding and smiling at the right moments. The sudden mention of *Monaco Mail* infiltrated her subconscious and brought her back to full alert.

'Did you say *Monaco Mail*?' she asked. 'This is a coincidence. I am meeting editor Abigail tomorrow about my blog.'

'That's nice,' said Dimitri. 'I did meet a grim-faced journalist there this morning.'

'Oh, was it Abigail?'

'I've no idea, but she was blonde if that helps.'

'Why did you go to *Monaco Mail?*'

'I'm doing some advertising with them to raise awareness for my private-jet-charter company. I'm becoming too well known for my gambling interests and that's not ideal just before the renewal of my *carte de séjour*,' said Dimitri, referring to Monaco's stringent residency visa system.

'You have a private-jet company?'

'Yes, it's a sideline. Anyway, as I was saying, my other reason for going to the *Monaco Mail* was to meet Hank Vert. Though he's best known around town as a publisher, he's actually a very successful broker of fine art.'

'Uh huh.'

'It seems he may have found a buyer for that Rodigliani painting in my dining room, you know the *Nude Blonde* one.'

Polina feigned acknowledgement with a nod of her head.

'I'm very pleased with €8 million,' continued Dimitri. 'Particularly given that the recent valuation was only €7 million.'

Polina noted the €1 million difference with interest.

'I've agreed to the terms, and it looks like we have a deal,' said Dimitri.

'This is good. I am very happy for you,' said Polina as she tried to remember what other artwork she'd seen in his home and on his yacht, and what collective value might be hanging on his walls.

The doorman at Dior welcomed them into the cool, hushed tones of the salon.

'I'm planning a special dinner for the two of us tomorrow night,' said Dimitri. 'Why don't you buy yourself a new dress on me? You can wear it to dine with me tomorrow.'

Polina gave him a radiant smile in reply.

'I'll be in the American Bar. Call me when they're ready for payment,' he said, turning to leave before adding over his shoulder as the doormen held the door open for him. 'Oh, by the way, don't get anything low-key. I want you looking hot.'

The discreet shop assistant pretended not to have heard the remark and approached Polina to greet her.

'*Bonjour Mademoiselle*. I adore your boots. They are beautiful.'

Polina accepted the compliment with a tight smile and slight nod of her head to make the disparity in their respective positions clear.

'I would like dress for evening. Very special. I see new season first.'

'*Bien sûr*,' said the shop assistant. 'Please, follow me.'

An hour later, Dimitri returned to settle the bill for the new dress, bag and matching shoes and to arrange delivery of the packages to the concierge at Polina's apartment. High from her shopping experience, Polina bade a bright farewell to the Dior staff and linked her arm through Dimitri's as they stepped out into the bright daylight of a picture-perfect Mediterranean day.

The Instagram moment was spoiled by a tall, overly tanned man bumping into them as he jumped out of a VW Beetle. As he slammed shut the car door, he shouted towards the driver: '*Merde!* You're an idiot, Lucinda.'

'I'd need to be sitting inside a chauffeured Bentley to put up with that sort of behaviour,' thought Polina, looking at an elegant, older woman inside the car and shuddering.

4

Barbara

Lunch with the FT: 58-year-old Barbara Esson on workplace diversity in the male-fuelled energy industry

BARBARA SIPPED FROM HER *QUEEN BEE* MUG, A GIFT FROM her daughter, as she skimmed the *FT* article on her phone, fresh from her recent industry jamboree in Norway. She slipped off her kitten heels as she stretched out her legs on the David Linley *Savile* cream sofa of her Roccabella apartment.

Meeting Barbara, Chairman of the Esson Group is not for the faint hearted. 'Good,' she thought. She'd hoped to put that intrusive little journalist in his place. *With one glance at the layered bob, steel-grey sleeveless dress and well-preserved physique…* Barbara snorted. Funny, she couldn't recall when the fashion choices or implied age of her male counterparts were given such prominence in the financial press. She glanced at the photo of herself, '*Nae bad fur an auld quine* (Not bad for an old girl),' she thought instinctively in the Doric dialect of her native Aberdeen. The scribbler continued, ...*I knew that I could not exceed our agreed one-hour lunch date by one minute. An oil services conglomerate with offices in twenty countries and over €15 billion in annual revenue doesn't run itself.*

She was proud of her family's achievements and made sure the journalist knew where she came from: how her grandfather had built up a moderate marine engineering fortune and how her father had expanded the business after oil was discovered in the North Sea in 1970. Barbara took interest in her father's stories about the explosive, global growth prospects and personalities in the oil patch. Nevertheless, she was surprised when he brought her onto the board at the tender age of 26. She assumed an ill-defined ambassadorial role much to the chagrin of the seasoned independent directors. The Esson Group listed on the London Stock Exchange at the turn of the millennium, but disaster struck not long after. Competitors swirled around the company hoping to take advantage of the share price collapse and perceived leadership vacuum after her father's fatal heart attack. Barbara stood firm. It became clear she had inherited her father's business acumen. And now, two decades later, no one could match her timing at outmanoeuvring rivals in the boom-bust oil industry.

'Ha!' She loved the final phrase: *Dismiss Barbara Esson as a lucky product of nepotism at your peril.* The only part of the feature that rankled her was about succession. She'd pushed to the back of her mind her worries about who would take over her empire. Certainly not her only daughter Sophie. She felt pain when she thought about Sophie's lack of drive. Maybe it was her fault. In giving her everything, she had taken away her grit. She winced when she thought about Sophie's sales role, at the Harry Grigoryan art gallery in Mayfair, that was going nowhere. It wasn't as if she were in it for her love of art. 'You're not supposed to like it. You're supposed to *own* it,' Sophie said bluntly, when Barbara baulked at the incomprehensible artworks on display. And then there was that no-good son-in-law, Marcus. Any money Barbara gifted to Sophie was liable to end up in his degenerate grasp.

A message popped up on her phone from Lucinda, confirming tonight's dinner plans at Café de la Fontaine.

Hope you had a lovely trip. Leo difficult as ever. Café de la Fontaine at 8?

Barbara texted back: *I brought back some antlers for you to skewer Leo. Glass of Dom Pérignon chez moi first? My driver will take us to dinner.*

Of all Leo's wives, Lucinda was her favourite. Though Lucinda's dress sense veered towards the bohemian, Barbara basked in the glow of her ethereal, aristocratic beauty. They understood each other. A shared childhood attending elite British girls' boarding schools. A wry sense of humour. A disdain for Monaco's superficial extremes. Of course, Barbara liked to think she would never tolerate Leo's withering put-downs the way Lucinda did.

Her own marriage was a case in point. When she came back from one of her many work trips to find her husband cavorting at Jimmy'z with a woman half her age in full view of her friends, she'd been quick to serve him with divorce papers. Not that she hadn't strayed herself, but she would never have embarrassed him so publicly.

She hoped this evening's *tête-à-tête* with Lucinda wouldn't be too depressing. She was bored of listening to her droning on about Leo. After all, marital distress was part of the Monaco lifestyle. Too much time, money, and temptation made the principality an epicentre of car-crash marriages. Just like policemen, there was a divorcée on every corner.

·

THE DUSTING OF HER MAID, NORA, INTERRUPTED HER reverie.

'I left my favourite Chanel work suit in Aberdeen,' said Barbara. 'Can you go to Scotland and bring it back?'

'Yes, of course, Miss Esson,' said Nora. 'You know, my cousin's boss keeps the same of everything in different houses. In the same order too. Maybe it's a good idea for you.'

'Pfft, that would be a ridiculous extravagance,' said Barbara, turning back to the *FT* app.

Unpaid employees rage at Marcus Staples' WeFork: *luxury fast-food chain in trouble as rumours of embezzlement and insolvency fly*, loomed the headline.

'We can't all have the Midas touch. He better not come crying to me for money,' thought Barbara, annoyed by the spiralling scandal of her son-in-law Marcus' business. While employees were going for a second month unpaid, the British media were having a field day with all his gauche Instagram selfies on private jets and yachts.

Barbara didn't mind subsidising her daughter and husband's lavish lifestyle, but she had no intention of funding his floundering business. She decided that it was high time for her to take a closer look at his business dealings: starting with his Monaco headquarters that she'd never actually seen.

As she eased her souped-up Aston Martin DBS Volante into the rue du Gabian, she was unfavourably surprised by the unprepossessing office block. She parked the car and took the lift up to his fifth-floor office. Marcus was nowhere to be seen. A lone employee continued on the phone in Russian.

His pristine office was like a showroom. She didn't get the impression that any actual work was done there, though that was not necessarily a red flag. Many entrepreneurs across the spectrum from legit to nefarious rented basic premises simply to have a Monaco address.

She glanced at his excessively attractive secretary. These determined temptresses were prepared to sell their souls for a bejewelled life of material luxury. Fifty-year age gap? No problem. Language barrier? Even better. It wasn't a stretch to imagine Marcus was open to temptation. Her daughter deserved better.

'Excuse me,' said Barbara, cutting off the secretary's phone conversation mid-sentence. 'Where is Marcus Staples?'

The secretary replied that she knew neither where he was, nor when he might be back.

'Tell him that I want to see him this afternoon, 2 p.m. sharp at Le Roccabella,' said Barbara.

•

BARBARA FINISHED HER VIDEO CALL DISCUSSING HER forthcoming keynote speech at Davos on energy transition. She checked her inbox to find a grovelling email from Marcus. He'd attached an investment proposal ready for their 2 p.m. meeting.

She called her private banker and trusted confidant, Damian Buhle, available for her 24/7. Discretion and charm in a Brioni suit, Ghanian-born Damian was the consummate private banker with a roster of legitimately wealthy clients that were hard to come by in *Moscow-sur-Mer*. His bursary-funded Gordonstoun education had helped to smooth the path from Mampong to Monte Carlo via Mile End. He answered after the second ring.

'Damian, can you come over? I need a second opinion on Marcus' investment proposal before he turns up. He wants me to dig him out of the *WeFork* mess. What's new!'

Fifteen minutes later, Damian arrived at Barbara's flat.

'So, what have you heard?' said Barbara.

'Apparently Marcus has been to see every bank in Monaco this week trying to scrape together a rescue package,' said Damian, opening a bottle of Badoit water for each of them. 'Of course, he hasn't had any luck.'

'It doesn't make sense,' said Barbara. 'People flock to eat his overpriced burgers so there must be plenty of cash going into the business.'

'Yes, but he wouldn't be the first boss to treat his company like a personal piggy bank,' said Damian. 'I mean, he's always in the bank withdrawing tens of thousands in cash.'

'That explains the unpaid salaries, I suppose,' demurred Barbara. 'Could it just be incompetence?'

'It's a plausible theory,' concurred Damian.

Marcus knocked on the study door. He looked awful. His billowing white shirt was undone to the fourth button, and he was swaying. Though unshaven, he had applied the usual indecent amount of gel to his slicked-back hair. From ten feet away, Barbara could smell the alcohol.

'Buhle,' Marcus said curtly.

'Sit down,' said Barbara from behind her desk, in front of the bookcase showcasing family photos.

Debauchery isn't calorie lite, she thought, watching his paunch slide into a soft-leather tub chair. Had he blown the cash on the usual Monaco combination of gambling, girls, and cocaine?

She stood up to retrieve a solitary piece of paper from the printer. *WeFork*: *elevating fast food to a higher and a healthier level of consciousness.* A few colourful charts and half-a-dozen bullet points. Not worth the paper it was written on.

'Are you still banging that Swedish bird with the great rack?' Marcus asked Damian.

Damian ignored Marcus' question, while Barbara slowly ripped the piece of paper to shreds.

'Your business proposal, Marcus, is a pile of crap,' she said, throwing the remnants into the wastepaper basket. 'No financial projections, no company valuation, not even how much you're looking to raise. Never mind an explanation as to why there's a black hole in the first place.'

Marcus rambled on about the cost of beef, labour shortages, and climate change. Barbara held up her hand.

'All desperate corporate guff,' she said. 'I'm offended you think I'd be hoodwinked so easily. How much?'

Marcus paused.

'€100 million.'

'Jesus Christ!' said Barbara.

'Chicken feed to you,' said Marcus. 'You're worth ten times that.'

'There's absolutely no way I'd stump up that kind of money when you're spouting meaningless drivel. Show me your books, then we can talk.'

'Oh, come on, Barbara,' said Marcus. 'Don't be so sanctimonious. Not everyone was born with the whole bloody silver cutlery set in their mouth.'

'I'm not going to dignify that comment with a response.'

'You owe me,' said Marcus. 'I saved your life in Limone.'

Barbara winced as she remembered that weekend at the fashionable, Italian ski resort where fur-coat-wearing Monaco residents kept their wintertime second homes. Having returned from Asia that afternoon, she decided to visit her chalet on a last-minute whim. At just 85km from Monaco, it wouldn't be a long drive. But it was after midnight by the time she arrived. She went downstairs for a nightcap. She lit a cigarette. The jet lag and the mountain air made her drowsy. She awoke to Marcus' voice. Luckily, he'd stubbed out the cigarette before the sofa, and perhaps even the whole wooden chalet, could catch fire.

'You're clutching at straws,' she said. 'I'd just nodded off for a second.'

'Passed out cold after a carafe of limoncello, more like,' said Marcus.

'No remote possibility of funds,' said Barbara. 'The answer is no.'

•

AFTER MARCUS HAD BEEN DISPATCHED, DAMIAN LET OUT A quiet whistle.

'Well, he's obviously hiding something,' said Damian. 'I'd be very concerned about the veracity of any numbers he hands over.'

'Quite. I think we need to do some discrete digging into my dear son-in-law's activities.'

'Shall I get in touch with Sournois?' Damian asked.

Barbara nodded.

Pierre Sournois had been the Monaco chief of police until he resigned abruptly the previous year. No-one knew why, though rumours swirled that he got too cosy with a cohort of unsavoury Russian mafia dons. He still knew everything that was going on, and what he didn't know, he could soon find out.

Damian showed himself out, and Barbara reclined in her chair. Her mobile phone buzzed. *Marcus said your meeting went well. Thank you! Big hugs, Soph xxx.* Lying to her daughter. What a cad!

5

Abigail

ABIGAIL DROVE HER FIAT UNO TO THE HÔTEL DE PARIS. THE doorman opened the car door and took her keys.

'*Bonjour, Madame Hackett*,' he said cheerily, waving Abigail up the steps and through the revolving door. Her recent *Behind the Scenes* feature on Hôtel de Paris staff had defrosted the famous *froideur* of the doormen, whose smile was reserved normally for celebrities and VIPs. There was a new swagger in her stride as she strolled through the glass-ceilinged atrium with its 28 onyx columns.

Abigail wondered why Polina had insisted on meeting at the hotel's American Bar. Since arriving in Monaco, Abigail had been there a couple of evenings to drink champagne to live jazz piano. It had an alluring 1920s vibe if only you could ignore the clientele. That said, she had never seen it during the day. As the bright winter sun shone through the long windows, the shiny wood looked tacky; like an actor wearing stage makeup after the show was over.

She gazed from woman to woman searching for the photo fit of a beauty blogger: young, pretty, and well-manicured. That described every woman in the bar. However, most of them were sitting cozily with balding men squeezed tightly into their expensive suits. Then she noticed a woman alone at a window table. Her face was turned towards the casino. Her long blonde hair cascaded towards an impossibly slender waist. Her black, fitted suit almost skimmed her thighs; her crimson stilettos matched her nails. She turned towards the room and noticed Abigail. Her voluminous red lips opened to a smile.

'Hello,' she said. 'Are you from *Monaco Mail?* I'm Polina.'

'I'm Abigail Hackett. Nice to meet you.'

'So, tell me about your beauty blog,' continued Abigail, settling into the chair beside her.

'I start last year *Powder Puff.* I have 100,000 followers combine Instagram, Facebook…'

Polina started explaining her blog in detail. Amid the words tumbling ungrammatically out of her mouth, sentences lost their meaning. Abigail zoned out. She was at once repelled and fascinated. As she fixated upon her bee-stung lips, so obviously surgically enhanced, Abigail realised they'd met before.

She was thrown back to her first disorienting week in Monaco, in her one-bedroom Fontvieille apartment. It was one of those ubiquitous peach-coloured Monaco buildings. All marble floors and gold plugs. Her new boss Hank owned the flat. While Hank lived in the superior Seaside Plaza next door, he had bought this miniature flat for his wife to store her generous wardrobe of clothes. Since their split two years ago, the flat had remained empty. He loaned it to Abigail for free. It suited him to have a housekeeper to keep his assets safe and it didn't hurt for Abigail to feel indebted to him.

The flat had its own walk-in wardrobe so Abigail couldn't complain. After all, she had one friend who lived in a studio without even a window. Yet unlike her lucky sea-facing neighbour on the other side of the building, Abigail's flat looked straight into the apartment block across the road. While her neighbour gazed upon the superyachts in Cap d'Ail port, Abigail could view her hirsute neighbour plucking his nasal hairs from her balcony. Every building in Monaco had this same dichotomy of haves and have-nots.

Her shipment of boxes arrived that morning. As she unpacked slowly, she heard the whirr of a helicopter. With Monaco's helipad several doors down the street, this wasn't a surprising sound. Yet the whirr grew louder and louder, so Abigail looked out of her balcony. A helicopter carrying a palm tree hovered over her apartment block. Gazing up from her balcony, Abigail spotted the glamorous tenant from the penthouse apartment above:

'What you think? Only way to get palm tree onto terrace,' shouted the tenant.

What hit Abigail was the presumption, as solid as her neighbour's gold Rolex watch, that every rooftop terrace must have a palm tree. Abigail remembered how pretty she looked: apparently makeup-free and wearing a pair of flowing, silk pyjamas.

'What you think?'

The question sprang Abigail back to the American Bar.

'Oh, err, impressive social media stats. I think it would be good to join forces. We could set up links from our beauty pages to your beauty blog and vice versa.'

'Vice?'

'I mean we put links to each other's sites to get more visitors.'

Abigail was about to round up the meeting and get back to the office, when she found herself asking:

'So, what brought you here to Monaco in the first place? You could have been married to some handsome Belarusian with a couple of kids in tow by now.'

'I no want kids in Gomel. Too close Chernobyl. Too many sick babies.'

Perhaps it was the frankness of Abigail's question that prompted such a frank answer from Polina. Perhaps it was Abigail's uncanny ability to draw surprising confidences from strangers. Whatever the reason, Polina's admission drew Abigail in beyond the brazen red lipstick.

It was an hour later that Abigail came blinking into the sunlight from the Hôtel de Paris. She was running late for her *Principality Pooches'* photoshoot with Lucinda, Countess de Mortcerf.

As she waited for the concierge to bring her Fiat, she gazed upon the vista of Ferraris and Lamborghinis parked up in front of the neighbouring Casino de Monte Carlo. The Hôtel de Paris reserved these parking spaces for the most expensive cars. Her Fiat and other cars that didn't make the aesthetic cut were swept out of sight into a nearby car park.

She put her foot down as she drove up the boulevard Princesse Charlotte towards the Millefiori apartment block that loomed unattractively above the surrounding smaller buildings. It seemed an unlikely abode for a countess. Abigail reflected that Monaco must be the only place in the world where multi-millionaires chose to live in gilded, concrete cages. All the same, this countess lived on the 35th floor. The higher the floor, the bigger the wallet.

A beautiful, willowy woman with a distracted look opened the flat door.

'Hello, hello, Abigail,' said Lucinda in a charmingly girlish tone, then noting Abigail's puzzled glance: 'You expected the housekeeper, no doubt. She's off sick. Come and meet Peanut.'

Abigail was unfazed by dog owner eccentricities in Monaco. She had seen dogs with their own velvet dog palaces, diamante collars and designer jackets. Yet she smiled when she came into the living room to see the long, copper-haired dachshund lying on an oatmeal cushion in a leather, Chesterfield dog bed, looking nonchalantly at a bowl of treats. He looked like the Jamie Dornan of the dog world.

'When I die, I'd like to be reincarnated as your dog,' joked Abigail.

'Ha, yes. I like to spoil him. I feed him wheat-free dental oaties shipped from England. They're made with parsley and mint to avoid bad breath. Nothing worse than dog breath. By the way, do call me Lu,' Lucinda said, picking up a cigarette.

She lay back against the sofa cushions as Abigail turned on the tape recorder. Lucinda smoked and chattered about her posh English childhood, her teenage years at a British girls' boarding school that led to her late teens as a runway model for Alexander Lauren; dabbling in watercolours, hanging out with Prince Alfred of Liechtenstein and the hunting-shooting-fishing crowd, her aristocratic Belgian husband, Leo's fondness for cooking, and most of all her beloved dachshund. Abigail jotted down the occasional note. When she spoke of her husband, Lucinda became agitated – Abigail wondered if her cheeriness masked a troubled soul. Was Lucinda in her 30s or 40s? Her skin bore the faintest of lines. There was more than a touch of Norma Desmond in *Sunset Boulevard* about her conversation peppered with past modelling glories: name dropping fashion designers and long-forgotten shoots.

Abigail took in the living room with its wall-to-wall antiques and portrait paintings in gilded frames. The dining area was screened off with a room divider covered in Chinoiserie wallpaper. Behind Lucinda was a walnut commode scattered with family photos shot against the backdrop of a large country pile. There was one close-up of an older, though rakishly attractive man in hunting gear with a gun. Too old to be Lucinda's husband, her father no doubt. A modernistic painting above the commode looked oddly out of place among the family heirlooms. It was of a naked woman with lustrous blonde curls, a long neck, and weird blank eyes. It was at once beautiful and ugly.

'It's a Rodigliani,' said Lucinda. 'Leo bought it. He's always had a thing for nudes.'

'Rodigliani seems to be quite the thing in Monte Carlo. Funnily enough, my last meeting was with a lady whose boyfriend has just sold a Rodigliani,' said Abigail.

'It's called *Nude Blonde*.'

'Interesting,' said Abigail. 'It would be a good background for the photoshoot. Perhaps we could put Peanut on your knee here on the sofa in front?'

•

BACK IN THE CAR, ABIGAIL SPED AROUND THE FAMOUS Formula One hairpin bend beside the Fairmont Hotel on her way down to the beachside avenue Princesse Grace.

At the far end lay the illustrious Roccabella where billionaires, beach babes and other assorted B-words lived. From its nondescript mud-coloured façade, it was hard to work out what all the fuss was about. Yet it was a building that worked better from the inside. With its unimpeded view of the Mediterranean Sea, it was also one of the few buildings along the stretch not to be affected by the construction work on the new manmade island, Portier Cove.

Roccabella was also home to the Scottish magnate, Barbara Esson: her last *Principality Pooches* interviewee of the day. As Abigail parked her car, she reflected that she was always rushing around. If she had been born with a face, limbs and family tree like Lucinda, she could have spent her days idling around looking sublime.

Having been let in by the housekeeper, Abigail waited in the living room for Barbara to finish a business call in her glassed-in home office. The housekeeper brought her a tray of Gyokuro green tea in a purple-clay teapot with an intricate bamboo leaf design. Abigail sipped tea as she admired the view, and the Westie sitting composedly on his green dog cushion with a tartan jacket on.

Finally, the glass door to the office opened and in came Barbara, trim and imperious in a burgundy tailored suit. On her way to shake hands with Abigail, she stopped to give her Westie an indulgent pat, then turned towards Abigail with a steely smile that didn't reach her grey eyes.

'So, you've met the scamp. He's called Laird.'

The two women shook hands, and Abigail introduced herself and *Monaco Mail* before turning on her tape recorder. Barbara expanded upon her eclectic business empire that stretched from oil to fishing and whisky. In a slightly bored manner, she touched upon corporate diversity as a woman in the oil industry. Abigail sensed her reticence and pushed her upon it.

'I cannot be criticised without someone citing sexism,' she mused. 'The corporate world focuses on ticking boxes when it should focus simply on talent.'

Barbara turned to pat Laird again.

'Is that your family tartan?' asked Abigail, motioning towards Laird's coat.

'It's from the Henderson clan in Shetland where my paternal grandfather was born. I grew up in a granite pile in Aberdeen myself.'

Barbara's eyes softened momentarily, before she continued primly: 'So, shall we get on with this photoshoot?'

As Abigail guided Barbara through the shoot, they chatted about her Business and French degree.

'Well, you've put both your degree subjects to good use,' said Abigail. 'I haven't used my Classics degree much.'

'Interesting. My mother studied Classics. Where did you go?'

'Manchester.'

'Bit of an oxymoron with Monaco,' said Barbara.

'Funnily enough, Manchester is more my vibe than Monaco. Even though I don't miss the weather,' said Abigail. 'Anyway, how do you fill your weekends?'

'I like to escape to my chalet in Limone. Not so much for skiing. More for the mountain air and the après-ski food.'

'Fondue washed down with some Limoncello?' said Abigail.

'Actually, my favourite is pasta with truffles. Mountain food isn't for skinny bitches,' said Barbara.

Abigail finished up with a shot of Barbara holding Laird on the balcony with the seascape below.

'All done in under half an hour. I think that's a record,' said Abigail, draining the last dregs of her tea. 'Thanks for the cuppa. This teapot is beautiful.'

'It's a Zisha teapot made by master potter Zhou Guizhen. I tend to drink *caffè stretto* myself.'

'I know how you feel. I need daily caffeine injections. Well, I'm off now with my daughter Daisy to her friend's birthday pool party. It's part of my research into how Monte Carlo ladies spend their days,' joked Abigail, packing away her camera.

'I've enjoyed our chat,' said Barbara. 'It's refreshing to meet non-airheads in Monaco.'

•

mathematical geoboard, Abigail drove towards Saint Roman and turned left at the traffic lights up a small street. The gates drew back to number three. She could hear the ripple of laughter. She wandered through the box hedge towards the pristine white villa that used to belong to a Formula One driver. On the terrace in front of a white-marble sculpture of the supermodel Madelyn Moss, birthday girl Aurora and her friends were splashing around in a one-foot-deep pool, surrounded by their nannies.

Hank's girlfriend, Serena, came rushing up in a turquoise kaftan and salon-coiffed black locks.

'Abigail, darling!'

'That's an unusual pool,' said Abigail.

'Isn't it awesome? You can choose the pool height at the press of a button. Would you like a glass of Cristal? You'll have to open it yourself.'

As Abigail headed towards the walk-in wine cellar, Serena held out her perfectly painted nails in explanation.

'My beautician cancelled on me this morning. Instead of my usual Shellac nails, I've just had to put on my own nail polish and it's still drying. It's Orange Sienna by Dior. I know it looks dreadful enough as it is, but I don't want to ruin it any further.'

Abigail decanted the ice into the bucket as Serena continued.

'You must stay for dinner. Daisy can have a sleepover with Aurora. I'm having some guests over so you really must stay.'

'I'm not sure this trouser suit will be up to one of your parties.'

'No worries,' said Serena. 'You can borrow one of my dresses.'

By 7 p.m., Aurora's guests had all left except Daisy who

was cuddled up on the sofa with Aurora munching on the last remnants of the Disneyland castle cake and watching TV. Out on the terrace, Serena's efficient housekeeper had commandeered a couple of the catering staff to help her ready the terrace for the evening party. The pool had disappeared at the press of a button and a long table appeared in its place. Next came sapphire-blue tableware, candelabra and knife rests by Monaco's best-known interior designer, Stella Montblanc. Together with her revered yacht-designer partner, Ethan Aspen, they were one of Monaco's power couples.

In Serena's bedroom, Abigail was trussed up awkwardly in a low-cut sequined mini dress and stilettos with Serena now doing the finishing touches to Abigail's hair and makeup.

'Gosh, isn't this fun? If I hadn't gone into modelling, I often think I'd have become a professional makeup artist. Hank says I can do the makeup when you're doing the photoshoot for your next celebrity interview. You should really ditch your glasses,' said Serena as she daubed on some purple eye shadow. 'I mean you're hiding your best asset. Look!'

At that moment, the doorbell rang so Serena rushed off to greet her guests. Abigail squinted at herself in the bedroom mirror. She looked like a hooker. But she couldn't afford to offend her boss' girlfriend. After all, she had promised Hank to look after Serena while he was away on business in Texas.

She meandered through the living room, where a Rothko painting dominated the fireplace, and onto the terrace. As guests began to arrive, the terrace blossomed with the foliage of sequins, diamonds, gold silk, and ruffles. Never could it be said that anyone underdressed for a party in Monte Carlo. Among the guests, she spotted the hunting-gear man from the photo at Lucinda's flat. His Façonnable shirt had one button too many undone as he chatted to a slim, silver-haired guy and two women wearing bodycon dresses designed to show off their boob jobs to the max. Abigail recognised one of the women as the evil chipmunk, Beth, from Serena's birthday party.

'Oh my God! It can't be…Abigail?'

Abigail turned to see Barbara with a young couple in tow. The woman looked like a younger, timider version of Barbara. Her plump companion, with slicked-back hair, shoved his hand forward to greet Abigail.

'Hi, I'm Marcus,' he said.

'Nice to meet you. I'm Serena's personal Barbie styling doll,' said Abigail, deadpan. 'Tonight, she's styled me as a Christmas-tree fairy.'

'How funny!' Marcus said, clicking his fingers at a waiter, who rushed over with a tray of champagne.

'I'm guessing you must be Barbara's daughter?' said Abigail, turning away from Marcus. 'I'm Abigail.'

'Where are my manners?' said Barbara. 'This is my daughter, Sophie and that's… well, her husband needs no introduction.'

'Let's have a toast — to love!' Marcus said, leering towards Abigail. 'What is love? It is the light of life. And marriage? It's the electricity bill.'

Sophie laughed nervously as Marcus continued.

'Why is masturbation like procrastination? It's all good until you realise that you're screwing yourself.'

Abigail and Barbara stalked off towards the house.

'I need a whisky,' said Barbara. 'If I hear one more smug, lecherous joke come out of that paid-for mouth, I might just punch out those perfect dental implants. Why are men in Monaco such tossers?'

'Quite literally in Marcus' case,' said Abigail.

'Gosh, don't print that, will you?' said Barbara,

'Don't worry, Barbara,' said Abigail. '*Monaco Mail* doesn't have a gossip column.'

Barbara strode into the wine cellar and came out empty-handed.

'Is there anything in this kitchen except champagne?'

Abigail offered to go to her car to retrieve the bottle of simgle malt that she had been given at last week's Monte Carlo Whisky Society event. Just then, Serena walked in.

'Abigail,' she cried. 'I've been looking for you. We're all sitting down for dinner. Come with me.'

Abigail followed dutifully to her seat beside one of the bodycon women she'd spotted earlier. She introduced herself as 'Victoria, but call me Tori'. As Abigail fought open a lobster, Victoria gushed about her glamorous life, at ease with her frumpy, fellow Brit.

As the evening and the champagne wore on, Victoria divulged her life story. It was a rags-to-riches fairy tale with a Monaco twist where Cinderella marries her sugar daddy. In Victoria's case, it had taken her no less than three husbands (and UK divorces) to amass her nine-figure fortune.

'Third time lucky,' noted Abigail. 'That's obviously where I've been going wrong. I've never even married once. So how did your third husband make his money?'

'Toilet roll,' said Victoria, glancing mischievously at Abigail as she cocked a brassy peroxide lock to one side.

Another bottle of champagne drew more tales of parties with Hollywood A-listers at her villa in Roquebrune-Cap-Martin, weekends aboard her yacht in St Barts, and her recent penchant for collecting art.

'Who do you collect?'

She leant over to whisper in Abigail's ear.

'Well, I just bought a Rodigliani for €16 million last month. Your boss Hank brokered the deal for me. He's hot, don't you think?'

'Which Rodigliani?'

'It's called *Nude Blonde*.'

Abigail choked.

'You alright?'

'Nothing to worry about — just choking on some lobster,' said Abigail regaining composure and thinking rapidly on her feet. 'I think we need some more champagne.'

'My kind of bab,' said Victoria, filling both their glasses.

Desserts and coffee arrived. The man in the Façonnable shirt sidled up to Victoria.

'Tori, you need to save me. I can't stand one more moment talking to that boring old bat that Serena sat me next to. Beth is looking for you too.'

The man noticed Abigail and smiled alluringly. Abigail greeted his gaze: 'Hi, I'm Abigail. I met your daughter Lucinda this afternoon.'

The man frowned as Victoria interjected: 'No, this is Lucinda's husband, Leo.'

Abigail escaped to her car to fetch the bottle of whisky and to change back into her trouser suit. She found Barbara standing at the edge of the terrace. Each with a glass of whisky in hand, Abigail and Barbara watched in companionable silence as the catering team dismantled the dining table. At the press of another button, the pool reappeared except at a two-metre depth this time. Suddenly Victoria came out of the house wearing a pale-pink negligée that barely covered her curves. Everyone watched as she promptly threw the negligée to the ground and jumped naked into the pool. Abigail watched Leo's face.

6

Polina

WITH A WARM FEELING OF ANTICIPATION, POLINA PREPARED to unveil the three Dior packages sitting on her dressing table. She started with the largest. Lifting the pleated tissue off the top, she unwrapped the champagne-coloured dress with its strapless organza and black body form stripes layered over silk. She felt the familiar thrill that a new outfit always gave her. Next from the dimpled white packages came black shoes and a miniature clutch bag. She compared the Paris Fashion Week runway photo on her phone to the items on her bed.

If designer clothes were a drug, she was an addict. Every purchase of high-end fashion drew her further from her humble beginnings. The more expensive the purchase, the greater her sense of security. She would never have to go back.

The ringing of the doorbell stopped Polina in her reverie. Precisely on time, her dream-team stylist duo had arrived. She opened the door to Jim, the very camp and very popular makeup artist: all smiles and frozen forehead. He was accompanied by Ezra, *coiffeur artistique* and specialist in the signature hairstyle that Monaco women requested — long, wavy, soft, and sexy. For the next two hours, they wove their magic, prolonging Polina's anticipation of the evening ahead.

'This calls for a reveal moment,' said Jim, brushing a final flick of powder over her made-up face.

'Yes! We'll have another glass of bubbly, while you dress,' said Ezra.

The finished result did not disappoint. Entering the room in her outfit, offset by the artful makeup and hair, brought 'oohs' and 'aahs' from Jim and Ezra along with complimentary comparisons to the Dior runway photo.

'We need selfies, darlings. Me first, pleeeze. Oh gorgeous, that's going straight to my social media. Come on, Ezra, your turn now,' said Jim.

'Remember to tag me,' Polina said, giving them generous tips commensurate with their level of enthusiasm, and their potential to help her. An opportunity to gain access to their social media followers shouldn't go to waste.

'Darling, your driver awaits,' said Jim, as he and Ezra took an arm each and escorted Polina downstairs to Dimitri's waiting chauffeur car.

The car crossed through the tunnel and left at the Port to ascend the avenue d'Ostende towards Dimitri's flat. With its somewhat misleading name, the Monte Carlo Palace apartment block he lived in was a cut above the council-flat chic that proliferated on this side of the Old Town. Polina rang the doorbell, expecting to see Dimitri on the other side. Instead, a worried-looking housekeeper opened the door.

'He's not back yet, sorry,' she said, opening the door fully and standing aside as Polina entered. 'You look very nice, all dressed up.'

'Where is he?' Polina barked as the two of them stood inside the polished marble entrance.

Before she could answer, the door opened again and Dimitri came rushing in. Looking relieved, the maid made a hasty departure.

'Oh good, I made it on time,' said Dimitri. 'I was at another function.'

Noting Polina's highly unimpressed look, he changed tack.

'*Moya dorogoy*,' he said. 'You look breathtaking. You chose the dress very well.'

The Russian endearment, *Moya dorogoy*, translated as both my dearest and expensive. Polina was never sure which translation Dimitri meant. Not that it mattered much. The important factor was the connection that their shared mother tongue brought. She put her annoyance behind her and focussed on the task at hand with a winning smile.

'Thank you, *moyo zolotse* (my gold),' replied Polina.

On the terrace, a table for two was set. The casino view was framed by a sea of flickering candles and fairy-light-lit trees. Perhaps the evening wasn't lost after all.

'Champagne?' he asked, lifting a bottle of vintage Dom Pérignon from the silver bucket.

'Yes, please,' said Polina.

'Here's to us,' Dimitri said, clinking his glass against hers. 'We will dine here tonight. I would like to talk with you about our future together.'

•

POLINA WOKE TO LOUD SNORING. DIMITRI LAY BESIDE HER. Memories of the night before drifted through her mind. She felt content. In an effort not to wake him, Polina raised herself silently on one elbow and reached for the velvet-covered box on the bedside table. Opening it gently, she admired the diamond engagement ring. Six carats. She could hardly believe her good fortune. The ring surpassed her expectations. Yet it was Dimitris' advance wedding gift that dazzled her. She looked at the number on the cheque again. €1 million. She relived the moment when he handed her the cheque.

'Polina,' he said. 'Now that we're engaged, I need to know that you are fully mine and fully committed to me. I hope you see this gift as my guarantee of our future together.'

'Or as a ball and chain,' thought Polina. This nagging thought was pushed aside as she read the amount on the cheque. For a brief moment, she felt suspended in time and space.

'The date is blank, because this cheque is yours to cash the day after we marry,' said Dimitri. 'I'll have my secretary make all the wedding arrangements this week. Then we'll know the exact date to go on the cheque.'

•

POLINA ENTERED THE HÔTEL HERMITAGE AND FOLLOWED the signs to the dog event in the Salon Excelsior. She knew she'd arrived at the right place when a dyed-pink poodle pranced past her, with a pearl choker around its neck and a piece of ham dangling from its mouth. Hot on its heels puffed a woman holding a matching pearl-studded lead.

'Princess, Princess, come here you naughty girl!'

Princess raced around the corner for privacy to gulp down her contraband before slinking back slowly with a guilty look.

A bemused Abigail Hackett stood at the entrance sipping champagne, while greeting guests and their canine companions.

'Hello, welcome to the madhouse,' Abigail said as she picked up the guest list in a distracted way.

Following her gaze, Polina noticed the errant Princess licking a ham sandwich clutched tightly in the hand of a small child. Abigail burst into giggles. Polina responded with an obligatory smile as she wondered at the British sense of humour.

'Hello Abigail,' said Polina. 'Good to meet you for blog meeting yesterday. I am excited for you to help me.'

Polina placed her handbag on the table and positioned her diamond clad hand atop it. Abigail noted the massive rock without comment.

'I'm sure it will be a very interesting experience for us both,' said Abigail.

'I come as guest of Leyla,' said Polina. 'She is over there.'

'Ah, the Tricks and Treats corner,' said Abigail, 'Rather short on the tricks, but very long on the treats.'

Not having a clue what she meant, Polina flashed her best smile in reply. It was a tactic that Polina favoured with complicated Brits and over-excited Americans.

'Leyla is chatting to Lucinda,' said Abigail. 'Do meet her, she's a lovely lady.'

'You look very happy,' said Leyla in greeting.

Polina wanted to tell her friend about the engagement, but she felt that Leyla deserved a private announcement so she air-kissed her on both cheeks.

'Yes, is good day,' said Polina. 'I am happy to come to dog show.'

'Polina, this is Lucinda and her dog is Peanut,' said Leyla. 'He is good colour, but too long for Louis Vuitton bag.'

'Hello Polina,' said Lucinda, before turning back to Leyla: 'Getting a dog will be the best decision of your life second only to…'

Lucinda stiffened mid-sentence as she looked toward the entrance.

'Oh my God, what is Leo doing here?'

'Who is Leo?' Polina asked.

'My husband,' said Lucinda.

Leo strode towards them.

'So this is where you are,' he said.

'Is there a problem?' Lucinda replied.

'I think you and I need to talk privately,' he said. 'Or, if you like, we can discuss our marital woes in front of these friends of yours.'

Leo curled his lip at Polina and Leyla. Taking his arm and mouthing 'sorry' over her shoulder, Lucinda directed Leo towards a quiet corner. There they continued their heated discussion in strained whispers that broke into full voice at frequent intervals. Polina shrugged her shoulders. She was perturbed neither by the marital spat, nor by the insinuation that she might be less than august company for Leo's wife. Nothing could disrupt her happiness.

'Leyla, I have exciting news,' said Polina, thrusting her dazzling six carats in front of Leyla's nose.

'He asked me last night,' continued Polina. 'I said "yes" of course, and you cannot believe what else — he gives me a cheque for €1 million to spend on honeymoon.'

Polina watched a struggle of conflicting emotions play over Leyla's face. A beaming smile won the day as Leyla said: 'That is wonderful, my good friend. You are luckiest girl in the world.'

Lucinda broke the moment by re-joining them with a faintly tear-stained face. She held Peanut close for hugs as she balanced her champagne glass in her free hand.

'Sorry about that,' said Lucinda. 'Leo and I were having a conversation.'

'No dogs here are match for Louis Vuitton bag so I go to Doggy Tinder corner,' said Leyla as she peeled off.

'Let's go look at the dog outfits,' Lucinda said. 'There's a section called Pawsome Outfits. Isn't that the cutest name?'

Polina shrugged agreement at Lucinda's faux-cheeriness. At least it involved designer clothing, even if the canine variety.

'Mummy, look. This is perfect for Laird. We must get it for our next Burns supper.'

Polina and Lucinda turned toward the voice.

'Oh, it's Barbara and Sophie,' Lucinda said, recognising the pair.

Polina slowed her pace a few steps behind Lucinda. She wasn't in a hurry to talk to her boss's wife and mother-in-law. She watched Barbara's animated daughter by the racks of designer togs for dogs, holding a tartan kilt reimagined for canine wear against their Westie.

'Hi Sophie!' cried Lucinda. 'You look wonderful as always. I love your Gianfranco Ferrari bag: Gianfranco gifted me one when I modelled for him in Milan.'

Lucinda embraced Sophie and then reached down to give their dog a loving pat. Polina heard Lucinda's voice change to a mellifluous doggy tone: 'Laird, who's a beautiful boy? Oh yes, you're my beautiful boy. Oh yes, you are.'

'Lucinda darling,' Sophie said as she fastened the kilt over Laird. 'We passed Leo with a face like thunder when we came in. He didn't even bother with a hello. Are you alright?'

'It's a long story, let's forget about him for now,' said Lucinda, back to her grown-up voice.

Glancing across the room, Polina noticed Leyla quietly departing the function.

'Hi Polina, nice to see you,' said Sophie.

The young woman smiled warmly as she departed to buy the kilt, leaving her with Lucinda and Barbara.

Polina noticed that Barbara was studiously avoiding eye contact. She had to admit that she felt a touch of admiration for the authority Barbara commanded. But like most powerful women she met — especially those past their physical prime

— she sensed that Barbara judged her as being too sexy and irritatingly attractive, automatically equating that to stupid and irrelevant.

Fortunately, Abigail joined the group, commandeering the champagne-bearing waiter on her way. 'Come on, girls, drinks all round!'

The waiter passed fresh glasses to each of the women.

'Well, Lucinda, Barbara, Polina: have you all met?' asked Abigail.

'We have indeed,' Barbara said as she turned to acknowledge Polina with a look of mischievous delight playing on her face.

'You work at my son-in-law's office, don't you?'

'Yes, I do,' Polina replied in a strong voice, doing her best to show Barbara that she was not intimidated by her.

'Well, I'm sure you and I will have a lot to talk about.'

'Oh, let's have a toast,' Lucinda said. 'Here's to dogs instead of men!'

'Cheers to that,' said Abigail, as they all clinked glasses and laughed.

•

IN THE BACK OF ROD'S CHAUFFEURED CAR, POLINA considered the WhatsApp messages from Leyla. Polina had ignored Leyla's first message with its apology for abandoning her at the dog event. She wasn't buying Leyla's excuse about an emergency plumbing leak. Now Leyla tried another tactic.

I take you for dinner. Let's go to Sass tonight, have drinks and dance.

Polina decided this message was Leyla's way of apologising, so she replied.

Yes okay. 10 p.m.? You make Sass booking and pick me up.

Leyla sent a thumbs up and kiss emoji. Polina closed the app.

Polina arrived at Rod's secret apartment. When he couldn't arrange out-of-town jaunts, he entertained her at this flat in the Park Palace, a prestigious *Carré d'Or* (Golden Square) building with discreet entrances. Today they were meeting to chat. Sitting on the sofa opposite from Rod, Polina revealed her engagement. She suppressed a proud smile at Rod's long whistle when she showed her ring.

'That's a whopper!' Rod exclaimed.

'Yes, it is six carats.'

'You'll be wanting to hold on to that, my sweet.'

Rod chuckled. Polina was grateful that she and Rod could be pragmatic about their arrangement.

'I want to talk with you, Rod, because we must be very careful before my wedding in one month.' Polina explained. 'And, after marriage, we must stop.'

'Funnily enough, I was planning a similar talk,' Rod said. 'My missus is giving me some grief, so I need to curtail extra-curricular activities for a while.'

'What happened?'

'Well, I don't suppose I'm the first man in Monaco to go for a sports massage with Miriam in Beausoleil and come home with a back-crack-and-sack wax job,' said Rod. 'Miriam is quite a friendly lady with her extra services.'

He laughed uproariously. Polina wasn't enamoured by Rod's base talk, but she was inured to it.

'I even got her to give me pedicures and manicures on the next visits to move the focus,' he continued. 'But Miriam gave it away by refusing to look my wife in the eye when we passed her along boulevard des Moulins,' Rod sighed.

'I shouldn't have tried to introduce them. Bloody Miriam made me look a right dick by completely blanking me.'

'Rod, you should ignore her if you are with wife,' Polina said.

'Yes, I know, but there's a bit of history with some intimate waxologists back in Australia. It all unravelled uncomfortably when my wife caught me out both times, so I was trying to throw her off the scent by making Miriam seem more legitimate.'

Polina sighed.

'You must learn to be, how do you say, discreet, Rod,' she said with a sweet smile as she wondered how on earth his wife put up with him.

•

POLINA AND LEYLA FOLLOWED THE WAITER TO THEIR outdoor table at Sass Café. A regular footpath by day, the makeshift terrace extended the restaurant's capacity in the evening, creating a see-and-be-seen opportunity for passers-by and diners alike.

Over a shared dish of elephant-ear-style schnitzel accompanied by multiple drinks, they sorted out what Leyla termed their 'misunderstanding' and were soon back on friendly terms.

'Good evening,' said a deep male voice behind Polina.

'Sergei.' Leyla stood up to greet her boyfriend with a lingering kiss on the lips.

'How's that boss of yours, Marcus Staples?' Sergei asked Polina as he air-kissed both her cheeks.

'Boss is good, thank you,' said Polina. She felt goose pimples on her arm. Sergei unnerved her.

Taking a nearby chair, Sergei settled himself at their table and called over the waiter.

'I'd like a bottle of Rémy Martin Cognac — the Louis XIII. And bring another table. This one is too small.'

The waiter's manner turned deferential with the €30,000 cognac order.

'Also bring *eau gazeuse*. Room temperature, not cold. And small bowl of ice,' said Leyla.

'God, woman! You don't put sparkling water in expensive cognac,' said Sergei.

'I drink it how I like,' said Leyla. 'If you cannot buy bottle for me to drink how I like, I buy my own drink.'

Unperturbed, Sergei ordered a bottle of her favourite vodka and mixers.

'Polina? What would you like?'

'I take champagne,' Polina said. Sergei responded by ordering a magnum of Cristal.

It wasn't long before people started dropping by the table to talk with Sergei. A couple of brutish types stayed a while and helped demolish the excessive array of drinks. Others merely said hello in passing, wanting to be acknowledged by him, or seen to be.

Finally, Sergei settled the massive bill as he left for a late-night meeting elsewhere. The girls wandered inside to indulge their love of dancing. After snaring a prime table in the music room near the piano, they danced on the banquet seats above the crowd, lost to the music. In the crowded space, Polina paid little attention to a group of fresh-faced young men who edged closer until they finally asked if they could share the girls' table, and what would they like to drink?

'Champagne,' the girls spoke in unison as they agreed to table-share, giving each other a look that said, 'Naive tourists — as if they'd ever have a chance with us.'

Bottles of rosé, champagne, vodka and mixers arrived at the table. The men shared the drinks generously with the girls as they danced alongside. Several hours of dancing and drinking later, Polina turned to Leyla:

'I feel dizzy. I need food. We go.'

Pretending to visit the ladies' room, the girls doubled back through the main restaurant and out the front door. This was their usual ruse to avoid awkward farewells to new male friends and to avoid dealing with the inevitable invitation to go on to Jimmy'z.

Outside, they got into a taxi at the curb and gave Polina's address. As the Mercedes purred through the quiet streets, they kicked off their shoes and slouched into the seat laughing drunkenly.

Suddenly, Polina was thrown across Leyla as the taxi driver made a U-turn. The driver was talking loudly on his phone.

'This is wrong way, where do you take us?' said Leyla.

'Back to Sass. You sort it out with them.'

'No, you take us home!' Polina shouted.

'Take us home, take us home!' Leyla screamed

'You should pay your bill,' the taxi driver yelled back.

'We did pay bill, you stupid man,' Polina shouted.

'My boyfriend is rich. He pays for everything,' Leyla shrieked.

Polina whispered to Leyla: 'Men who buy drinks at our table. I think they leave without paying.'

'Not my problem, your problem,' the taxi driver said.

The girls screamed in unison: 'Stop the car! Stop the car! Stop the car!'

Suddenly the taxi driver did stop the car. But he jumped out and locked all the doors. Polina and Leyla screamed and bashed the window glass until they spotted a duty policeman talking with the taxi driver and calling for backup.

'Oh, God,' said Leyla. 'I know what happens now. They put us in jail until morning to teach us lesson.'

'What?'

'It happens to everyone. No problem, but we will need breakfast,' said Leyla, pulling up a menu on her phone. 'Here, choose what you like.'

At the station, the girls were processed. Just before they were taken to the cells, a policeman appeared with two waiters, each carrying elaborate trays of breakfast food, coffee and juice.

'Mademoiselle Leyla?' the first waiter enquired.

'*Oui*,' Leyla replied.

'Your breakfast from the Hôtel de Paris, Mademoiselle,' said the first waiter.

'*Pardon Monsieur*,' said the second waiter. 'Where may we set out breakfast for the ladies?'

Polina snapped a close-up of the breakfast tray and posted it to her Instagram page with the caption: *A person who never made a mistake, never tried anything new.*

7

Lucinda

Lucinda was not going to let yesterday's public humiliation with Leo ruin it. Everyone has their bad days. She would put on a brave face and get on with things, like Barbara would.

Leo wasn't there when she returned home late last night. Nor was he in bed when she woke this morning. He must have gone for a late dinner with Frédéric after tennis and then got up early for one of his morning walks. But he was back home in his office now.

Sitting in bed in her dressing gown, Lucinda glanced at the collection of family portraits hanging on the wall opposite. The gilded frames couldn't hide the bulging-eyed ugliness of Leo's royal ancestors. How different from the beautiful family portraits that hung on the walls of her childhood home, Russell Hall.

'At least I have one family portrait here,' she thought, glancing at her green-eyed, British grandmother.

She would ask Abigail to email her an image from yesterday's *Principality Pooches* photoshoot to join the family portraits. She smiled as she walked into the kitchen. Hearing Leo's phone bleep on the counter, she glanced at the screen. A text from Victoria:

You coming for coffee?

Why would Victoria be texting Leo? Leo spent more and more time at Casa del Caffè, while Lucinda found the group rather boring. Lucinda preferred the newer Italian cafe, A Cantina, under the Park Palace, where they served cappuccinos with almond milk and a mini-sized, homemade chocolate fondant. The owners there loved Peanut and always made sure Lucinda had a good table.

'Leo,' Lucinda shouted towards the office door. 'Victoria just texted you.'

'Oh, right. Well, I'm not going to the cafe,' Leo shouted back, coming out of the office. 'I've got tennis.'

He put his coffee mug in the dishwasher, grabbed his racket from the closet, and put his Gauloises cigarettes in his tennis jacket.

'Tennis *again*?'

Leo kissed her head and shut the door behind him.

Lucinda had the flat to herself. How peaceful. She walked through the bedroom to the terrace. She breathed in the floral scents from the neighbouring terraces. A moment later, the wind blew in clouds from the La Turbie hillside and it grew dark. A two-minute hailstorm came out of nowhere. Huge ice splinters tumbled from the sky, and people screamed in the streets as they ran for shelter. One shard narrowly missed Peanut.

'My poor darling, are you okay?' Grabbing Peanut, she

rushed inside. 'Let's go downstairs and see whether Matthieu has any parcels for us today.'

The concierge, Matthieu, liked to chat and give her compliments about Peanut. As she grabbed her keys from the hall console, she remembered the stiff lock. She dallied to arrange for a locksmith that afternoon, before taking the lift downstairs.

'*Bonjour Madame. Comment allez-vous?*' said Matthieu, as Peanut ran over to his foot and started tugging the shoelace with his teeth.

'Peanut, stop it! Sorry, Matthieu. He's still such a puppy, aren't you, my darling?' said Lucinda. 'Are there any parcels for us? I'm expecting my friend Victoria to drop off a pack of bamboo straws.'

'Victoria?'

'The tall one with blonde hair.'

'I know who you mean. She was here the other day,' he said, tying up his shoelaces. 'Tuesday it was. But she didn't leave a package. She just went straight up to your flat. Maybe she left it there?'

'Tuesday? That doesn't make any sense,' thought Lucinda. 'I was in London on Tuesday so it couldn't have been Victoria. Matthieu must be mistaken.' But it was an easy mistake to make. Over 50% of Monaco women fit that description.

'I think you mean my friend Emily: she's tall with blonde hair,' said Lucinda. 'She's always popping around without calling first.'

Lucinda looked in her phone, found a photo of Emily, and showed it to Mathieu: 'That's Emily.'

'*Non, c'est pas elle.*' Matthieu shook his head.

Lucinda scrolled to a photo of Victoria, even though she was certain it wasn't her.

'You don't mean her, do you?'

'Yes, that's her.'

Why would Victoria visit her flat while she was away? Infidelity flitted through her mind. No. Victoria didn't even like Leo. Victoria wasn't Leo's type either. He hated peroxide blondes and breast implants. 'You can feel fake boobs right away,' he liked to complain. 'They feel like foreign objects sliding beneath the skin.' Leo liked Lucinda's long figure and her pert breasts, which had never breastfed, and her bottom, even if he'd not seen them for a while. Victoria must have been visiting someone else; no doubt her Russian friend who lived on the 36th floor, and who had paid a fortune to have the Venetian lagoon painted on their leather-lined walls.

At that moment, she spotted Peanut in the lift. The doors closed before she could reach them. The lift went up to the 12th floor and stopped. She slammed the button several times.

'Don't worry,' said Matthieu. 'I see Peanut on the camera being stroked by two women. He's on his way down in the lift now.'

Two attractive women carried Peanut out the lift. Both young and dirty blonde. She had not seen them before. Dressed in head-to-toe Gucci, teetering on sky-high stiletto heels, and speaking some Slavic language, they fussed over Peanut. As she grabbed Peanut into her arms, she could smell a strong musky perfume on him.

•

THE HAILSTORM HAD SUBSIDED BY THE TIME LUCINDA WENT out for her doctor's appointment. Although her hair still looked thick, she'd been losing hair lately. It was stress, no doubt. Emily had recommended Dr Hammami's surgery in the French border town of Beausoleil. Despite the lack of a formal national boundary, there was a clear delineation in aesthetic terms from Monaco's toy-town immaculate streets to France's pavements strewn with litter.

She went upstairs to a dark waiting room crowded with patients. Every seat was taken so she hovered by the doorway. Eventually a receptionist called her name. She walked towards the lobby where an olive-skinned man with glossy black hair greeted her.

'Hello, I'm Dr Hammami,' he said. 'Come this way.'

Before she could enter the treatment room, Dr Hammami said:

'Oh, fuck! There's a woman in there in her underwear. I forgot all about her. She's been there for ages. Wait outside while I sort her out.' And then he slammed the door in her face.

Five minutes later, Dr Hammami ushered Lucinda back into the room. Without taking notes, he asked about her medical history.

'What's the problem today?' he said.

Lucinda described her worries about her recent hair loss. He started writing out a prescription before she'd even finished. Then, without a word, Dr Hammami went up behind her and started running his fingers through her hair. It felt strangely intimate, almost flirtatious. All of a sudden, he grabbed two large handfuls of her hair and pulled hard.

'Yes, it falls,' he said, looking at his hands. He went back to his prescription in silence. The door burst open. A teenage boy ran into the room with neither a knock nor an apology.

'I need some money,' the boy said.

While Lucinda looked on, the boy chatted to Dr Hammami for a few minutes about his plans to go out with his friends. Eventually Dr Hammami handed over some euros and the boy left.

'Kids,' said Dr Hammami, shrugging, before finishing his prescription and handing it over. 'It's for your hair.'

'What is it?' Lucinda said.

'It's for your hair,' he said.

'I know, but what is it?' Lucinda insisted.

'It's for your hair,' he yelled.

After escaping from Dr Hammami's surgery, Lucinda ambled through the open-air fruit and vegetable market when she saw Polina coming up the avenue Saint-Charles staircase.

'Hello, Lucinda,' said Polina.

'Oh! Hi, Polina. Sorry, I was a bit distracted. I didn't notice you.'

'Am I in Beausoleil?' said Polina.

'Almost. Once you cross the street behind me, you will be,' Lucinda said.

'I go to Doctor Hammami and I must cross border.'

Lucinda laughed. 'I'm sorry to laugh, Polina. I don't think of it as a border. What a coincidence though! I've just seen him. It was a rather strange experience.'

'What happens?'

Lucinda recounted her hair-raising experience with Doctor Hammami. Polina looked shocked.

'Not sure I go to Doctor Hammami now,' Polina said.

'You should be fine, as long as you Google his prescriptions before you take them,' Lucinda said.

'I only want sleeping tablets,' said Polina. 'And I know the ones I want.'

'Then he's the perfect choice,' Lucinda said. 'Writing prescriptions is his forte.'

She walked to her twice-weekly hair blow-dry on boulevard des Moulins. It had taken a long time for her to find an acceptable hairdresser in Monaco. They were a decade behind the latest products and styles available in New York and London. One time, her Monaco hairdresser applied henna to dye her roots 'more naturally'. Luckily, she mentioned the henna before getting her highlights at London's Richard Ward salon, where they warned her that bleaching henna-dyed hair could make her hair turn green, and even smoke. After that, she only went to Monaco hairdressers for haircuts and blow-dries, while Peanut sat on her knee.

An hour later, with her hair now bouncing beautifully, she took a meandering walk back home through the casino gardens. Everywhere in Monaco was easy to reach on foot. It was strange that so many people took their cars for journeys within a principality around the size of London's Hyde Park. She dallied with some local dog owners, as Peanut greeted their dogs by sniffing their behinds. She strolled past the designer shops in the One Monte Carlo district. Along avenue Princesse Alice, she spotted Leo, Beth and Victoria at the cafe, drinking coffee, smoking and laughing.

'Wasn't Leo at tennis? Should I join them?' she asked herself, before continuing back to Le Millefiori. 'No, they haven't spotted me. Anyway, I have to be back in time for the locksmith.'

Five minutes later, back at her flat, the doorbell rang.

'*Entrez, entrez, merci d'être venu,*' said Lucinda, ushering the locksmith in.

'Jacques Médecin,' he said. 'Call me Jacques.'

'*Enchantée,*' said Lucinda, pondering whether to reply with her first name. 'Can I get you a drink? A glass of water. Some tea, perhaps?'

'*Non, merci.*'

'Is yours a family business?' said Lucinda.

'Yes, my grandfather set it up.'

'You must have some good stories, fixing people's locks.'

He smiled conspiratorially as he sat on the floor, removing the old lock.

'Yes, but I couldn't say.'

'I won't tell anybody, I promise,' said Lucinda. 'I'm so happy you're here.'

She went to her iPod, stopped the playlist and switched to *Radio Paradise*, a radio station from California before returning. Norah Jones' *Chasing Pirates* started playing.

'Your lock is original. As old as the building,' Jacques continued. 'From the 1960s. You can break into a flat with a lock like this using just a credit card.'

'A credit card?' said Lucinda.

'That's right,' he said. 'I caught two women recently using a credit card to get into a flat with the same lock you have. They were well dressed, so no one would suspect them. They walked in as if they lived in the building.'

'Here? In Monaco?' Lucinda thought about the two young women exiting the lift. 'Strange, I haven't read anything in the *Monaco Mail* about it.'

He explained his company's policy of informing only those involved. *Monaco Mail* never reported on such news. Like suicides, which were rather common. Who needed to die a slow death from pills with alcohol, when you could fall to your immediate death from high terraces across the principality? Such incidents, like break-ins, were kept quiet. Monaco did not like bad press.

'Of course, some burglars don't even bother to pick locks. Last week, a van went to a hotel in Fontvieille, and collected several suitcases from the concierge,' continued the locksmith. 'They just stole the guests' belongings right from under their noses.'

'*Voilà*, all done,' he said, as he polished the lock. 'And here are your four sets of keys.'

'*Magnifique*, thank you so much. How much do I owe you?'

'We'll send you a bill in the post.'

'Wonderful. I can't tell you how much safer I feel.'

She put the spare sets of keys next to the front door ready for Leo. He wouldn't know about the lock change, so she decided to stay in.

Peanut followed her to the wine fridge, where she grabbed a bottle of Miraval rosé. Drinking alone was a habit she'd acquired. She never used to drink on her own before she moved to Monaco. A cigarette hung from her mouth as she fished out some ice cubes and picked up an ashtray overflowing with cigarette butts on her way to the terrace. She settled onto the cushioned bench, facing the Tête de Chien, and poured herself a glass. How life had changed since she had moved to Monaco and married Leo.

She remembered her first weekend with Leo in Monaco five years ago. Leo was living in a vast flat: one of only two buildings with a lift in the Old Town, known as *Le Rocher*. They went for a scooter ride. She felt giddy as a girl on the back of his powerful Suzuki Burgman 400, riding down avenue de la Quarantine, with the view of Port Hercules on the right. She held onto his strong body, smelling him. Even now, sex seemed to be the only way he could express his love for her. Their diminishing sex life never felt vacuous. Though it was a rare occurrence now. When they first had sex, it was non-stop. He said it was like coming home. She never felt like it was home, but she was happy at the time.

Hours passed in a blur of rosé. Her inebriation eased the pain of her predicament. It was dark. She looked up to see fireworks: a regular sight in Monaco during fine weather. She drew Peanut close to feel less alone.

8

Barbara

AWAKENED BY HER MOBILE RINGING ON THE BEDSIDE TABLE, Barbara rolled across her helipad-sized bed and answered.

'Hello, darling. You're up early.'

She flopped back into a luxurious mound of wrinkle-preventing satin pillows and listened languidly for a few moments. As Sophie began telling her about Marcus' plans for them to cruise to the Cap d'Antibes for lunch, Barbara sat bolt upright.

'What planet are the pair of you on? Burning 10,000 litres of fuel is an odd thing for a man with money problems to do. Especially now the Serious Fraud Office is breathing down his neck.'

'We made last-minute plans to meet friends at the Eden-Roc. Besides, the sea air will clear Marcus' head. I'll just have to grin and bear it with my seasickness.'

Three years earlier, Sophie had given Marcus a Mangusta Sport 104 for his 30th birthday. At 32 metres long with four cabins and a four-man crew, *Play Buoy* was a comparative tiddler compared to the colossal gin palaces that dominated the Monaco port. All the same, it was stylish and fast.

'Must be nice to have a magic money tree,' Barbara said.

After the call, Barbara lay in bed contemplating her next course of action. How could she find the truth behind Marcus' outrageous €100-million demand? She took some comfort that her daughter's significant marital assets were owned by the Esson family trust. Nevertheless, Barbara reckoned that Marcus' financial vortex meant that it wouldn't be long before the odd painting or piece of jewellery disappeared. She exhaled slowly. Perhaps it was time to turn off the taps. If she stopped their lavish monthly stipend and froze the array of credit cards, Marcus might be compelled to come clean.

Imagining *Play Buoy's* 2,600 brake horsepower engines revving up to head to Antibes, Barbara burst out of bed with a sense of purpose. Marcus' short absence from Monaco would be an ideal opportunity for some further snooping.

•

NORA HAD LAID OUT A BREAKFAST SPREAD ON THE TERRACE and, with perfect timing, placed a fresh cup of coffee on the table as Barbara sat down with her iPad. Barbara checked the oil price and scrolled through the news headlines. As she signalled to Nora for a refill, her mobile rang. It was Damian.

'Good morning. How are you?'

'Been better,' Barbara replied. 'No sign of an explanation from Marcus and now they're swanning around on the boat.'

'Can't say I'm surprised, but we may have a breakthrough. Does the name Sergei Kukushkin mean anything to you?'

'Nothing. Should it?'

Barbara tore a piece off the fresh almond croissant, while Damian recounted how the resourceful ex-police chief Sournois had uncovered a promising lead. Marcus' movements around the security-camera-infested principality were easy to establish, even more so in his Bianco-Icarus Lamborghini Huracán. While an endless stream of celeb-spotting tourists took selfies beside his parked car, Marcus would often hold court inside the Hôtel de Paris. Beyond the jovial greetings with a steady procession of people in the American Bar, security camera footage showed that he spent a considerable amount of time with one man in particular.

'I've forwarded you an email from Sournois,' Damian continued. 'Check out the photo of Kukushkin. He checked into the Hôtel de Paris last night. Apparently, he's a big spender at the casino, but he hasn't been able to get a *carte de sejour*.'

Barbara opened the email and clicked on the attachment. The grainy image showed Marcus enjoying the aroma of a torpedo-sized cigar and offering one to the man opposite.

'God, he even manages to look smug on CCTV.'

Barbara peered at the cigar recipient, a heavy-set man with a crew cut and spade-like hands.

'So, that's Kukushkin? He looks like a bouncer.'

'Yes. Sournois is finding out more from his Russian contacts. He said you have to be pretty dodgy if you can't get a residency permit in Monaco.'

Damian let his sentence trail off.

'Sophie and Marcus are social butterflies,' mused Barbara. 'But I can't imagine them being friends with a boorish, shell-suit-wearing mobster.'

Barbara peered at the other figures in the image. 'I recognise the blonde. I think I'll pay Marcus' office another visit.'

•

FINDING MARCUS' OFFICE LOCKED, BARBARA WAITED IN HER car outside for a few minutes until she saw Polina strut into the building. Five minutes later, Barbara entered Marcus' office. Polina did not look up from her desk. She was fixated on her left hand which was hovering motionless above her keyboard.

'Hello again! Olina, isn't it?' said Barbara.

Barbara liked the power play of mistaking the names of inconsequential people. Despite her white Valentino midi dress and orange Birkin bag, Barbara felt understated compared to the dolled-up secretary. Polina was squeezed into a hot pink Hervé Léger dress that left little to the imagination.

'More work-the-pole than corporate attire,' thought Barbara, noting Polina's lilac-encased front zip could open all the way down.

Barbara explained that she was considering investing in *WeFork*. Nodding towards two large filing cabinets, she asked if she could inspect some documents.

'You help Marcus?'

'Yes, of course. We're family,' Barbara replied with a disingenuous smile.

Polina retrieved a set of keys from a drawer, switching them from right to left hand so that Barbara couldn't fail to notice the gigantic diamond engagement ring on Polina's hand.

'Congratulations,' said Barbara as she rationalised that Marcus might not be sleeping with Polina after all.

'Thank you,' Polina replied, her eyes drawn to the dazzling gem. 'I say to Dimitri — nothing too big!'

With a flick of her hair, Polina turned back to her screen. Barbara rummaged through the filing cabinets. To Barbara's surprise, the drawers were empty except for a transparent bag of pills and MuscleMax protein supplements.

'There's nothing here,' said Barbara.

Polina looked up and volunteered that most of the accounts and other legal documents were held by Marcus' business partner. In all the years Barbara had known Marcus, he never alluded to any business partner. Why not?

Polina opened the cabinet under her desk and produced a bulging folder with 'Legal Stuff' scrawled across it. Barbara sifted quickly through the stack of papers. It wasn't long before she came across a contract between two signatories, namely Marcus Francis Staples and Sergei Ivanovich Kukushkin. A cursory glance through the pages showed Barbara that this was a one-sided agreement.

'Marcus,' Barbara hissed quietly. 'You bloody fool.'

Polina made no objection when Barbara said she was going to borrow the folder. Barbara thanked the dutiful secretary and added airily that there was no need to tell Marcus she had stopped by.

•

THOUGH BARBARA AND DAMIAN HAD NO SHORTAGE OF underlings to unpick *WeFork*'s byzantine structure, the delicate nature of the task meant that they pored over the documents themselves for hours in Barbara's study. A sorry picture emerged. Any half-decent accountant could have predicted *WeFork*'s financial implosion — the entity that Marcus owned at any rate.

'*WeFork* is an unholy mess!' Barbara lamented. 'This Kukushkin crook sure found a convenient dope in Marcus.'

'Yep,' Damian agreed. 'On the surface, *WeFork* is a roaring success, but the financial stresses have been growing each year. The trouble is that gullible Marcus doesn't own any of the physical property assets.'

He rotated his notepad to show Barbara a simple organisation chart he had drawn up.

'Simply put, the Russian controls the so-called *PropCo* through offshore vehicles that provide the usual veil of anonymity, and Marcus owns the *OpCo*, the operating company.'

Damian stubbed his calculator quickly and gave a short chuckle.

'It's incredible, the *OpCo* is paying extortionate rents to the *PropCo*. Why didn't Marcus query the eye-watering yields Kukushkin was earning?'

'Because he's an idiot,' Barbara noted bitterly.

'And flashy Marcus routinely withdrew massive dividends from the *OpCo* and now it's gone bust,' Damian observed.

He showed Barbara a rudimentary cash flow history. Over a few short years, liquidity at the *OpCo* drained quickly and Marcus resorted to bank loans to shore up the company finances. When lenders refused to extend any more credit, *WeFork OpCo* couldn't pay its employees and Marcus was pilloried publicly for sucking the company dry.

'It gets better,' said Damian, enjoying the corporate vivisection.

'The *OpCo* has now failed to pay rent to the *PropCo*. I can't imagine Kukushkin's happy that his cash cow is in peril or that *WeFork*'s financial black hole has caught the attention of the fraud squad.'

'So, not only has Marcus got into bed with a mobster, he's also a shockingly bad businessman,' Barbara grimaced. 'I don't know which is worse.'

She rested her elbows on the desk and rubbed her temples. Barbara had never seen anything quite like it and she worked in the murky oil industry.

'The numbers still don't add up. Where did Marcus pluck the €100-million figure from? It seems way too high.'

After sifting through legal letters, bank statements and printed out email exchanges, Damian found the answer.

'Check out this proposal. Understandably, Kukushkin wants to avoid the scrutiny of the UK authorities and needs to terminate the arrangement quickly and discreetly.'

Damian slid a piece of paper across the desk towards Barbara.

'He's demanding Marcus buy the property assets for €100 million or else,' said Damian. 'Since Kukushkin's acquisition cost was around €180 million, selling at such a massive discount screams of money laundering.'

'Quite,' said Barbara.

'It's not exactly a charitable gesture either,' said Damian. 'By my reckoning, Kukushkin has extracted over €200 million in rent over the past six years.'

'So, Marcus has nothing to sell or pledge as collateral. His house of cards is on the brink,' said Barbara, with the twitch of a smile. 'Shame.'

Damian nodded in agreement as he gathered up the paperwork.

'Obviously, Marcus hoped to inject fresh capital into the brand. But no sane investor would touch this ruinous corporate structure. Your instinct was correct. You are Marcus' last resort.'

It had just turned 6 p.m. Barbara entrusted Damian to return the damning folder to the *WeFork* office. She retired to the terrace with a revitalising gin and tonic. As a business quandary, it was quite clear cut. Marcus was incompetent, possibly to the point of criminality, and would be summarily dismissed if he were Barbara's employee. Alas, she couldn't sack Marcus as her son-in-law.

'Thank God they have yet to breed,' thought Barbara.

Her mind turned to dinner with Lucinda. Barbara had made a last-minute decision to invite Abigail. She hoped the young journo's peppiness would lighten the mood if the model-cum-aristocrat was more emotionally needy than usual. She mused how different generations fraternising with ease was a hallmark of the eclectic Monaco social merry-go-round. Barbara found mixing with younger people made her feel youthful, and she took pleasure in their rapturous enthralment with her wealth and wisdom. As long as they didn't refer to her as 'Sophie's Mum' as one younger acquaintance had recently.

•

AFTER CONSUMING UNLADYLIKE-SIZED PORTIONS OF FIERY beef rendang and buckets of red wine, the three women relocated to the sitting room in search of an ashtray and a *digestif.*

'I've given up trying to give up,' Barbara said, puffing on a cigarette. 'Thankfully, I've got great genes. My mother had a beautiful complexion. She always wore sunscreen, even in winter.'

'White flatters my face too,' she added, motioning her white shirt.

'Lucky you,' Abigail remarked. Lucinda suppressed a smile.

Barbara's wrinkle-free face came courtesy of the renowned cosmetic surgeon Dr Pfersching in Geneva. Though Botox and fillers were readily available in Monaco, Barbara didn't want to bump into people she knew at a local clinic – one of the most common awkward encounters in the principality. Regular visits to her aunt's Lake Annecy villa were a convenient cover for 'restorative' pit-stops to ward off any drooping. The doctor was kind enough to treat Barbara in a suite at a discreet lakeside hotel. Barbara didn't do waiting rooms and couldn't stomach even a lowly receptionist knowing that her 'great genes' had a helping hand.

'Your white shirt is classic Alexander Lauren,' said Lucinda.

'It reminds me of Alexander's infamous black-and-white collection when the fashion magazine editor Alexia Winston walked out of his runway show as he'd employed strippers on the catwalk.'

'Thanks,' said Barbara. 'So, how do you like working for Hank '*the per*' Vert?'

Abigail stifled a giggle. 'Hmm, how to answer that question diplomatically?'

'Ach, diplomacy is overrated,' Barbara said. 'Besides he's no friend of mine. Have you ever met his twins? They're about Sophie's age.'

'No,' Abigail replied. 'It's hard to keep track of his conquests and offspring. But his youngest, Aurora, is best friends with my daughter Daisy.'

Barbara swirled her brandy, took a sip and settled back into the sofa.

'Gavin and I were visiting my parents one summer in the early 90s before we moved here permanently. We went to the Rascasse after dinner one evening. They used to have great live bands.'

Barbara's mind flitted back to the time when she was happily married, but she quashed any nostalgic feelings and returned to the story of her first encounter with aspiring art dealer extraordinaire, Hank Vert.

'We were talking to a Canadian bloke, when a friend of his sauntered over and introduced himself as Hank. The three guys started chatting, so I said hello to Hank's companion, a beautiful, young woman who introduced herself as Justyna, Hank's dog walker. She couldn't have been any more than eighteen or nineteen.'

'Hank has always been an unrepentant lech,' said Abigail.

'Hank beamed at me, saying: "I hear you're new parents. My wife is pregnant with twins." So I asked him when the babies were due. He replied: "She's in labour right now!" and tilted his head up in the direction of the hospital. The hormonal new mother in me just blurted out, "If my husband was out gallivanting, when I was giving birth to his child, I'd chop his legs off."'

'Good for you,' said Abigail. 'How did he react?'

'Like I'd slapped him in the face with a wet kipper. He disappeared promptly into the crowd, though I saw him leaving the bar around 2 a.m. hand-in-hand with his 'dog walker'.'

'There's no shortage of cads in Monaco,' said Abigail. 'Though Hank makes most of them look like choirboys.'

'Must be something in the water,' Lucinda said. 'All the men here are rotters.'

'*Princeps viventium, humilis moribus*, as my mother used to say,' said Barbara.

'Is that your family spell?' Lucinda giggled.

'No. It means 'high living, low morals'.'

Barbara turned to Abigail.

'My mother's Classics degree comes in handy from time to time. Anyway, Hank gave me a wide berth, until he traded in his wife for a younger model. Then he tried for years to charm me into buying overpriced art.'

'Sounds like classic Hank,' said Abigail. 'Back to your original question, he's a tyrannical arsehole.'

Abigail drained her glass, then shrugged: 'But I have bills to pay.'

Announcing it was bedtime, Barbara escorted Abigail and Lucinda to the lift. They were startled when the lift doors opened and Marcus emerged. He gave the departing guests no more than a cursory glance. Lucinda mouthed, 'You okay?' as they stepped into the lift.

Barbara retreated to her doorway without inviting Marcus inside. His dilated pupils announced his drunkenness. Barbara was not in the least surprised to see him empty-handed.

'I don't see any financial records.'

'Why the fuck did you freeze our credit cards? Sophie is really pissed off.'

Barbara smiled as she imagined Marcus' humiliation when it came to pay for his sumptuous lunch at the Eden-Roc.

'Look, are you going to give me the money or not? *WeFork* is a great company. We've been voted the best burger chain in Europe two years in a row.'

'Awards don't pay bills, Marcus. Let me save you from embarrassing yourself further, you deluded prat. *WeFork* is insolvent. It's finished.'

Barbara cut off Marcus as he attempted another plea: 'Who in their right mind would invest €100 million with your ownership structure and rip-off leases? I might as well go to the Hôtel de Paris and hand over the money to that gangster Kukushkin!'

Beads of sweat appeared on Marcus' forehead.

'Look, Sergei is a rough chap, but he's a businessman. Yes, he wants €100 million. But in return for the freeholds to all his properties. It's a bloody good price. He's desperate to avoid the police digging around his affairs. We could end up business partners. Sophie would love that.'

'I don't go into business with liars and frauds.'

'Then I'm a dead man.'

'Oh, spare me the theatrics.'

As Barbara slammed the heavy-duty door in his face, Marcus thrust out his foot to keep the door ajar.

'Always knew you were a bitch, Barbara. But throwing your daughter's husband to the wolves, that's pretty fucking cold.'

'Oh, don't play the family card. You've lied to us for years.'

Marcus retreated from the doorway. He kept his back to her while waiting for the lift. Once inside, he turned to face Barbara. As the doors glided shut, Marcus looked her in the eye and gave a barely discernible shake of his head.

'You can't take it with you, Barbara.'

'God, you're an asshole.' Impulsively, Barbara darted to the lift and yelled into the closed doors, 'and you're *fat!*'

Barbara poured another brandy and checked her phone. Damian had emailed to say that one of Monaco's Russian oligarchs was hosting a lavish party aboard his superyacht that evening. It would be heaving with his compatriots, including Kukushkin. The well-connected, ex-police chief Sournois had secured an invite. It was a golden opportunity to size up Kukushkin and determine how big a threat he posed to the extended Esson clan. Sournois promised to provide an update the following day.

'*Excellent,*' Barbara replied. '*Marcus' day of reckoning isn't far off.*'

Barbara enjoyed being one step ahead of her adversaries and Marcus was no exception. She liked to see him squirm. That said, the alleged violent threats from Kukushkin concerned her. She couldn't chance her daughter being at risk if things took a nasty turn. Before heading to bed, Barbara texted her.

Hi darling, Sorry! Must have been a tech glitch. Spoke to the bank to correct. Aberdeen Art Gallery's new wing is opening this week. I can't go to the VIP reception, something's come up at work, but someone from the family should go. I've sorted a PJ to pick you up tomorrow morning, so you'll make it on time. I'll forward you the details. Call me when you arrive. x

The private jet departing from Nice airport had been booked weeks ago for Barbara herself. As a generous benefactor, she had been looking forward to lording it up at the gallery on home soil, but the event was a convenient ruse to spirit Sophie out of Monaco until the *WeFork* situation was resolved. Her daughter would be in her element talking artspeak for a few days. She wouldn't notice the Esson Group security detail keeping a discreet eye on her.

Sophie replied five minutes later. *Hi, at Sass. Sounds fab! I'll pack my thermals lol. S xxx*

Barbara was satisfied to see no signs of dissent from her daughter. In her dressing room, she calmly applied a range of age-defying Crème de la Mer creams. Her ascendancy had been challenged before, but her son-in-law's defiance didn't feel like a contest.

'For all your swagger, Marcus,' thought Barbara. 'You're just a pig-ignorant amateur.'

9

Polina

POLINA STOOD STILL ON THE DAIS, WHILE THE TWO assistants did up the myriad tiny buttons that ran down the back of her wedding dress. A vague atmosphere of tension pervaded the room as they worked briskly, overseen by Christobelle Jensen.

A regular fixture on the social scene of Monaco's higher echelons, Ms Jensen had built her couture business by showcasing eye-catching gowns on her own fabulous figure at events alongside the rich and famous. The cachet of couture garments hand-crafted in Monaco set her brand apart. At eye-watering prices, it was an exclusive service for a lucky few, including Polina.

She had convinced Dimitri: 'Is so convenient I can do fittings in Monaco, not travel to Paris. But I think she will say no and I am shy. She will say not enough time. Can you help me?'

Dimitri, or rather his PA, made everything possible. The moneyed power of Dimitri Namilov smoothed over any deadline concerns.

Buttoning completed; the shop assistants stood back to allow Polina an uninterrupted view in the 360° mirrors. Plunging low at the front, and even lower at the back, the jewel-encrusted lace clung to her body in a mermaid silhouette, fanning out from the knee and extending into a small train at the back.

After a prolonged silence, Polina glanced towards the anxious face of her dress designer.

'Dress is good. Is big improvement since all my changes. I am happy now.'

Christobelle responded with a bright smile, while the two assistants glanced at each other with relief.

'Now you can take dress off,' Polina directed them.

The two assistants stepped forward to gently unbutton and remove the dress, revealing Polina's cream-silk La Perla lingerie. Once they left the room, she dressed again in a Gucci dress and four-inch heels. At €2,000, the dress was one of the cheapest in her wardrobe. It was a daytime staple that she came back to time and again, although she avoided tallying up the total cost of her outfit on days that she wore it. The black-and-gold shift dress was knitted all over with the iconic interlinked double Gs to make the designer logo clear.

Holding the door ajar, Christobelle bid farewell. Polina was too busy messaging Dimitri's driver with a blunt '*COME NOW HURRY*' to respond. Time was running short, and she needed to go shopping before her lunch.

'Louis Vuitton,' Polina told the driver, establishing hierarchy in a no-nonsense voice as he opened the rear door for her.

'*Oui, Mademoiselle.*'

As usual, the Louis Vuitton boutique's temptations made her run over time. But Polina had a peace offering in hand as she made her way across to the Hôtel de Paris. In the American Bar, Leyla was sitting at their favourite spot by the window. Her new dog-carrier bag was placed on the table. Several elderly patrons crowded around with their own miniature pooches in tow. They spoke in silly voices to the bundle of brown fluff inside.

Noting Leyla's scowl at her late arrival, Polina held up one of her Louis Vuitton shopping bags in apology.

'Is gift for dog,' Polina announced happily, as she approached the table.

She set the package down to greet Leyla with an air kiss to each cheek, which the small crowd thankfully took as a cue to return to their own tables.

'This is dog,' said Leyla, as she indicated the handbag. 'Name is BowWow.'

'Hello, BowWow,' Polina paused, wondering what else one could say to a canine. Then she waved her hand towards the large shopping bag: 'Open gift.'

Leyla unwrapped the elaborate packaging to uncover a dog collar and lead in matching LV monogram print.

'Oh, I love it. Is perfect gift,' squealed Leyla. 'It matches dog-carrier bag.'

'Yes, I know!' replied Polina. 'We can go back to shop to have BowWow engraved on collar — no extra charge.'

Polina changed the conversation: 'Today was last fitting for wedding dress.'

'Good,' Leyla said, distracted as she changed the dog to its new collar and lead. She held up the squirming LV-clad puppy alongside its matching designer bag for the benefit of the other mutt owners in the bar, provoking a smattering of applause.

Raising her voice above the din, Polina ploughed on in a loud voice.

'Dmitri has surprise honeymoon for me. I only know is Caribbean.'

Leyla stopped fiddling with the dog accessories momentarily and turned to Polina.

'Did you know your client Rod goes to Caribbean sex island?' she said, matching Polina in loud volume.

There was an awkward silence. The American Bar dog set started fussing with their dogs and looking studiously in the other direction.

'What is sex island?' Polina asked in an urgent whisper.

'Is holiday resort on private island, where men go by themselves because girls are already there,' Leyla explained, in a matter-of-fact voice.

'When man arrives,' she continued, 'he selects girl he likes best, and girl stays with him for all holiday. She sleeps in his bed and goes to restaurant with him, just like a wife or girlfriend. If he doesn't like girl, he puts her back and takes another one.'

'How do you know Rod goes there?' Polina asked.

'I have friend who worked on island. She met Monaco man there and became his wife. Now she is rich Monaco housewife.'

'Clever woman.'

'Yes, and she sees Rod walking on street in Monaco and recognises him from island.'

Polina wasn't surprised. Monaco men were so predictable.

•

POLINA AWOKE IN HER LE MÉRIDIEN HOTEL SUITE. A RAY OF sunshine came through a small gap in the curtains, heralding an auspicious start to her wedding day. She peeked at wedding preparations on the beach terrace outside. An army of workers scurried around setting up sound equipment and lighting, setting out chairs in rows and covering a long, arched walkway with flowers.

How her fortunes had changed! She reflected with pride that no one else from Gomel had ever married a billionaire. Yet at the edge of her mind a different thought, or rather a hazy feeling, mingled regret with sadness, and even repulsion. Polina had trained her mind to ban any thoughts about Dimitri's bulky frame, his controlling manner, or his age. She must never let that nagging genie of thoughts out of the bottle. As always, she pushed the uncomfortable feeling away and concentrated her mind upon the security and status she would soon be enjoying as Dimitri's wife.

'You must be so happy,' Leyla gushed later that day as they dined on fresh lobster at the wedding banquet for 50 guests, most of whom Polina hadn't met before. 'Wedding was beautiful and now you are married woman.'

'Yes, but I am not properly married woman yet,' replied Polina. 'Today is just for tradition and party.'

Leyla raised her eyebrow.

'Marriage will only be official when we do ceremony at La Mairie and sign papers,' Polina continued, referring to the legal requirement for a Monaco marriage. 'You're invited, remember?'

'Of course, I remember,' said Leyla, 'I buy new dresses for both, but I did not know that beach wedding is not the legal marriage.'

•

THE NEXT MORNING, POLINA WAS AWOKEN BY DIMITRI standing by the side of the bed in a white towelling robe.

'Come on sleepyhead. Breakfast is ready on the terrace. Come and join me.'

'What time is it?'

'Eleven o'clock. You've had more than enough sleep. Up you get. I've been working for the last four hours.'

'Alright,' Polina agreed in a drowsy voice.

Still half asleep, she went to the bathroom and spritzed her face with cold water. She brushed her hair and twisted it into a casual bun. Next, she applied a natural, undetectable foundation and a light spray of perfume.

'Beautiful,' Dimitri said, as she took her seat opposite him on the sunny terrace. 'You're exactly how I like a woman to look in the morning.'

After a leisurely breakfast, Dimitri had a meeting with a business associate.

'Spend some time at the spa, relax, order anything you want,' he said. 'I'll be back in a few hours, and we can have a late lunch together.'

Polina flopped onto the bed in her hotel suite and scrolled through her social media feeds. She was enjoying the solitude after yesterday's socialising. Eventually, she rose and took a shower before dressing in her 'day-after-wedding' outfit.

Twirling in front of the mirror, Polina admired the Zimmerman dress. The print featured Dimitri's favourite flowers: red roses. They were scattered upon a powder-blue background with delicate lace edging. It had a feminine, sexy vibe thanks to the low plunging neckline and short hemline. She reached for her phone to take some selfies before reclining innocently on the bed.

She posted a shot on her Instagram feed with the caption: *Love and a red rose can't be hid.*

•

TWO HOURS LATER, THE DOOR FLUNG OPEN. DIMITRI'S FACE was screwed up in anger.

'You're a scheming, conniving tart!' he yelled.

'What are you saying, darling?' Polina cried.

'Do you think I'm stupid? You're nothing but a tart.'

'What do you mean? I'm a model. Who have you been talking to?'

'God, how did I not see it?' he said, striking his head. 'It all adds up. You've made me look a complete fool — a laughing stock.'

'Please Dimitri, *moyo zolotse*, you must calm down.'

'Oh my God, are you for real? You just don't get it, do you? Your game is up! I know who you are. You're nothing but a high-class hooker! Thank God I found out before we're legally married.'

For a few moments, they stared at one another, neither sure what to say next. Changing to a calm, controlled voice, Dimitri broke the silence.

'I. Want. That. Cheque. Polina, go and get it *now* and give it back to me.'

'The cheque is mine,' said Polina, collecting two dresses from the wardrobe and smoothing them into her bag. 'You gave it to me and I'm going to put it in the bank.'

'No, you won't. And even if you do try to bank it, I'll be taking the funds out of my account.'

Polina held her chin high as she zipped up her bag.

'You will never have that money, Polina!' he screamed to her back. She had left the room.

•

POLINA ARRIVED AT HER APARTMENT AND SANK ONTO THE sofa. She stared straight ahead, oblivious to her surroundings. She could barely remember the drive from the hotel. Perhaps Dimitri would message to say it was all a mistake and to come back? No. He would never take her back. Even so, she picked up her phone and checked her messages. Nothing from Dimitri, but several messages from Rod. Strange, given that their arrangement had now ended.

She clicked on the first message: *Honeymoon trouble?*

Then the second: *Guess who I saw at Menton Marina today? Your brand-new hubby at a cafe deep in conversation with an attractive woman.*

Polina's hands shook as she messaged him back.

What woman? What did she look like?

Rod replied: *Good looking. Young. Tall with long, dark hair. Nicely dressed like you. Quite sexy actually.*

Rod interpreted Polina's silence the wrong way.

Sorry, but you asked!

Polina felt hot and cold all over. Could it be Leyla? No, there had to be another explanation. Perhaps the woman Dimitri met was a private detective? Dimitri was a control freak, after all. Yet the description matched Leyla. She tried to think of reasons why Leyla would want to ruin Polina's opportunity to leave the escort world behind, marry a billionaire and cash a €1-million cheque. As the reality dawned on her, she almost laughed out loud. It was so obvious. Even so, it was difficult to imagine that her closest friend would sell her out.

Bizarrely, Polina's phone beeped with a message from Leyla.

Hello darling friend. I am SO happy for you. The wedding was beautiful. You were beautiful. I bring your wedding gift to ceremony at Le Mairie. Big kiss X

Polina was confused at Leyla's unusually effusive message. Surely this meant that Leyla was innocent. Or the opposite?

•

AS SOON AS POLINA STEPPED INTO THE BANK, SHE KNEW Dimitri had got there first. His private banker — *their* private banker — Damian Buhle emerged from his office immediately and invited her in.

'How can I help you, Polina?'

'I am here to bank cheque.'

Damien spoke in a wooden voice. 'I'm instructed by my client that he no longer wishes to gift you the funds indicated on the cheque. It was given under agreed circumstances which have now changed, and he would like you to hand the cheque over for destruction.'

'Circumstances do not change!' Polina shot back. 'If you do not bank cheque, I talk to your boss that you do not accept cheque. You are my banker too.'

Damian paused to consider the situation while Polina stared him out.

'Okay, I don't have much choice here,' said Damian. 'I will bank the cheque, Polina. But I should mention that Dimitri has removed all funds from that account. The two of you will have to sort it out through the legal process.'

•

MARCUS LOOKED UP WITH MILD SURPRISE AS POLINA arrived for work the next morning.

'I thought you were supposed to be doing your town-hall wedding thing today and leaving for your honeymoon.'

'I have problem, Marcus.'

'So it would seem. Sorry to hear it. Coffee?'

'Strong coffee, Marcus. Double espresso.'

'That bad, huh?'

Polina paused before continuing. 'Wedding is cancelled. Worse, he wants cheque for €1 million back.'

'Oh no, that's awful. This must be very difficult for you, Polina.'

'Is very difficult,' she said quietly through her tears.

'You need that money, right?'

'Yes. I will be single woman with no husband and no boyfriend to help me.'

Marcus looked at Polina carefully.

'What if I said I had an easy way for you to earn a very large amount of money. €500,000 in fact.'

Polina's eyes widened as she moved closer.

'There is a person giving me grief just like Dimitri is doing to you.'

He paused. Polina gave him a sympathetic look so he continued.

'She won't help fund the *WeFork* business, which desperately needs an injection of cash, even though she has loads of money.'

'Barbara?'

'Yes, Barbara,' said Marcus. 'I've got Sergei Kukushkin piling the pressure on me to pay a large sum of money. Frankly, Polina, I'm very concerned. Those guys don't fuck around. They mean business.'

'Marcus, this is bad,' said Polina. 'You do not want Sergei as enemy. You must pay him.'

'Yes, I know, but try telling Madame Uppity that. She'd rather put her family in danger than help me out. I know you'll understand after what Dimitri has done to you.'

Polina nodded. She knew how it felt to be at the mercy of a more powerful figure.

'I'll come to the point, Polina. I need you to help me hire a person to take care of Barbara for good. With her out of the picture, the family finances could be used for the good of all, without the interference of her high-and-mighty-ness controlling our lives.'

Polina's jaw dropped.

'There's no danger to you,' Marcus hurried on. 'You just need to meet the person recommended to me and make the arrangement. That's all there is to it. And you'll be €500,000 the richer for it.'

Polina felt temptation and fear. She needed €500,000 now that Dimitri had turned off the money tap. But this was murder. She could go to prison as an accessory. She didn't like the way Barbara looked down on her, but that wasn't a reason to kill her. But was her own life in danger now that she had knowledge of Marcus' plan?

'By the way,' Marcus smirked at her, 'I know about your handgun. I've seen it in your bag.'

'I need to think, Marcus,' Polina said, rushing out the door.

•

BACK HOME, POLINA KICKED OFF HER SHOES AND RETURNED to the misery of her sofa. She dabbed her tears with multiple tissues and threw the crushed damp pieces on an ever-growing pile on the coffee table. Who could she trust in this tangled Monaco web?

Dimitri hated her, that was clear.

She didn't know if Leyla was her best friend or worst enemy.

Her boss was prepared to make her an accomplice to murder by asking her to hire a hitman.

Even her banker wasn't on her side.

It dawned on her that the only person in Monaco she could trust was a woman she barely knew.

•

ABIGAIL SWUNG HER APARTMENT DOOR OPEN AND SMILED when she saw Polina.

'Hello, Polina. Gosh, are you okay?'

As Polina fought to control her trembling bottom lip, Abigail pulled her inside and closed the door.

'Come into the kitchen and I'll make a nice cup of tea. Let's see, Earl Grey or English Breakfast?'

'Um, I have what you have,' Polina replied, not comprehending either option.

Settled on the sofa with steaming mugs of tea, Abigail asked gently what was troubling her.

'Oh, Abigail, everything is big mess. Dimitri dump me after marriage day but not real marriage only beach one. And my €1-million cheque is maybe cancelled. This is big problem already, but Marcus gives me more big problems. Marcus say Sergei comes after him for money and Barbara won't give money so Marcus asks me to help do murder plot. Yes, I want €500,000, but Barbara is not mafia. She is not type of person you murder about money.'

'Oh my God!' said Abigail. 'Polina, take a deep breath. Shall we start at the beginning?'

Abigail's expert questioning helped Polina to gather her thoughts and describe the events of the last few days in a cohesive and detailed manner.

'Thank you so much for coming to me,' Abigail said as Polina's story came to an end. 'At least, we can warn Barbara and help keep her safe.'

They sat in silence for a few moments as Polina inspected her tear-stained makeup in her compact mirror, dabbing at the black streaks under her eyes.

Suddenly Abigail sprang into action.

'Polina, I'd like you to tell Marcus that you need some time off to recover from your broken engagement. Go back to your apartment and pack a bag for a stay in the countryside.'

'I don't like countryside.'

'I think my olive farm may change your mind about that. It's a beautiful place where you can relax and unwind after these awful shocks you've had. My aunt and daughter are there and will make you welcome.'

'But my €1-million cheque,' said Polina.

'I think we should deal with the murder plot first, don't you?'

Though she disagreed with Abigail's priorities, Polina felt relieved to have a friend who listened and seemed to care. She'd never had that before in Monaco.

'Okay, I go to farm and think.'

'Good, that's settled then.'

Polina was silent for a moment.

'Abigail?'

'Yes, Polina. What is it?'

'I am scared for Barbara,' Polina swallowed hard. 'Marcus had crazy look in his eyes.'

10

Lucinda

'WHAT THE FUCK!' LEO WALKED IN WITH HIS TENNIS RACKET.
'You changed the keys and didn't even tell me.'

Lucinda rubbed her eyes. The doorbell had woken her. It was 10:30 a.m.

'Hello, darling! Oh yes, I wanted to tell you I had to change the lock, but you didn't come home last night. I was here all evening waiting for you. Is everything okay?' asked Lucinda.

'I stayed over at James' flat. I didn't want to disturb you. And then Frédéric booked tennis this morning,' said Leo.

'Take a look at the new lock. It's so much safer.'

'What a waste of time. There are no burglars in Monaco.'

Leo walked into the bedroom. He was not drenched in sweat, as he usually was after tennis. But then it was mild outside, and he'd probably had a coffee at the Cap d'Ail Tennis Club, while cooling off.

'How was tennis?'

'Terrible. Frédéric beat me two sets to love. What do you think about going to the beach this afternoon?'

'What a lovely idea! Shall we go to La Rose des Vents after lunch and play backgammon over some rosé? We can bring Peanut.'

'I thought we could go to Miami Plage. It's livelier.'

Since when did Leo like lively? Miami Plage was Monaco's oldest private beach and restaurant, but it was always packed. They normally went to the quieter, dog-friendly La Rose des Vents.

'I suppose Peanut will be fine on his own for a few hours. Won't you, darling?'

Lucinda went to the bedroom to gather her yellow La Perla bikini, white kaftan and two striped cotton foutas that Alexander Lauren had gifted her after a poolside photoshoot at his fabled white villa in Roquebrune-Cap-Martin, along with Leo's latest read: E L James' *Fifty Shades Freed*, and her copy of the latest *Harper's Bazaar*. She put everything into her handwoven beach bag with dangling coloured pom poms ready for later. Then she dressed into her Lululemon gym wear ready for a workout at Billie's Bootcamp with Victoria.

'I'm going to the barber,' he said. 'See you at the beach at 1:30 p.m.?'

Leo had a French translation of Laura May's *Journey to Healing* under his arm. Was everyone in Monaco reading this self-help book? She took *Fifty Shades Freed* out of the bag.

'Yes, I should get there around then after Billie's Bootcamp. Maybe you can drop me off on your way? I need to go to the place des Moulins cashpoint.'

'Sorry, running late for my appointment,' Leo said, slamming the door behind him.

•

minute walk from the French border town of Cap d'Ail where Billie's Bootcamp was run. She was looking forward to grabbing a coffee with Victoria beforehand at the nearby beachside cafe, Lamparo. Victoria was there already with a plastic folder in front of her. Usually, Lucinda was the early one.

'Could you do me a huge favour?' said Victoria. 'Could you pass your eye over Pandora's CV?'

Pandora was Victoria's overly-pampered daughter.

'Not even any small talk before asking for a favour,' thought Lucinda, before replying: 'Of course I'll have a look later.'

'Thanks. How are you getting on with the book I left with the concierge?'

'You mean the book about healing your life?'

Victoria nodded.

'Not very far,' said Lucinda. 'Do you know what is very strange? Leo is reading the same book in French. He normally hates self-help books.'

Ignoring Lucinda's observation, Victoria scrolled on her phone for a photo and then showed it to her friend. 'Look at my Womb Wisdom Retreat last weekend.'

'Are you naked? Is that mud?'

'Yes, isn't it great?' said Victoria, showing her another photo.

'It looks like a girl-on-girl orgy,' said Lucinda.

'Nothing of the sort,' said Victoria. 'It was amazing though. I feel like a completely new woman. Awakened, embodied and complete. A genuine wholeness. It's all about hearing the innate intelligence of the natural world. About a sensory awareness in deep communication with the source of life. About experiencing your body as an expression of Mother Earth. It's very humbling.'

Lucinda opted against her usual cappuccino and *pain aux*

raisins in favour of a slimming-in-a-bikini espresso.

'I'm already booked for their Summer Solstice retreat next year. You should come too,' said Victoria. 'It will help get you out of your funk.' Then, finally noticing her friend's deflated air: 'How are you doing?'

'Today has been okay so far. Leo suggested we go to Miami Plage. Just the two of us.'

'And all of us. I'm going with Beth, James, and Amy,' said Victoria, taking a drag on her Marlboro Light.

Those happy hours until sundown with Leo, playing backgammon over glasses of rosé, evaporated.

'Does James even work?' said Lucinda.

'Sure, but not when Beth puts on a bikini, if he can help it.'

'Tell me, is that young trainer still keeping you extra fit?' Lucinda was referring to Victoria's latest squeeze.

'No, that's over,' said Victoria, signalling to the attractive Italian waiter for the bill.

'Don't you want to get changed for Billie's Bootcamp now?' said Lucinda. Victoria was wearing a beach dress.

'Sorry, I'm rushing to a doctor's appointment,' said Victoria. 'I'll meet you at the beach later.'

Lucinda dawdled alone towards the Pointe des Douaniers on a promontory hewn from volcanic rocks and lulled, usually, by a gentle breeze. This seaside spot was a desirable location for her twice-a-week exercise ritual. Billie's Bootcamp was run by a husband-and-wife team who sported matching year-round tans and bleached-blonde mohawks. They both seemed to be on speed, pushing everyone too far without correcting their form. Regulars dropped out after suffering from injuries and were replaced by a steady stream of new recruits. Lucinda liked the obstacle courses, but she wasn't so keen on burpees.

'Come on, Countess. You call that your top speed? Let's

have ten more burpees,' shouted Billie, as the veins popped out of his oversized arms.

Lucinda was sad that Victoria hadn't come. It had been her idea to go together in the first place. Still, it was easier to box with her new sparring partner than broad-shouldered Victoria. Last time Lucinda came with her, her boxing gloves could barely contain Victoria's powerful jabs. 'Hey, I like my face,' Lucinda had teased to no avail.

An hour later, Lucinda took the bus to Larvotto. She walked along the beachside promenade towards Miami Plage. Sweaty after her workout, she nipped into the changing rooms to take a shower and change into her bikini and kaftan before joining the others.

Lying on a sunbed was the toned figure of Victoria, cigarette in hand.

'I really should quit,' thought Lucinda, as she noticed the deep, vertical smoker's lines around Victoria's mouth in the raw sunlight.

Beside Victoria was a silver bucket filled with ice and a magnum of Domaines Ott rosé. On the adjoining sunbed was Beth. She perched alluringly in her bikini bottoms, while chatting to two other bare-breasted women, who Lucinda did not know, but whose faces she had seen out and about in Monaco. James and Leo lounged on neighbouring sunbeds, sipping their drinks, and enjoying the topless theatre around them.

Lucinda said hello to everyone, put on her sunglasses, put up her parasol and lay on her fouta. With the sound of conversation and children's laughter in the background, she started to flick through *Harper's Bazaar*.

A while later, Leo shouted to Lucinda: 'What would you like to drink, darling?'

'An iced coffee would be lovely, thank you.'

Lucinda took out the backgammon game: a pastime they could enjoy together without arguing, though neither was especially good. She closed her eyes. She felt the breeze on her face and the sun on her arms. 'How lucky am I to live in such a desirable place. So why aren't I happy?' she thought, drifting to sleep under the shade of the parasol.

She awoke to the sound of Leo, laughing and cursing in French, and to the smell of pizza. The backgammon was laid out on the table next to Victoria's sunbed, Leo faced her, perching on Beth's sunbed. They both puffed on cigarettes as they played together.

'What time is it?' said Lucinda, feeling disoriented. The sun was setting, and the smell of pizza made her hungry.

'Hey baby,' said Leo, turning towards her. 'I am going back up to the flat to make us dinner.'

He hadn't called her baby in a while.

'Do you mind taking Peanut out?'

'Sure.' He kissed her, grabbed the backgammon, his cigarettes, phone, and keys.

There were now several empty wine bottles around, among half a dozen glasses.

'Is there any wine left?' Lucinda asked. 'I might have a glass.'

'Awake, at last,' said Victoria, pouring wine into a clean glass. 'Drink up and let's go for a swim.'

•

SHE STROLLED BACK HOME, CRISS-CROSSING ACROSS THE French border into place de la Crémaillière, and back up some stairs to the Millefiori in Monaco. She felt happy for once. As she entered the flat, she smelt garlic. Leo was cooking his prawn pasta with chili, coriander and garlic. Her favourite. After a long soak in the bathtub, she put on her bathrobe and joined

Leo in the kitchen. While he cooked, she finished reading *Harper's Bazaar* with a glass of rosé in hand.

The doorbell rang. Leo rushed to open the door. From the kitchen, she could hear him let someone in and then some words she couldn't make out. Moments later, a young girl walked in; 18 years old at the most with long, straight, dark-blonde hair and in business attire. An envelope in her hand, she walked straight to Lucinda and handed it to her.

'*Il faut signer*,' said the girl, gesturing to the envelope and proffering a pen.

'What's this? Who are you?'

Leo smiled, as he approached within inches of Lucinda's nose.

'I'm divorcing you.'

Lucinda froze. Lost for words. The girl watched, waiting for the document to be signed so she could leave. Lucinda stared at the Montblanc pen. She couldn't think straight. Her only focus was how to get this girl out of her flat. Lucinda wanted to resent her, even though the girl was just doing her job. Of course, Lucinda had no choice — she had to sign to make her leave.

Struck by the urgency of her business-like manner, Lucinda opened the envelope. Inside was a document in French. It was a court order to appear before a *tribunal* in a few weeks' time.

Her hand acted independently of her body. As Lucinda signed, Leo turned and went onto the terrace to light a cigarette. The young girl thanked her, unemotional, and left as swiftly as she had appeared.

She stood speechless for a few seconds. Then she stumbled to the terrace, took one of Leo's unfiltered Gauloises cigarettes, lit it, and sunk onto the bench. An overwhelming feeling of nausea started in her stomach and ended in her throat.

11

Barbara

BARBARA MAINTAINED A BRISK PACE ALONG THE COASTAL path between Cap d'Ail and Plage Mala, a picturesque beach nestled in an amphitheatre, pausing only when Laird met a fragrant *derrière* to sniff. Barbara worked out at a gym with an overenthusiastic personal trainer twice a week, but preferred outdoor pursuits to keep in shape. This 10-kilometre route beside Monaco was a highlight of living on the Riviera. The calm seas and sunshine soothed her turmoil after last night's heated encounter with Marcus.

Since the waves lapped the shoreline gently, Barbara ignored a 'No Entry' sign and continued on the original precarious path towards Plage Mala. Descending the steep, undulating steps, Barbara was greeted by a chaotic scene on the pebbly beach. Several policemen marshalled a handful of distressed beachgoers and a *gendarmerie maritime* boat bobbed in the sea near the shore. A white forensic tent had been erected near the water's edge.

'Oh my God! Someone must have drowned,' thought Barbara. 'Some people overestimate their own ability.'

Refreshed after her bracing walk, despite the gruesome scene on the beach, Barbara settled down behind her desk. The next few hours flew by as she reduced her inbox back to zero and took business updates from various Esson Group lieutenants around the world. By mid-afternoon, she needed a caffeine hit. Barbara arranged to meet Lucinda at Il Calcio: a no-frills cafe on the boulevard des Moulins that served excellent Italian coffee.

Laird and Peanut were more enthusiastic to see each other than the two weary friends. As Lucinda described the gut-wrenching moment that Leo served her with divorce papers, Barbara recalled her own separation. Monaco was medieval when it came to divorce. Many divorcées were trapped in the Lilliputian principality and could only see their children at the will of their ex-husbands. Of course, her own split had been an anomaly: her control of the purse strings meant that her husband had fled voluntarily.

'I can recommend a pit-bull of a lawyer,' said Barbara. 'You'll need one.'

'Leo says it's all my fault. I'm impossible to live with apparently,' Lucinda sighed, offering Barbara a cigarette to keep her company. 'Oh, let's talk about something else. How's business?'

Lucinda was one of the few Monaco housewives who enquired about Barbara's work. Most found it perturbing that someone in their midst had a job. As a new mum, Barbara recalled declining the mums' post-school-run coffee because she had work to do. The standard response was an unnecessarily sympathetic: 'Oh, poor you!'

'Well, today the board was updated about an insurgency threatening oil installations in West Africa, an impending hurricane in the Gulf of Mexico, bribery allegations in Brazil, and the attempted theft of our patented thermal treatment technology. Never a dull moment in the oil industry!'

'Compare that to my day spent staring at the bedroom ceiling.' Lucinda's eyes welled up. 'What would Alexander think of my life now?'

'Believe me, personal troubles are no less trying than professional ones,' said Barbara. 'Work is a walk in the park compared to dealing with Marcus at the moment.'

'I wasn't sure if you'd want to talk about him,' Lucinda replied. 'I don't know much about his business.'

'Neither does he.'

When Lucinda went to the *tabac* to buy another pack of cigarettes, Barbara fished her phone from her bag to check for messages. Ten missed calls. Nothing particularly unusual. But why were six of them from Abigail? Barbara dialled 121 to hear her voicemail.

Hi Barbara, it's Abigail. I, um, need to speak to you rather urgently. It's probably nothing. A case of crossed wires, I'm sure, but can I see you as soon as possible? Call me back! Thanks, bye.

Perhaps Abigail needed to fact check something for the pooch article? When she returned from the *tabac*, Lucinda suggested a cheeky glass of wine and bask in the late-afternoon sunshine. Barbara agreed and summoned Abigail to join them.

Ten minutes later, Abigail's car screeched to a halt near the cafe. She zipped into a newly-vacant parking spot, much to the fury of an old man in an ancient Saab who had been eyeing up the space. Abigail jumped out of her dinky Fiat Uno that bore many duelling scars from driving in the South of France. She ignored blithely the volley of abuse from the apoplectic Frenchman. Barbara and Lucinda looked on amused as Abigail glanced back at her foe, shrugged her shoulders and shouted innocently, '*Non comprendez!*'

'Making friends with the locals?' Barbara asked.

'Sorry to interrupt,' said Abigail.

'Not at all. Have a seat,' Barbara flagged a waiter to bring over another chair to the table since her Hermès Kelly bag currently occupied the spare chair and would not be demoted to the pavement. 'Glass of wine?'

'No, thank you. Actually, yes, please,' Abigail sat down, glanced at Lucinda and turned to Barbara, 'I have something quite delicate, and probably ludicrous in all honesty, to discuss with you.'

'Would you like me to leave?' said Lucinda.

'It's fine. Stay. But you may have to sign a non-disclosure agreement.' Barbara smiled at Lucinda.

'Look, this is going to sound crazy, and I don't want to get anyone in trouble,' began Abigail.

The waiter arrived with a glass of white wine. Abigail took a big gulp of the cheap plonk as Barbara and Lucinda looked at her expectantly.

'I don't want to alarm you and I know this sounds so far-fetched, slanderous even,' continued Abigail. 'But I was told that Marcus wants to hire a hitman.'

'What?' said Barbara. 'Who on earth told you that?'

'Polina. We're actually neighbours, though I don't know her well. She turned up on my doorstep and blurted out that Marcus had offered her money to hire a hitman.'

Abigail took another quick sip of wine. 'Apparently a mafia type is after Marcus. I think Polina is genuinely afraid about getting caught in the crossfire. Not literally, I hope.'

'Oh, come off it!' Barbara let out a nervous laugh, which Lucinda instinctively copied after a pause.

Abigail looked sheepish.

'Look,' said Barbara. 'Please don't broadcast this, but Marcus *is* having difficulties with a Russian business partner. I found this out recently and the situation is, shall we say, in flux. But I doubt even he would do something *that* daft. He's too much of a coward.'

'Are you sure?' Abigail paused. 'It's only because Polina said that the hitman's intended target is *you*.'

Lucinda choked on her wine. Barbara's eyes narrowed as she casually lit a cigarette.

'Could you tell Olina that I'm sure Marcus was just mouthing off after a few too many, and I'd appreciate it if she keeps her trap shut.' Barbara arched an eyebrow at Abigail. 'I don't want to read about this nonsense in the *Monaco Mail* either.'

'Of course not,' said Abigail. 'I came here to warn you, not get a scoop.'

'It's probably just a big misunderstanding. All the same, I feel duty bound to protect her so I'm taking her to my Grasse farm. I left her packing a bag ready for the olive harvest tomorrow. Under any other circumstances, I'd invite you both over.'

'Oh, I'd love to join you,' said Barbara. 'I think Olina and I should have a little chat.'

'Count me in,' said a tipsy Lucinda. 'Safety in numbers.'

Barbara raised her glass as she thought: 'Am I really going to confront my capricious son-in-law and a Russian mobster with a bimbo, an ex-model, and a journalist at the local rag in my corner?'

Barbara returned to her apartment and busied herself by choosing an outfit for the olive farm outing. Despite her brave face in front of Abigail and Lucinda, she felt anxious.

'Don't be so paranoid. Marcus is a moron, not a murderer,' she told herself firmly.

Barbara was irritated by her mental fragility. A long, hot soak would restore her usual feeling of omnipotence. An hour and a half later, poised and pink, she threw on a robe. She was ready to give Damian a call.

'Hello, Barbara. Everything okay?' Damian shouted above the music.

'Are you out gallivanting?' said Barbara.

'Yes, I'm at Jack's,' said Damian.

'On a date, no doubt,' said Barbara.

'Not for much longer,' said Damian. 'When I came back from the gents, I saw her googling how much my watch is worth.'

Barbara chuckled.

'Anyway, it's good that you called,' said Damian. 'Listen. I have some bad news…'

'Tell me.'

'Sournois is dead. His body was found washed ashore at Plage Mala this morning. Apparently, he sustained horrific injuries from a propeller.'

The grisly scene on the beach that morning must have been the recovery of the ex-police chief's body. Could this day get any more macabre?

'Good God! Did he go to that Russian yacht party last night?'

'Yes. Would you believe that the €200-million-yacht's security cameras weren't working and that no witnesses have come forward? Of course, there are lots of rumours swirling. One of my more reliable competitors was on board and thinks he saw Sournois leaving on a tender with someone matching Kukushkin's description and a couple of his henchmen.'

Barbara shook her head. This *WeFork* fiasco was spiralling out of control. 'Is this a terrible coincidence or was Sournois killed because he was asking about *WeFork*?'

Damian chose his words carefully. 'I think it would be complacent to assume it was a tragic accident.'

Barbara's scepticism about the hitman plot dissolved. She paced rapidly up and down her bedroom. 'Let's hope Sournois didn't reveal he was snooping on my behalf. I wonder if Marcus has heard about this.'

'I couldn't give a fork about *WeFork* going kaput or Marcus' safety. I'm concerned for yours.'

Barbara fished out a set of keys from her bedside table as she spoke. 'Hmm. Rumour has it that Marcus thinks bumping off his minted mother-in-law will solve all his problems.'

'Are you serious?'

'Why settle for €100 million? He might as well try and hit the jackpot,' Barbara gave a lukewarm chuckle.

'This isn't a laughing matter. I'm coming over.'

'Oh, there's no need. I'm unlocking the gun cupboard as we speak.'

Barbara wedged her phone between her ear and neck whilst she retrieved her Purdey shotgun. Upon examining the empty chambers, she looked inside her cartridge bag. It was empty. Barbara pushed her concerns to one side.

'I can take care of myself, Damian.'

Barbara hung up and walked through to the sitting room where she perched on an armchair with a whisky and the shotgun. The apartment was cloaked in darkness save for the pale glow emanating from a few scattered lamps. Despite the late hour, Barbara was too wired to feel drowsy as the *WeFork* saga consumed her.

Sometime later, Barbara's pulse quickened as she detected faint, deliberate footsteps approaching. A hooded figure crept slowly into the sitting room, moving around with a sense of familiarity. From her vantage point in the shadows, Barbara watched the man retrieve a chunky Murano ashtray and newspapers from under the coffee table. He deposited a packet of cigarettes from his pocket onto the table before heading over to a silver tray loaded with decanters. The intruder's gloved hand poured a large measure of brandy and downed it in one go before refilling the crystal glass. The brandy was then carefully poured over the pile of newspapers scattered around the ashtray.

'An accidental fire,' Barbara thought. 'Not very original.'

The man turned towards the hallway leading to the bedrooms, his breathing now deep and rapid. At that moment, Barbara flicked on a light switch. The hood slid off the would-be assassin's head as he spun around to see Barbara sitting in the corner, a shotgun in her hands.

'Bit late for a social call, Marcus.'

'What the fuck! Stop pointing that thing at me!' Marcus took a step towards Barbara.

'Stop right there,' Barbara turned off the safety catch. 'I won't miss from this distance.'

'You wouldn't dare kill me,' said Marcus, remaining glued to the spot.

'You're right. I don't want your brains splattered across my expensive wallpaper. I'm aiming about three feet lower.'

Marcus flinched.

'I think the police would be very sympathetic if I mistook you for an intruder. You can kiss *WeFork* and the highlife goodbye. If you don't want Sophie to hear about this desperate little stunt, you'll do exactly as I say.'

'You can't bully us.'

'Since you are insolvent and I can stop your allowance permanently, you will do exactly as you're told, you pathetic cretin,' said Barbara. 'And right now, you're going on a little trip.'

'What do you mean?'

'Oh, I thought you might want to reboot your career. Would you consider the energy industry?'

'You mean work for you?'

'Starting at the bottom of course. In fact, there's a vacancy for a cleaner on an oil rig west of Shetland. You can start in a couple of days.'

'No fucking way.'

'Yes fucking way.'

Barbara thought Marcus was about to speak, but he launched himself across the room with a feral ferocity that took her by surprise. Despite knowing it was futile, Barbara instinctively pulled the trigger as Marcus lunged for the weapon.

Click.

Marcus' eyes bulged with deranged glee as he found his hands unexpectedly gripping the barrel of an unloaded gun. He wrenched it out of Barbara's hands with ease and tossed the redundant prop across the room. Marcus rose to his full height over his recoiling mother-in-law and glared down at her with malignant triumph. Without warning, he viciously cracked the back of his hand across Barbara's face sending her sprawling and dazed onto the floor. Barbara's bluff had failed, and she felt an unfamiliar sensation overwhelm her. Fear.

'Marcus, don't. Please.' Barbara tasted metal as blood flooded her mouth.

Marcus pondered the request for a brief moment, before dishing out a sharp kick to Barbara's ribs, her cry of pain eliciting a satisfied sneer. Marcus used his foot to flip her onto her back. During the assault, Barbara's robe loosened.

Marcus snorted. 'Nice tits, Barbara. Must have cost a fortune.'

Barbara fought the pain to cover herself and salvage an ounce of dignity. But her rage could not conquer the powerlessness she felt as she unsuccessfully fought back tears. Marcus dragged Barbara roughly over to the sofa. The agonising pain in her ribs prevented her from putting up a fight. Marcus turned his attention to the pool of brandy-soaked papers on the coffee table and retrieved a lighter from his jacket pocket.

Barbara gurned as she raised herself onto one elbow. 'I'll give you anything you want. Anything.'

Marcus sat down gently on the sofa and looked scornfully at the bruised and bloodied Barbara. Like a cartoon villain, his face twisted with scorn and hatred as he smirked: 'Are you begging me?'

'Yes. I'm begging you.' Barbara's voice was barely a whisper. 'And I promise you, I won't tell Sophie about this.'

'Oh, your little princess knows exactly what's going on. You see, unlike you, she doesn't put money before family.'

'I don't believe you, you bloody liar.'

With a guttural yell, Barbara tried to unleash a volley of punches. But she was no match for Marcus. He slapped her again and grabbed the nearest cushion. With two firm hands, he pressed the dense cushion over Barbara's face with lethal intent. Barbara squirmed with muffled cries. As her lungs screamed for oxygen and her arms flailed around, Barbara was desperate to grasp salvation out of thin air. Her charmed life did not flash before her eyes. There was no calming white light to walk toward. Only fear, pain and a looming blackness.

On the brink of losing consciousness, the cushion suddenly flew off Barbara's face. In a confused state, she took several rasping gasps of air. Barbara gingerly lifted her head as far as she could manage. She saw Marcus on all fours with Damian raining blow upon blow with the butt of the shotgun. Barbara eyed the weighty glass ashtray in her line of sight and thought how good it would look embedded in Marcus' skull. But she couldn't move.

When Damian raised the shotgun to administer another

blow, Marcus sank his teeth deep into his assailant's calf. The urbane banker roared in pain while Marcus quickly rose to his knees. In the most unsportsmanlike fashion, Marcus unleashed a powerful uppercut, striking Damian directly between his legs. Damian let out a barely audible high-pitched screech as he crumpled into a foetal position.

Marcus staggered towards the front door. Upon seeing that neither Barbara nor Damian was in pursuit, he turned to bark:

'Before you even think about calling the police. Remember, if I go down, Sophie goes down with me.'

Barbara heard a vase in the hallway smash on the marble floor before the front door slammed shut. Barbara clasped her throbbing head in her shaking hands and dry heaved. Damian winced as he crawled onto the settee and put his arms around her. For the first time in her adult life, she sobbed uncontrollably.

Eventually Damian took control. After rummaging around in the kitchen, he returned with an improvised ice pack, two glasses of whisky and some painkillers. He discovered an unperturbed Laird locked in the utility room. Barbara applied the ice pack to the ghoulish left side of her face and washed down the painkillers with some whisky. She felt devoid of energy.

'Barbara? Barbara?' Damian touched her gently on the shoulder. He pulled his mobile phone out of his jacket pocket. 'I'm calling an ambulance and the police.'

Barbara snapped out of her stupor and looked up at Damian. 'Don't you dare!'

'Barbara, this isn't some high-stakes corporate takeover. That bastard tried to kill you.'

Damian sat beside Barbara. 'And I want him charged with grievous bollocky harm.'

'He won't get away with this,' said Barbara, the colour

returning to the non-bruised side of her face. 'But the police will only drag Sophie into this mess.'

'Come on Barbara, Marcus is only trying to protect himself. Sophie doesn't have a harmful bone in her body. He only said that to rile you.'

'Well, it worked. Christ, my own daughter?'

For the second time that tumultuous evening, a foreign emotion once again engulfed Barbara. Doubt. The thought that her only child could be complicit in a murder plot made her nauseous. She burst into tears again.

'It's okay, it's okay,' Damian consoled her. 'Look, I won't call the police. For now. But I'm not leaving here until I've arranged a bodyguard, alright?'

Barbara nodded feebly. Damian stood up and called his bank's head of security.

Barbara drained her glass of whisky and shambled through to her ensuite bathroom. She stared at her unrecognisable reflection, disgusted by the red, puffy eyes and blackened cheeks smeared with dried blood and snot. Barbara gripped the sink as her legs threatened to give way.

'Pull yourself together, you stupid bitch,' she said to herself.

But the words made no difference, and she slumped slowly onto the floor.

12

Abigail

'HERMÈS CROCODILE HANDBAGS NEED THEIR OWN passports to travel,' said Camille Marceau as she pincered salmon sushi into her mouth.

Abigail was interviewing Camille, the director of Monaco's best-known auction house, over lunch at Capocaccia. Abigail wasn't sure whether to be more shocked that a handbag required its own passport (as crocodiles are an endangered species) or that this particular crocodile Hermès handbag encrusted with orange diamonds had been auctioned for over €100,000.

With her petite figure and raven hair swept into a ponytail, Camille was Monaco's answer to a Bond girl. Having worked for a decade at a Parisian intelligence agency before moving to Southern France, she admitted a lifelong fascination with crime. Abigail reflected that no one could be better placed to navigate collectors through the shark-infested waters of the art world than Camille.

Half an hour later as the interview wound to a close, Abigail rose and grabbed her suit jacket from the back of her chair. As she turned back, she saw a fleeting smile pass Camille's face as if she were remembering something funny. After the interview, Abigail took her time walking home. As she meandered down avenue Princess Alice, she heard a wolf whistle. Abigail looked up to see a team of workmen smirking down at her from some scaffolding above. She hadn't expected her trouser suit to attract such attention. The workmen were putting new striped awnings onto the freshly cleaned façade of one of Monaco's nondescript 1970s apartment blocks. Monaco was littered with such building sites. Local politics decreed that historic villas were cherry-picked for demolition, while modern high-rise blocks were destined for never-ending renovations that only half-concealed the ugliness of their original architecture.

'The architectural version of the plastic surgery favoured by Monaco residents,' thought Abigail with a smile.

Abigail had a lot on her mind. She reflected on the past 24 hours' staggering chain of events. Three tales that combined a heady cocktail of sex, money and power.

First, there was the suspected infidelity of Lucinda's husband. Such ageing lotharios were sadly two a penny in the principality. Abigail felt piqued by the impossible standards of beauty imposed upon Monaco women: to be stunning at all times, to never show the slightest signs of age, and most importantly to be slim, yet full-breasted. At that moment, she passed by Botero's Rubenesque statues of Adam and Eve. They seemed like a gentle, artistic protest against the principality's obsession with dieting.

Then there was Polina's fiancé: that hypocritical blowhard who failed to accept that his own dubious dating choice carried as much blame as his fiancé's career choice. Abigail pondered: how could a man get engaged to someone whom he knew so little about? And how was it possible that he never once suspected any financial motivation behind a stunning young woman 'falling in love' with a much older, wealthy man? No doubt, Polina's fiancé was duped by his own ego.

Finally, there was Barbara's son-in-law and his hitman plot: extreme even by Monaco standards. Obviously, Marcus' incompetence and arrogance had combined to produce his catastrophic business affairs. Yet that a failing business should spiral into a murder plot revealed Marcus' true Faustian nature. He wanted money and power at any cost. If anyone could control the situation, Abigail felt sure that Barbara would be the one. After all, no one else in Monaco turned the tables so successfully upon the male sex as the redoubtable Barbara.

Back at her Fontvieille flat, Abigail took off her suit jacket and grabbed a pair of jeans and a jumper from the wardrobe. As she glanced in the wardrobe mirror, she noticed a chartreuse lacy thong protruding from the back of her tailored trousers. She winced with horror as she realised that she had spent the whole day showing off such luridly embarrassing knickers: a gift from a colour-blind ex-boyfriend. She blushed as she thought of the workmen's smirks and worse still of the elegant Camille. What must she have thought?

At that moment the doorbell rang. It was Polina. She'd obviously been crying again. Her normally immaculate mascara pooled around the edges of her eyes giving her an unlikely Alice-Cooper-dressed-in-Dior look.

'You'd better wash your face before we leave,' said Abigail. 'I'll meet you outside the lobby. I'm just going to bring the car round from the garage.'

Ten minutes later, Polina stepped gingerly into the passenger seat of Abigail's Fiat Uno to avoid soiling her cream

Dior suit. She looked into the mirror to check upon her mascara situation, while Abigail lugged Polina's two gigantic Louis Vuitton suitcases into the boot and threw her own rucksack onto the back seat. Abigail slammed on the pedal to pick up Daisy from her birthday party in Port Hercules. They queued for a while behind the usual army of Range Rovers and other 4x4s that flat-dwelling Monaco mums favour for their quarter-of-a-mile commutes — as if they didn't realize that such vehicles were designed for life in the Scottish Highlands.

They eventually arrived in front of the superyacht where Daisy's friend was holding her fifth birthday. Unlikely though it might seem, superyachts were the gold standard for kids' parties in Monaco. More surprising than the location was the lengths to which some mothers would go to outshine their offspring. In the La La Land of Monaco, themed birthdays weren't just about the kids, but also about the tiger moms vying for gorgeousness dressed up as a cowgirl or Jessica Rabbit. As Abigail was escorted onto the yacht by a steward, she recognised the birthday mum as Beth, the ubiquitous evil chipmunk. Dancing around a pole in the middle of the deck, Beth was dolled up as Wonder Woman complete with blue-starred hot pants and knock-out boobs. On the other hand, it took Abigail a further ten minutes to discover the birthday girl cowering below deck and playing with Daisy. The birthday girl tugged uncomfortably at the gaudy pink bows of her Little Bo Peep bonnet as Daisy said goodbye.

Once she had settled Daisy into the car with Polina (now thoroughly restored to immaculateness), she took the A8 motorway west. If Abigail slammed on the pedal, she would make it home in less than an hour. She turned off the motorway and wound through byroads towards her Grasse farmhouse. Abigail dubbed this area 'curbanside': that rural-urban fusion where villages merged into an endless scenic townscape. Finally, she passed through the rusty gates and down the winding drive lined with linden trees towards the 18th-century stone bastide. Her aunt Julia and her Irish wolfhound Lupa greeted them at the door.

'I have a pot of fresh bolognese waiting for you.'

Daisy dragged Polina into the garden, while Abigail joined Julia in the kitchen.

'Here, you look like you need this,' said Julia, handing over a glass of rosé.

'Yup; rough day,' said Abigail, slugging back the glass.

'I don't know how you handle the Monaco circus,' said Julia.

Abigail stood watching Julia prepare the pasta on the aga. On her left was the original *mangeoire* where the animals grazed in centuries gone by. It reminded Abigail of a simple lifestyle that had been lost forever. What used to be a vital element of the household economy was now merely a receptacle for their gleaming stainless-steel pots and pans. Modern-day sophistication had rendered them all Marie Antoinette playing the pretty spectacle of ersatz farmhouse simplicity. Yet Julia kept Abigail grounded as she had always done. She was Abigail's antidote to Monaco.

Without Julia helping to look after Daisy, Abigail would never have been able to take up the job with *Monaco Mail*. And it was only thanks to Julia's encouragement that she'd plucked up the courage to make the move to Southern France in the first place. When Abigail inherited this dilapidated olive farm from her Belgian father, it was Julia who persuaded her to move down here rather than sell up. It was Julia who took on the task of slowly renovating the farmhouse, buying a chicken coop for the garden and inspiring Abigail to try *permaculture* (no fertilisers, no plough, no weeding, but lots of straw) upon their organic vegetable garden. All the same, Abigail still sneaked in an occasional, guilty dose of Roundup when the weeds grew out of control.

Abigail took a plastic beaker of milk out to Daisy who sat in the olive grove picking flowers. Abigail laid out a blanket for Polina to sit upon and they sat in silence making daisy chains. Beside them, the olive tree canopy had grown heavy with *cailletier* olives. Though small compared to their luscious Italian counterparts, these black Niçoise olives were well suited for crushing into extra-virgin olive oil. With over 100 olive trees, they had enough olives for their own pressing at Huilerie Sainte Anne: the 300-year-old olive mill that was the last traditional mill still operating in the nearby backcountry. The ripe olives had started to fall upon the nets laid out on the ground beneath the trees. Tomorrow was the day of their harvest.

•

ABIGAIL WOKE AT 8 A.M. WITH THE GLARING NOVEMBER SUN shining through her diaphanous curtains. She slung on a pair of corduroy jeans and a baggy green jumper before heading downstairs to the kitchen. Here she found Daisy munching on fresh figs and Julia brewing up some mulled wine. She could smell the roast lamb brisket that had been cooking in the aga overnight. She grabbed a bowl of homemade muesli as she waited for their newfound friends who had all volunteered at the last minute to harvest the olives with the bribe of payment in cans of extra-virgin olive oil.

At that moment, Polina swept downstairs. In a black bodycon dress, red stilettos and matching lipstick, she looked like she'd stepped straight out of *La Dolce Vita*.

'Well, the local lads are in for a treat today,' said Julia.

First to arrive in her white VW Beetle was Lucinda with the lead of her beloved long-haired dachshund Peanut in one hand

and a bottle of champagne in the other. Abigail considered this British aristocrat as her elegant alter ego: always resplendent in silk scarves and Tropezian sandals. Today though she looked uncharacteristically tired and her shirt a little crumpled.

As Lucinda and Abigail chatted, the kitchen door swung open with her boss' girlfriend Serena and her copy editor Rob. With Hank away on another work trip, Abigail had commandeered Rob to chauffeur the car-less Serena to the olive harvest.

'Hello Abi,' cooed Serena, throwing her arms around Abigail. 'I've brought some of my tofu escalopes with black olive salsa verde.'

'I'm guessing no lamb brisket for you then,' said Julia tartly.

'Absolutely not. I've been a vegan for six years now,' said Serena.

Julia grimaced towards Abigail as Serena lectured Julia about meat-production pollution and her vegan diet saving the planet, though Serena did admit a fondness for lemon sole.

'So, you don't mind killing sole then,' said Julia. 'Even though 90% of the world's fish stocks are fully exploited, overexploited or depleted? Perhaps sole is less cute than lamb?'

Julia was one of the few women who made Abigail look positively diplomatic. Abigail steered Serena towards Lucinda who was busy popping champagne corks and opening bottles of rosé. Abigail went to the door to greet their closest neighbour, Jean-Pierre. This retired factory worker had spent four decades working in nearby Grasse for the Fragonard perfume factory where he had become Grasse's inter-factory *Pétanque* (French bowls) champion. Having lost his wife to cancer the year before, he had grown close to Julia. He taught her how to play *Pétanque* and even how to make *vin d'orange*. Whenever Julia was away, he would collect the post and take care of the chickens.

More *Grassois* followed: the plumber, the butcher, the florist and other villagers that Abigail and Julia had befriended in the last six months. They came bearing Southern French gifts: rosemary-sprinkled *fougasse* bread and almond-and-orange *calisson* candies. They grouped together on the terrace with glasses of rosé in hand as they swapped gossip of village life.

The last to arrive was the formidable Barbara Esson, who arrived in a chauffeur-driven Bentley. With her tartan-clad Westie, Laird, on a lead, she stalked gingerly across the gravel drive and into the bastide. She looked around with her critical eye and arched an eyebrow towards the collected villagers as if expecting them to bow down before her. Julia stifled a giggle.

With the whole party assembled, Abigail took them over to the olive grove where ladders had been set up beneath a dozen trees. Each family took a different tree: one would collect the fallen olives, another would pick olives from the lower branches, and yet another would climb the ladder to pick the highest olives. As they embarked upon collecting olives, Barbara surveyed the scene imperiously from the terrace balcony. Meanwhile, Polina surprised everyone by whipping off her stilettos, borrowing some wellington boots and shimmying up a ladder to collect a bucket full of olives: much to the enjoyment of the local lads who gazed smirkingly up her dress.

An hour later, the ground was awash with buckets brimming with olives. Then there was a cheer as a tractor pulled into the drive with a tree shaker. This hydraulic arm would grab hold of the tree trunk and shake the tree mechanically while the olives fell to the ground. It reminded Abigail of a robot arm on a slot machine. It was there to do the lion's share of the work as the remaining trees would be harvested over the following week with the tree shaker.

'At last, the work force,' cried Barbara.

The friends washed their olive-stained hands in a makeshift

basin of water before gathering on the terrace for lunch. Julia brought out the brisket along with BBQ sausages, platters of roasted root vegetables from parsnips to Jerusalem artichoke and potatoes *boulangères* (roasted with onions and sprinkled with rosemary). Lunch rolled on to more bottles of rosé. One group splintered off to play *Pétanque* with Jean-Pierre taking the lead, while Serena and Rob wandered off by themselves into the olive grove with a bottle of rosé in hand.

Lucinda and Abigail sneaked off to the kitchen to find Barbara downing a glass of single malt. Now that Barbara had taken off her sunglasses, Abigail noticed her puffed-up face. No amount of foundation could cover the bruises.

'I know it's a little early for whisky, but I need some reinforcement after last night.'

'Me too,' said Lucinda.

They all grabbed shots of whisky as Barbara debriefed them both on the night before with her murderous son-in-law. Then Lucinda took the floor sobbing through a box of tissues as she told them all about Leo. Abigail listened to this black comedy of events that seemed too over-the-top to be true.

Lucinda lit a cigarette: 'You know the only thing that Leo ever introduced me to was smoking. It's ironic that such a pan-European socialite ended up leeching off my friends.'

Polina appeared with her mobile phone in hand and an aloof manner. Abigail invited her to join them in shots of whisky. Polina seemed reluctant as she mumbled something about waiting for a phone call from her friend Leyla.

'My banker Damian was chatting to me yesterday,' said Barbara. 'He mentioned that a client of his wanted to cancel a wedding-gift cheque for €1 million.'

Polina flinched.

'Apparently, his fiancé's best friend told him that his wife-to-be was a high-class hooker. Although Damian didn't mention any names, it didn't take much to put two and two together.'

Suddenly all efforts at composure were lost. Polina hurled her phone across the kitchen. There was a smash as the phone knocked over a tray of champagne glasses on the kitchen counter, and shards of glass shattered over the floor. She screeched out a jumble of words about lies and jealousy. Piecing together the verbal scattergun: it seemed that Leyla had been jealous of Polina's engagement and her modelling work, so had decided to tell 'lies' about her. She ended her diatribe with the words: 'Dimitri is cockroach.'

'A dim cockroach at that,' observed Barbara.

Abigail sought to dial down the emotions as she turned the conversation to Lucinda's recent photoshoot for *Monaco Mail*. She opened up her ever-present laptop and dug out one of the shots.

'Look,' said Abigail. 'Don't you love the backdrop of that painting?'

All four women looked towards the laptop as Polina remarked:

'I know that painting — Dimitri sold for €8 million.'

'I think you've added too many zeros,' said Lucinda. 'Leo doesn't have that kind of money for art anymore.'

'Actually, I heard it was sold for double that amount. €16 million, wasn't it?' said Abigail.

Abigail paused as she wondered how to broach the delicate matter of Victoria paying for the painting hanging in Leo and Lucinda's flat. Yet Polina insisted upon the amount of €8 million. She went into detail about how she had seen a blond with a leopard-skin dress arrive at Dimitri's flat to view the painting and that the next day, an art dealer ('Hank who owns *Monaco Mail*') had come over again to give Dimitri a cheque for precisely €8 million.

'Was the woman's name Victoria, by any chance?' demanded Lucinda.

Polina nodded.

'Wait... Victoria bought a €16-million painting for Leo as a romantic gift?' said Barbara.

'I'm not sure my husband is worth that much,' said Lucinda.

'If the painting was bought for €8 million and then sold a few weeks later for double that amount,' said Abigail 'that means my demonic boss, who hasn't paid anybody's wages for two months, has a sideline as an art fraudster.'

'Well, that's all of us fucked,' summed up Barbara. 'What the hell do we do now?'

Part Two

REVENGE

13

Lucinda

'SHALL WE SPOIL OURSELVES WITH A GLASS OF RUINART?'
said Lucinda.

Lucinda and Emily sat down on the outdoor terrace at
La Voile d'Or overlooking the St-Jean-Cap-Ferrat port. Emily
smoothed her silk crepe dress, hanging her pastel-pink Gucci
bag on the chair, while Lucinda removed her taupe silk kimono
to reveal a Forte-Forte blouse over skinny jeans, and settled
Peanut at her feet. They could have been in London's Notting
Hill — very bohemian for the expat Riviera crowd.

'Well, *I'm* having one,' said Lucinda.

The waiter overheard, and walked over, smiling
conspiratorially. '*Bonjour Mesdemoiselles, un verre de champagne?
Ou deux?*'

'*Deux!*' said Emily.

Lucinda was relieved. She didn't want to drink on her own.

'I cannot believe how bloody blind I was,' said Lucinda. 'You know Mathieu, the concierge who flirts with me? He told me point blank that Victoria came to our apartment to see Leo while I was in London the other week.'

'No!' Emily's eyes widened as she gave Lucinda her full attention.

'Yes. She was in our apartment and neither she nor Leo said a word.' She fingered the diamond heart necklace that Leo had given her in better days. 'He told me he didn't even like fake boobs.'

'Oh Lu…'

'And that's not all. There's this painting of a nude in our flat. Long story, but Leo didn't buy it. Victoria did. And it's in our flat.'

'That doesn't make any sense.'

The waiter arrived with two glasses of champagne, which he placed on round coasters with the hotel's logo.

'The thought of it just makes me feel sick,' said Lucinda.

'Yeah, I can imagine,' said Emily, gulping down her champagne and staring unblinkingly at Lucinda. 'Please don't take this the wrong way, Lu. But I have to admit, I couldn't bear meeting you and Leo together recently. He always puts you down. It's really upsetting.'

'Why didn't you tell me?' Lucinda asked.

Emily deftly changed the conversation.

•

LUCINDA DROVE HOME PAST THE TRAIN STATION ENTRANCE on boulevard Princesse Charlotte. The grand 19th-century houses, with port views, were hidden behind foliage from this busy Monaco thoroughfare.

As she approached her street, the front of her chest

tightened. It had been a relief to spend time at Abigail's with her three troubled book-club friends, playing *pétanque* in the olive grove to the sound of cicadas. The restorative glasses of Ruinart with Emily had helped too. But now they were back in Monaco, nothing could block out the reality. It took all of her energy to manoeuvre down the helter-skelter carpark, past Monegasque, Dutch and Swiss number plates to her space at minus five. Peanut whimpered with excitement. They were home.

Moments flashed through her memory. All those times Leo had given Victoria the cold shoulder. And vice versa. That hot afternoon at the beach when Leo and Victoria played backgammon. The dinner party at Frédéric and Caroline's when Victoria chided Leo for being rude. And now the painting. A spectacularly expensive masterpiece gifted by Victoria to Leo. In their flat. An ugly painting. An ugly truth.

•

SHE EXITED THE LIFT ON THE 35TH FLOOR, WHERE SHE bumped into the son of her Monegasque neighbour with dementia. She was known to wander around the corridors of Le Millefiori naked.

'*Bonjour Monsieur. Comment va votre mère?*'

'She's going downhill. Age is a steady decline, until we become completely dependent, like babies,' said the man, only a few years older than Lucinda.

'I'm so sorry.' A moment of remorse for someone other than herself: a welcome distraction from her own ordeal.

'By the way,' he continued, 'you should know that my mother's flat was burgled when I was out for lunch with her yesterday. They managed to pick the lock. They took some jewels and cash. She didn't really have anything of value. I thought you should know.'

She looked at the door lock on his mother's flat. It was the original 1960s lock just like the one Lucinda recently replaced in her apartment. She felt slightly reassured. Her mind turned to the two suspicious women she'd seen leaving the building the other day.

'I will have to find a place for her somewhere where she can be properly cared for. This can't go on.'

'It must be difficult for you,' said Lucinda, bidding her neighbour farewell.

Lucinda wished the conversation could have continued, rather than having to face what was behind her own door. She turned the key. Silence. And then the sound of Leo's voice, speaking French. She took a deep breath and exhaled slowly, before speaking.

'When were you going to tell me?' Lucinda said.

'I'll call you back,' he told the person on the other end of the line.

'Tell you what?' he said, looking slightly nervous.

'About you and Victoria,' she said.

'What are you talking about?' He closed his laptop.

'I know everything. About her. About the painting. It's hers. Not yours. Not ours.'

Leo sipped his gin martini.

'It was Beth's idea, not mine, not Victoria's. Everyone knows you get over emotional. And now look at you. You're overreacting. Just as we all thought you would.'

Lucinda noticed a blank space where a grand family portrait used to hang.

'It is just a little favour to Victoria,' continued Leo. 'While she is moving things around. We knew you would take it badly.'

'You lied to me,' she said quietly.

'Just a little white lie.'

'What about Victoria?'

'What about her?'

'I know she's been here.'

Leo kept his poker face.

'I should have known better,' said Lucinda. 'What girlfriend or wife have you *not* cheated on?'

'Don't be ridiculous? There is no one else. I just don't want to be married to *you*.'

Lucinda had not read the divorce papers. Only 11 pages long. But she couldn't bring herself to read them.

'Cleo,' said Leo. 'I didn't cheat on Cleo.'

'The wife who took you to the cleaners?'

Somehow this revelation roused Lucinda from her paralysis.

'The wife who's the reason you refuse to live in the UK ever again? The wife who was so attached to your family heirlooms that she insisted she keep them all? The wife who insists on keeping your silly title to this day even though it doesn't hold legally? She's the *only* one you didn't cheat on?'

'Yes.'

How could she have been such a fool? How could she have left her first husband for him? She thought back to the weekend she first met Leo at a boar shoot near Coburg in Germany. A group of rich South Americans had paid a fortune to shoot wild boar. But the swine turned out to be more domesticated than wild. And the boars were also enormous: as big as cars and several times bigger than any seen in France or Italy. It made for a disappointing shoot. There were only two women on the shoot: Lucinda and Leo's third wife Laura. The two of them with their spouses were the only ones drinking gin martinis. That fateful Saturday evening, Leo seduced Lucinda into a clinch on top of the walnut sideboard beneath the deer antlers. Unfortunately, Laura caught them *in flagrante*.

'Listen, I haven't got time to fight. I have an appointment. Will you take Peanut out to poop before you go out?' said Lucinda, kissing Peanut as she left.

•

SHE ARRIVED AT THE FONTVIEILLE LAW OFFICE OF MARIE Morales, a.k.a. 'the rottweiler'. The door looked like a massive bank vault from a *James Bond* film.

'So Monaco can be modern when it wants to be,' Lucinda thought to herself, imagining the scandalous stories filed behind that heavy door.

She pressed the buzzer on the left. A camera stared down at her from a corner in the ceiling. Seconds later, a young girl answered.

'I have an appointment with Madame Morales. My name is Lucinda. Lucinda Kiddington.'

The young girl ushered her in with minimal politeness. She walked Lucinda to a small waiting room dotted with red-and-white geraniums: a patriotic nod towards the red-and-white Monaco flag. Lucinda despised geraniums. She waited for at least 20 minutes: leafing through assorted gossip magazines and staring at the geraniums, before the lawyer finally walked in. Unsmiling and expensively dressed, just as she expected.

Lucinda took her copy of the signed court order out of her bag and passed it on to Madame Morales. She explained that she had been served these papers a few days earlier.

There was a long silence.

'Looking at this, he appears to be blaming you for the divorce.'

'He said it was amicable. I'm sorry, I haven't even had a chance to look at this properly. I've been out of sorts.'

'Well, this is far from amicable. I imagine that he must have some evidence. No doubt he has *attestations*: witness statements testifying to your 'faults'. I would say that he's been planning this for a while.'

Lucinda was shocked.

'Look, to save yourself some money,' said Madame Morales. 'Google the legal articles mentioned in the documents, and you'll see why this isn't an amicable affair.'

Lucinda remained silent.

'Is there anyone else?' said Madame Morales.

'No, of course not.'

'And what about your husband?'

'He says there is no one else.'

'What about you? What do you want?'

That was a good question. What did she want? The question felt rather existential. She didn't want to divorce. She wanted things to go back to the way they were, but that was a long time ago. Clearly, she was not prepared for this meeting: neither emotionally, nor in a practical sense. Lucinda watched her €500 fee fly away into nothingness in the space of this brief meeting.

Madame Morales appeared annoyed at having her time wasted. She suggested Lucinda have a 'good think'. She did not find the lawyer empathetic. If this was meant to be the most feminist lawyer in the principality, what was the average lawyer in Monaco like?

No, she just had to toughen up. She recalled the wise words of her father when — as a child — she complained once about a compassionless surgeon, operating on her little finger: 'Lucinda, darling. We're paying him to be your doctor, not to be your friend.'

'I don't want to divorce. I want to make it work.'

'Right. Well, I suggest you tell him so. You've got a few weeks before you're called before a judge. Your husband will have his lawyer. Assuming you would like to proceed in this fashion, you should go alone. As in, without representation. You could suggest that you both have more time before making any rash decision. It says here that he would like to separate formally as soon as possible. Things move quickly here. You could ask the judge to give you a few months to work on your relationship together. That is what you call amicable.'

Lucinda listened. She was tired. She hadn't eaten a proper breakfast that morning.

'Have a think and let me know what you decide. Be aware that Monaco is patriarchal. You are not in France or England. His word is more important than yours. And these testimonials, which he will have organised by now, are considered more important than his opinion, and yours of course.'

'How can I protect myself?'

'I'm afraid there isn't much you can do. This is Monaco. There are benefits to living here, and then there are disadvantages. If you're expecting to be treated fairly, don't. You are aware that men have the rights when it comes to children, until they reach adulthood? Not the mothers. Otherwise, Monaco would be a matriarchy. Have you signed a *Contrat de Mariage*?'

'Yes, I signed a contract saying I wouldn't ask for any family heirlooms should we decide to divorce. I have no problem with that. The heirlooms aren't mine.'

'Bottom line,' continued Madame Morales. 'If he gives you both more time, then you have something to work with. If not, you need to work on getting your own testimonials.'

•

LUCINDA WAS LOST IN THOUGHT WHEN SHE REACHED THE door of the flat and heard Peanut whimpering. It smelled foul. She opened the door to discover a trail of dark thick diarrhoea leading from the kitchen all the way to Peanut's bed in the sitting room. Even Beans' poo incident at Caroline's dinner party was a picnic compared to this.

'Oh my God,' she said out loud. 'He didn't take you out, did he?'

Lucinda was furious. Leo must have left without taking out Peanut, who was clearly ill, not to mention distressed. She picked him up and took him downstairs to the grass beside their apartment block. Peanut walked uncomfortably, while she dialled Leo's mobile.

'Yes?'

'You forgot to take Peanut out. Poor thing has shat all over the flat. Where are you?'

'I'm at the Mercedes showroom in Fontvieille.'

'What do you mean you are at Mercedes? What are you doing at Mercedes?'

'The Bluetooth was not in sync with my iPhone. I needed them to have a look at it.'

'How could you just leave him like that? Peanut is obviously ill. Poor thing is shitting dark liquid poo everywhere. It stinks. I need your help here.'

This idea of making the marriage work was not off to a great start. Some acquaintances arrived at the Millefiori, staring at the brown marks on Lucinda's blouse from carrying Peanut.

'Come home now.' Her voice screamed into her mobile and from the car's speakers at high volume into the Mercedes showroom for everyone to hear, prompting the salesman next to Leo to turn down the volume in the car, as she continued. 'There is shit everywhere.'

'Good news,' said Leo. 'The Bluetooth is working.'

Lucinda hung up. Back in the flat, she placed a miserable Peanut in the empty bathtub and closed the door. She cleaned up the mess as best she could, while Peanut cried from behind the door. Minutes later, she opened the door to find Peanut had climbed out of the bath. Not only was he now completely covered in diarrhoea, but there were also poo paw prints all over the floor and the inside of the door. Her life, her flat, it was all shit.

•

WITH THE FLAT AND PEANUT BOTH CLEANED UP, THERE WAS still no sign of Leo. Deciding to have a look at the court order, she went to the office. The desk had side-by-side stations: the right side for Leo, the left side for Lucinda. Her desk looked like chaos, but she knew where everything was. Papers would often fall from Leo's side onto her side. Usually, she'd move his paperwork carefully over to his side. Today, she just shoved it all over, not caring that half the stuff fell onto the floor. As she tossed his stapler to his side, it hit his keyboard, prompting his computer to turn on. She saw a tab on his computer that read hopeandwisdom.com. When she clicked on it, it was a locked account. That piqued her curiosity, so she went into her computer and googled *Hope and Wisdom*.

'Mutually Beneficial Relationships…No strings attached… Sign up to *Hope and Wisdom* now.'

She clicked on 'Learn More.'

'An arrangement is where people are direct with one another and stop wasting time…Money isn't an issue… thus they are generous when it comes to supporting a Sugar Baby…'

Again, she clicked on 'Learn More,' as she held her breath.

'Many traditional relationships fail because there is not enough give, and too much take. Every successful relationship is an arrangement between two parties. In business, partners sign business agreements that outline their objectives and expectations. *Hope and Wisdom* is your dating solution.'

She usually did not smoke in the office. 'Fuck it,' she thought, as she opened the door to the terrace and lit a cigarette. A wet, newly clean Peanut came over and had a thorough shake before turning in a circle and sitting next to Lucinda's feet.

She looked at the court order on her desk. It was an official ordinance stating that Leo wanted to divorce her and informing her that she was to meet with him and his lawyer in front of a judge at the Palais de Justice, Monaco's courthouse next to the cathedral in the Old Town. In three weeks. Attached were copies of their residency cards, passports, and wedding documents. Leo asked for sole occupancy of the flat.

She googled 'Article 197 du code civil.' There were three reasons for using this article for divorce in Monegasque civil law:

1. Infidelity
2. Abuse
3. A criminal conviction making the marriage intolerable

Nothing made sense. Their marriage hadn't been plain sailing for months, but why had he not sat down and talked to her? And what on earth compelled him to open an account with hopeandwisdom.com? They hadn't slept together much for the past year, but still. What exactly was his relationship with Victoria? Was there any point in trying to make this work? It was hard to do anything when he was not even around. But she couldn't give up yet. She couldn't face two failed marriages. She had to give it another chance. She decided she would go before the judge by herself, and request three to six months to try and work things out. That was reasonable, wasn't it? The judge would have to have a heart of steel to not grant that request.

•

SHE SPENT THE NEXT FEW DAYS GETTING LOST IN THE world of *The Count of Monte Cristo*. It was a welcome diversion.

Leo was absent a lot of the time. Aside from this adventure novel, Peanut distracted her as did occasional chats over drinks with acquaintances. But she was most looking forward to the book club meeting.

When she did manage to see Leo, he was obviously avoiding her.

'Why don't we go to a therapist?' she asked.

'It's too late.'

'But we have never spoken about this. You just hurled abuse at me.'

It was clear that he wanted out and he wanted out now. She felt desperate to make her marriage work, but she did not want to be insulted either. She looked at this man sitting opposite her, and his familiar face, and realised he was now a stranger. But she couldn't face the reality of their break-up yet.

When the evening of the meeting arrived, she grabbed her well-used copy of *The Count of Monte Cristo,* kissed Peanut, gave him a treat, and told him: 'I'll be back with you as soon as possible, my love,' and closed the door behind her.

14

Abigail

ABIGAIL PERCHED HERSELF ON A STOOL AT THE GOLD-mosaiced Salle Blanche bar. She yanked up the bodice of her black dress self-consciously and slipped off the right heel of her tight Louboutin stiletto. Her outfit had been lent by Serena, who was on a fruitless mission to 'Monaco' her. Abigail wondered why her publisher Hank had organised an evening out at the Monte Carlo Casino for the *Monaco Mail* editorial team when he'd given neither Rob nor herself more than a cursory glance since they arrived. She could hear Hank's Ottawa Valley twang from a distance as he held court at the French roulette table. Next to him sat Dimitri Nalimov whose posterior spilled onto a second seat. The two of them exchanged lewd jokes as they vied for victory with ever-increasing piles of casino chips. A gold-lamé-clad brunette approached the table. Hank flashed his newly whitened teeth in welcome.

'A gin and tonic for your thoughts.'

Abigail turned to see a slender, well-dressed man smiling at her. She recognised him as Barbara's banker.

'Damian, isn't it?' said Abigail as she acquiesced to the drink.

'Look at those dazzling white incisors,' said Damian, nodding towards Hank. 'Quite the crocodile.'

'Indeed, he fits in perfectly with all the other reptiles here. No wonder this casino is his second home.'

They sat down at a table with their drinks as they watched the VIP gamblers play. Some sat on the glass-enclosed Salle Blanche terrace that looked up towards the stars and out towards the Mediterranean Sea. Others sat beneath a gigantic Belle-Epoque painting of three naked courtesans. Her copy editor Rob arrived and minutes later, Serena. Rob was jubilant from a win on the slot machines in the Salle des Amériques. So what if the slot machines were looked down upon by high rollers. Rob was unperturbed by snobbery.

'Don't tell my mum I missed the family Friday-night meal for a gambling session,' said Rob. 'All in the name of work, I suppose.'

The four of them laughed over a bottle of rosé champagne that they put onto Hank's bill. Only Serena seemed a little downcast: perhaps she had spotted Hank dribbling over the brunette at the roulette table. While Rob regaled them with tales of his winning slot-machine punches, he laid his hand gently on Serena's back in silent reassurance. Abigail listened, sipping her champagne and pondering the irony that international Monaco residents like themselves were allowed to gamble in Monte Carlo, while local Monegasques were banned by law from the sport.

'Serena, how long have you been here?'

They all turned to see Hank looking glassy-eyed from too many vodka martinis.

'Come and join us,' continued Hank, tossing his hand imperiously in the direction of the French roulette table.

'I'm in the middle of a conversation,' said Serena.

Hank noticed Rob's hand on Serena's shoulder.

'Rob, your babysitting duty is over. You can bugger off.'

Rob sat still. So did Serena. In an attempt to quell the rebellion, Hank manhandled Serena clumsily off her chair. Rob grabbed his arms to stop him.

'Get your fucking hand off my arm,' said Hank. 'Remember, I pay your salary.'

'Actually, you haven't paid anyone's salary for the last six weeks,' said Rob.

'Leave now, you moron, before I sack you,' said Hank.

'I'll save you the bother,' said Rob. 'I quit.'

In his fury, Hank swung around to punch Rob in the mouth. Flecks of blood spattered as Rob fell to the floor. Damian rushed to grab Hank from the back and stop him lunging again towards Rob. Arriving at the fracas, the casino security guards grabbed Hank and frogmarched him efficiently out of the casino.

'*Connards*,' Hank shouted, kicking one of the guards in the shin.

Abigail and Damian followed the security guards, who bestowed on Hank the dubious honour of a lifetime ban from the Monte Carlo Casino. Still high from the drama, Abigail and Damian wandered home together towards Fontvieille where they both lived. Abigail felt at ease with Damian. Passing by the Automobile Club of Monaco, they noticed an unusual window dressing. Live porn. The security guard must have switched channels from the usual motorsports, forgetting about the street-window TV projection.

'Welcome to window undressing in Monte Carlo,' giggled Abigail.

•

'WINNING IS 100% IN YOUR HEAD,' SAID ADAM MCCOULTY.
'You have to understand how to deliver the killer blow.'

Abigail struggled to concentrate through the fuzz of her
hangover. She was interviewing Formula One driver McCoulty
over lunch. With *Monaco Mail's* entertainment budget only
stretching to fast food, McCoulty had been magnanimous
about dining at a burger joint, Grubers, on the pedestrianised
rue Princesse Caroline.

'It was one of those crawl-through-the-floor moments,'
said McCoulty, describing his most embarrassing race moment
when he shunted his car just ten minutes into a race. 'I won
the race, but with my car in broken parts.' McCoulty was
refreshingly honest about the sacrifices that entire families made
towards Formula One success. Some parents mortgaged their
house to finance their child's fledgling driving careers, while
many racing drivers spent more time with their engineering
teams than their own family.

As McCoulty spoke, Abigail scribbled notes in shorthand.
With a microphone attached to her phone recording the
interview, notes were redundant. But they were a useful pretext
for her bashfulness. Known to her friends as one of the world's
worst drivers, Abigail knew next to nothing about the world
of motor-racing. She'd prepared for the interview by cooking
dinner for two petrolhead friends who'd given her the lowdown
on racing lingo as she plied them with bolognese. She scattered
her questions with references to 'G-forces', 'traction control'
and 'engine mapping'. Abigail smiled at the irony when
McCoulty complimented her on her racing knowledge.

Interview over, Abigail was running late for a meeting
with her art-auction friend, Camille Marceau. She raced uphill
towards the central shopping district in Monte Carlo, the most

central of Monaco's eight districts, and the only one that any foreigner knew about. In her hurry, she tripped and broke her shoe heel.

She toyed briefly with the idea of buying Super Glue to fix the heel, but realised she'd be even more late. Instead, she hobbled on one heel into Mada One — the new luxury fast-food cafe dreamt up by a Michelin-starred chef inspired by his Caribbean roots. She spotted Camille in a window seat, smiling at her in amusement. Abigail wondered if every meeting with Camille would involve a sartorial humiliation. Apologising for her lateness and her ridiculous appearance, Abigail got down to business.

'I need your help,' said Abigail.

This phrase divides Monaco. Many nouveau-riche Monaco residents recoil when asked to help others: except for photo opportunities to show off their good work. But old-time Monegasques still believe in *noblesse oblige*. Abigail surmised that Camille belonged to the latter camp. Abigail laid bare her financial worries and all those other unpaid *Monaco Mail* employees. She explained Hank's art fraud, and finally put forward her proposal for a sting operation.

'You do know that my intelligence-service days are long behind me,' said Camille casually lighting a Gauloise blonde cigarette.

Abigail paused, wondering how best to respond, as Camille smiled.

'Bien sûr, I'm happy to make an exception when it comes to a *connard* like Vert.'

'Con…art: that seems apt,' said Abigail.

•

LEAVING MADA ONE CAFÉ, ABIGAIL HOBBLED TOWARDS THE boulevard des Moulins for her next appointment with Dr

Pimpant. In Monte Carlo, every woman has a gynaecologist. And no gynaecologist was more sought-after in the principality than Dr Pimpant: Monaco's very own Dr McDreamy. Every woman wanted him, and his five-year waiting list proved it.

New mums had been known to literally swoon over his *rééducation périnéale* course involving muscle electrostimulation of the vaginal area with a smooth, oval instrument that vibrated. One of the most extraordinary aspects of this postnatal course (dubbed the 'Mum's dildo course') was that it was all paid for by Monaco's national health service. Never could it be said that Monaco failed to keep its perineums in tip-top shape. No incontinence pants needed for Monegasque women. Although she wasn't a new mum, Abigail had been recommended for the course due to an issue with her pelvic floor — she sometimes leaked a little when laughing — that had dogged her since Daisy's birth. She was lucky enough to jump the line via a senior contact at the Princesse Grace Hospital.

On her way to the appointment, Abigail nipped into a shoe shop to buy a new pair of pumps. The leopard skin-print ballerina shoes were neither her usual style, nor her usual price range. But she couldn't face meeting Dr Pimpant hobbling in a broken heel. With her fancy new togs at odds with the dullness of her suit, Abigail arrived at the doorway to the discreet first-floor surgery above the Baby Dior boutique. She pressed the intercom. Waiting for an answer, she scanned the spotless shop display of designer-baby apparel. Everything from cashmere bodysuits to fur-lined ski suits with four-figure price tags. It made Abigail furious to imagine tens of thousands of euros being spent on a toddler's wardrobe that would be outgrown within months. Yet all thoughts of extravagant waste were forgotten when the door catch released, and Abigail drifted upstairs to Gynaecology Heaven.

An hour later, Abigail returned blinkingly to the street

and switched her phone back on. Five messages bleeped at her: all from Hank. She had avoided the office all day. After the night before, she couldn't face a showdown with Hank. She texted back a feeble message about her Formula One interview running over and about various office errands. She promised a meeting with him first thing the next morning.

She raced back to the apartment to set the scene for their first book club meeting. They had all agreed that meeting at her flat would be the best way to avoid any interruptions as no one ever visited Abigail at her flat. The Memmo Center was too austere in its perfection to suit Abigail, who preferred a more worn-in aesthetic. The white-tiled kitchen floor showed every speck of dirt and screamed high maintenance, while her bargain-discount clothes felt like an insult to the wood-panelled, walk-in wardrobe. Whenever Abigail entered the lobby, the concierge would glare at her as if she were lowering the tone of the building.

After a quick shower, Abigail prepared the essentials: a bottle of rosé in the fridge and a copy of *The Count of Monte Cristo* on the coffee table. At 7 p.m. precisely, the doorbell rang with the arrival of Polina and Lucinda. Not a minute early, not a minute late. Barbara followed 20 minutes later with a bottle of single malt in her fist like a baby's dummy. Settling down upon the linen sofas, they exchanged gossip, avoiding the topic of revenge. Abigail regaled them all with her night out at the Monte Carlo Casino and the TV show at the Automobile Club of Monaco.

'The ACM is so eccentric,' agreed Barbara. 'When I joined, I was sent an introductory booklet with all the rules that read: 'No children under 16 may dine in the restaurant, but dogs are welcome.' I was so tempted to turn up with Laird and demand a four-course canine dinner for him.'

Then Lucinda took centre-stage with a tale about suicide.

A month ago, Leo's friend Frédéric shot himself in an apparent suicide. His wife Caroline was visiting her parents in Brussels when it happened.

'Now the insurance firm is asking questions,' said Lucinda.

The crime scene raised doubts. The positioning of the gun seemed off for a suicide. Rumours were starting to surface about the dubious state of their marriage. Allegedly, Caroline was having an affair with her tennis coach, Arthur.

'And now the insurance firm has just found out that Arthur was on vacation in Southern France at the time of Frédéric's death,' said Lucinda.

'Maybe Caroline was playing the long game,' said Barbara.

'Gosh! Sounds a bit far-fetched,' said Abigail. 'I've met Caroline and she seems more Stepford wife than murder mastermind.'

Barbara laughed gleefully: 'Well, I nearly murdered Angie Guilder last week when we went to Jeanne's 40th birthday.'

The well-liked Monaco socialite Jeanne's birthday guest list comprised most of Monaco's alpha females. None were as pushy as Angie Guilder, whose main claim to fame was her husband's film-production company that filled their Villefranche-sur-Mer villa at weekends with A-list Hollywood stars.

'Angie suggested we share a birthday present for Jeanne,' said Barbara. 'It seemed like a good idea. What I didn't realise was that Angie's idea of a suitable 40th-birthday present would be a traffic-cone-orange crocodile Gucci handbag at an eye-watering €2,500.'

'Only in Monaco,' said Abigail.

'Yeah, but that's not the worst,' said Barbara, taking a slug of her whisky. 'When we get to Alain Ducasse's Louis XV restaurant, Angie starts sneering about the house wine on the table. Then she grabs the wine menu and orders a €10,000 bottle of vintage Château Latour.'

'Wow, that's a generous gift,' said Lucinda.

'Yeah, I thought so too. But then Angie looks at me and says — I kid you not — "Jeanne will be paying for the Latour, not me."'

'What? She put the wine on Jeanne's bill?'

'Yup! She spouted some rubbish about 'revenge for Jeanne not inviting our husbands to her 40th.' Can you believe it?'

Nothing in Monaco shocked Abigail anymore. She had witnessed more outrageous behaviour in 18 months living in this tax-free square mile than in two decades living in London. Abigail smiled at how disparate women became friends here. Within the expat world of Monaco, it wasn't unusual for unlikely friendships to form. The lack of social choice in this tiny principality broke down the usual divides of education and socio-economic status.

With many husbands working abroad from Monday to Friday, women were often left to fend for themselves. These abandoned women referred jokingly to themselves as the 'Monaco widows'. At the best of times, kindness and camaraderie replaced commonality as they forged strong friendships. At the worst of times, female friends were merely frenemies in the endless fight to secure the prize of an unattached Monaco male.

As the evening drew on, the wine, whisky and gossip helped to ease the awkwardness. Finally, they broached the topic of retribution. They chatted back and forth about how they would help each other achieve their mutual goal of revenge. They discussed taking Polina's ex-fiancé to court over the uncashed cheque; setting a honey trap for Leo and making Victoria share the pain of infidelity that she had caused Lucinda; revealing Hank's art fraud through a complex sting operation; and devising a plan to eject Marcus from Sophie's life.

By the end of the evening, they dreamt up a master plan

for revenge worthy of Alexandre Dumas himself. Were their own moral codes warped by Monaco's looking-glass world enough not to question their own vindictive motivations? Were they too intent upon vengeance to dwell upon any unexpected and unwanted consequences? As she pondered these questions, Abigail thought of Dumas' own words: 'He who pours out vengeance runs the risk of tasting a bitter draught.' And then she put her qualms to one side.

15

Polina

POLINA LEANT BACK IN HER TERRACE CHAIR AND PRESSED *submit*. There! Her profile was now live on the *Hope and Wisdom* website: a new sugar-daddy website with a rapidly growing following.

Reeling in men was second nature to Polina. Easy as shooting fish in a barrel. It was all about making him feel desired and understood, along with a tantalising glimpse of what would be on offer if he behaved well. She knew that men seldom let on to their wives what they really liked in the bedroom: a reticence that rapidly disappeared when it came to paid encounters. Abigail's suggestion that Lucinda give them some hints about Leo's sexual predilections for the sugar-daddy sting had been rather naive in that regard. It just goes to show that education doesn't equal street smarts. Poor Lucinda! How she had squirmed at the conversation. Of course, Polina would ignore everything Lucinda said about Leo. Romantic gestures, gourmet cooking and flat chests were not going to be the hook in this fishing contest. But then, as the conversation wandered off topic, Polina struck gold.

'Have any more artworks gone missing from the flat?' Abigail asked Lucinda in a sympathetic tone.

'Yes, another family portrait disappeared. But I've had a rather good find.'

'Oh, do tell.'

'I found Leo's long-lost Marilyn Monroe collection.'

'Err, did I hear that correctly?' Abigail said.

'Yes, it's an odd one I must admit,' Lucinda said, with a slightly embarrassed laugh. 'But not without value as I understand it. He's been buying select pieces for years.'

She continued, 'I'm sure you know the famous dress from the *Seven Year Itch* that blows upwards when Marilyn stands over a subway vent?'

'Yes, of course. It's iconic.'

'Well, Leo once flew to LA to bid on that dress at Julien's Auctions.'

'Goodness! He really is a fan, isn't he?' Abigail said, stifling a giggle.

Lucinda began to giggle as well. 'He missed out on the dress, but he did come home with a pair of her stockings, a bra and her kitchen telephone from 1961.'

Lucinda and Abigail fell about laughing, but Polina became excited.

'Is perfect! Perfect for *Hope and Wisdom* photo! I have beautiful photo being Marilyn in white dress! Look, I show you. I find on phone.'

Scrolling through her phone, Polina found the photo she wanted, and enlarged it.

'Look, see! I make good Marilyn.'

'Oh my, that's amazing,' said Abigail.

They all admired the image of Polina; unrecognisable as Marilyn Monroe in a platinum wig, holding down the front of her white halter neck dress as the breeze beneath blew it upwards.

'Now is easy to make Leo want me on *Hope and Wisdom*,' Polina said.

'I don't doubt it,' Lucinda said, 'It's the perfect disguise. He'll never make the connection between you as Dutch Marilyn living in Amsterdam and the woman he saw briefly at the dog event.'

•

POLINA AND ABIGAIL PAUSED OUTSIDE THE LEGAL OFFICE that housed the merciless Madame Anne-Sophie Chamet.

SPECIALISTS IN FAMILY AND COMMERCIAL LAW read the description above the lawyers' names on the signboard.

'How very sensible,' Abigail mused as she stopped to read. 'Divorce and money make the perfect marriage for a lawyer, don't you think? Or would that qualify as an oxymoron?'

Polina was becoming used to Abigail's clever little quips. They went right over her head. But there was something very warm in her manner that gave Polina a feeling of being valued and cared for, even when they weren't communicating on the same level.

Pushing the button for the third floor, they entered the mirrored lift. Polina noticed that Abigail was more smartly dressed than usual. Even so, there was only so much you could do with a Zara suit, and it didn't help that she appeared to be wearing unmatched shoes. It was beyond Polina's comprehension how Abigail could make such an error. By comparison, Polina was feeling fabulous in her white suit of high-waist shorts and slim-fit blazer. Her cleavage-revealing silk top gave a splash of bright yellow, while the ensemble was set off by tanned legs and strappy white heels.

'Before we go in, I should mention that this lawyer is known for being eccentric and unpredictable,' said Abigail, ignoring their reflection. 'But I do think she's your best chance for taking on Dimitri.'

Polina nodded acknowledgement, as she applied a quick top-up of lip gloss in the mirror.

'No one knows where her personal moral compass is pointed and there's no rhyme nor reason to the cases she takes on. But she's fond of the high-profile ones and is very adept at dealing with international media.'

Polina swallowed hard as the lift pinged their arrival. This was the first time the words 'international media' had been mentioned.

They announced themselves to the attractive French receptionist, who gave them a thorough look-over before ushering them into the meeting room. Polina's internal antenna for receiving attention hummed with satisfaction, until she came face to face with the force of nature known as Madame Chamet. Dressed in a 1990s power suit that no businesswoman other than French or Monegasque would consider wearing, Madame Chamet was a tiny, wiry package of energy with brunette pixie hair and questioning eyes. The lawyer exchanged rapid-fire introductions, before waving them toward some chairs with a flick of her hand and taking a seat herself.

'Please, sit.'

Allowing a silence, she looked from one to the other with a steady gaze until Polina cast her eyes downward and Abigail jiggled her legs nervously. Satisfied that she'd made her superior position known, she addressed herself to Abigail.

'Thank you for the thorough briefing you sent me, Madame Hackett. I have familiarised myself with your email and I think it is all very clear.'

Then she turned to Polina and took a deep breath.

'Mademoiselle Petrova.'

'Yes,' came Polina's reply, in a voice weaker than she'd have liked.

'I would now like to hear about this in your own words. I'd like you to tell me how you came to be given a cheque for €1 million by Monsieur Dimitri Nalimov, and why he later refused to honour it. Take your time and try not to leave out any details. Let's begin with how you met him...'

The lawyer listened intently, making occasional notes as Polina described her whirlwind 'romance', her move to Monaco, and the surprise engagement. She described their wedding at Le Méridien, and how their legal marriage ceremony at La Mairie was prevented by a troublemaker telling stories to Dimitri.

As she came to the end of her story, Abigail gave Polina a tight smile of encouragement as they waited for Madame Chamet's verdict.

'Well, to put it in simple terms, Mademoiselle Petrova, the cheque is an instrument contingent to the accessibility of funds, through the drawee's acknowledgement to...' Seeing Polina's confusion, Madame Chamet stopped.

'He cannot give you a cheque and then refuse to honour it because he doesn't like something that you did,' she continued. 'From what you describe, he gave you this cheque as unconditional financial security. That aside, there is no such thing as a *conditional* cheque anyway in the eyes of the law.'

'Yes! Is my cheque for promise of happy life and he should not take it away,' Polina said.

Madame Chamet looked at Polina thoughtfully as she

lightly drummed the fingers of one hand on her desk. Presently she spoke.

'I will take this case.'

Polina exchanged a delighted look with Abigail.

'Madame, I thank you,' Polina said, remembering Abigail's advice that she should try to use 'thank you' more often.

'It's just two small words, but it opens doors, Polina. You'll see what a difference it makes in our culture,' Abigail had explained.

'Now,' said Madame Chamet. 'We will start softly, softly first: try to reach an agreement, keep the details confidential, and so on. Yet, I do not think that will work. *Non, non*, it will not. Monsieur Namilov will be motivated by emotions more than logic. It can't be avoided: we will be seeing him in the courtroom. It will be everywhere in the media.'

Undeterred by the tear trickling down Polina's face, Madame Chamet continued.

'We have an expression in French; *avoir la moutarde qui monte au nez* which means to have the mustard climbing up to the nose. When a man feels he's been chopped off at the… Well, you know, if you hurt his ego, it makes him very angry, like hot mustard in the nose. You should be under no illusions, Mademoiselle Petrova, this is going to be a rough ride.'

•

POLINA LOOKED AGAIN AT THE COST ESTIMATION AND Terms of Engagement letters from Madame Chamet. She had no idea it could be so expensive. How could a lawyer justify charging so much? Frankly, she wasn't ready to think about the reality of supporting herself financially, so soon after the eclipse of her golden ticket. It was too depressing. Putting the letter aside, she logged onto the hopeandwisdom.com site. There were 35 replies already.

Polina flicked through the responses. While looking for Leo, she was also assessing suitability for her own needs. Adeptly, she cast aside each one as she considered their profiles. Delete, delete, delete, delete. Suddenly Polina stopped. She should have known to expect this. There in all his glory was Rod. The quintessential badly behaved Monaco man. Delete. When, and if needs must, she'd contact Rod directly, without the added effort of a Dutch accent and a Marilyn-Monroe-inspired romp. At least her disguise was working well. There was no sign of Leo as yet. Her profile had only been live for a few hours. He'd be in touch in due course, she was sure of that.

•

POLINA WONDERED HOW A CALL FROM BARBARA TO arrange a meeting turned into a lecture about her finances.

'It's quite simple Polina, you need more money coming in than going out, or at least the same amount coming in as going out,' said Barbara.

Polina detected a slight slur to her words. Was she drunk?

'Yes, but is very hard with big apartment rent and cost to live the life in Monaco. And now I have court case.'

'I don't disagree that your apartment is an excessive indulgence. But as you're tied into a contract, there's no point in us going there.'

Polina thought how easy it would be to hit the *end* button and finish the call.

'You need to sit down with pen and paper and draw two columns on the page,' she continued. 'The first column is called In and the second column is called Out. Are you with me, Polina?'

'Yes.'

'In the first column, write down all the ways you earn an

income and think about how you could increase that income. Could you get some more *modelling* work for example?' There was the merest hint of sarcasm behind Barbara's question, as she continued. 'In the second column, make a list of all the expenses that you could cut down on. Restaurants, for example. Perhaps you could go out say, twice per week instead of six times? Chauffeured cars are another one. Maybe you could take taxis, or even jump on a Monaco bus from time to time. I do! It's true, I really do.'

'Okay, she's definitely had one drink too many,' thought Polina as Barbara continued her monologue.

'...Clothes shopping: you could choose to not purchase any clothes, shoes or bags, for the next few months. You've got so many, and it would be a major saving.'

Polina had zoned out of Barbara's lecture, until this mention of reducing her monthly clothes bill brought her back with crystal clarity. Barbara paused when she heard Polina's sharp intake of breath.

'Thank you, Barbara,' Polina said in a sickly-sweet voice, remembering Abigail's advice about those two little words. 'Is so good all book club womans need each other and help each other so much.'

With that, she ended the call. Polina was not a two-column list type of girl and certainly not when it involved spending less money on clothes. Barbara needed a lesson in reading her audience. In the mood for some light relief, Polina logged onto hopeandwisdom.com. And there he was. Leo had taken the bait. Taking a quick look at his response, he seemed smitten by her image and extremely keen to meet in Amsterdam. High on a sense of achievement, Polina scrolled to the book club WhatsApp group for a call with Abigail, Barbara, and Lucinda.

Barbara picked up first. 'Hi Polina, I'm so pleased you

called back. I actually thought you'd intended to hang up on me just now.'

Polina rolled her eyes. Luckily Abigail and Lucinda saved Polina from dealing with more tipsy lectures from Barbara. As soon as they were all on the line, Polina burst out with her news.

'I did it. I hook Leo on hopeandwisdom.com. He never sees a woman he likes so much and will come to Amsterdam urgent.'

Silence fell. A moment later, small sobs could be heard down the line. Abigail stepped in.

'Oh Lucinda, darling, this must be awfully upsetting for you. I know it won't make the hurt any less. But it does show you the type of man he really is, doesn't it?'

Lucinda sobbed louder in reply.

'Polina, you've done a brilliant job. You do know it's not personal, don't you? It's just upsetting for Lucinda to know that her husband could behave this way,' Abigail continued. 'I expect we'll all suffer some upset on our path to revenge. But just think how wonderful it will be when everything comes to fruition. What a glorious 'fuck you' to the men who've betrayed us!'

'Yes, you're right, Abigail,' Lucinda spoke between sniffs. 'And I do love being part of this supportive group. Polina: I'm upset with Leo, not you. I'm really grateful for all that you're prepared to do so that I can avenge that rotten so-and-so.'

'Right then,' said Barbara. 'I expect you three will be off to Amsterdam quite soon.'

'Surely, you're coming too, Barbara?' Lucinda asked.

'No, I'm not.'

'We'd appreciate if your secretary would make the travel arrangements for us, Barbara, as previously agreed,' said Abigail.

'Yesh, yesh, alright. I'll have her call you,' Barbara drawled.

'Oh my God,' Lucinda whispered. 'It's really happening.'

•

POLINA CONTEMPLATED THE LONG LIST OF UNANSWERED messages from Leyla on her phone. Her former friend seemed keen to give her side of the story. The messages hadn't stopped since Dimitri ditched her. Leyla's dinner, lunch and coffee invitations were all ignored. Polina clicked on the video attachment in the most recent message.

'Hello Aunty Polina!' said Leyla's children, Erdem and Aylin, in sing-song unison. 'Please come to our friends' birthday parties with us on Saturday.'

They blew kisses to the camera and gave comic, pleading eyes before reaching a hand forward to stop the recording.

Making up with Leyla was the most difficult task she'd been given in the revenge plan. How she despised that woman. Though the distraction of the kids' parties was preferable to lunch listening to Leyla's lies.

Her phone pinged with a new message: *Thank you for watching video. Will you come?*

Recoiling at Leyla's stalker-like message, Polina tapped her reply slowly.

Yes, I come. Send me details, but no talk about Dimitri or breakup.

•

POLINA AND LEYLA SAT ON CHAIRS BESIDE A FOOTBALL pitch in the grounds of an enormous villa, high atop Cap Ferrat with views extending over the Mediterranean towards Nice airport in one direction, and Cap d'Ail, Roquebrune and Italy in the other. Waiters came by offering morning drinks and pastries on silver trays to the hundred or so parents accompanying their children at the birthday party.

Mesmerised by the grandeur, Leyla and Polina did their best to look nonchalant. But their conversation was the opposite.

'This is biggest house I see in my life,' Polina said. 'Who is birthday boy?'

'Mateo. Today will be football tournament with 60 boys invited to play on teams.'

'Sixty!' Polina said, as she took in the mock village fair being enjoyed by parents and siblings of the football partygoers.

Leyla lowered her voice to a murmur. 'At school, they whisper the father is Italian mafia.'

'Maybe Sergei knows him,' Polina said, with a butter-wouldn't-melt smile.

The tension of the moment was broken by Leyla's 10-year-old son Erdem returning from the house with his 59 fellow party friends. All were now fully kitted out in brand new football jerseys of various Italian teams, complete with their name and number on the back. They were even wearing new shorts and socks.

'Look Aunty Polina,' said Erdem, pointing to his black-and-white jersey, 'I'm playing for Juventus.'

Erdem raced off to join his teammates and the round-robin matches began. Polina and Leyla watched the match. At one point, the birthday boy Mateo conceded a penalty. He threw himself upon the ground in a tantrum. With his screams ignored, he scrambled up to shove a player on the opposing team to the ground. He proceeded to bite the player on the arm before the referee intervened. A minute later, the penalty decision was reversed, and the match resumed.

At lunchtime, Polina and Leyla followed the other spectators to the terrace where large, round tables were chock-a-block with platters of Italian food and bottles of first-growth claret.

'Children's party is better than adults,' Polina observed, snapping a selfie and posting it to her Instagram page with a caption she copied from a friend's page: *Life is like a camera. Focus on what is important. Capture the good times. Develop from the negatives. And if things don't work out, take another shot.*

The day ended with a prize giving. Mr Mafia (as Leyla dubbed him) appeared behind dark sunglasses. With stern handshakes, he handed out commemorative medals and trophy cups. As a delighted Erdem came running over to show his medallion, they were distracted by a woman's voice.

'Come, children! Take, take!'

They turned to see a woman lifting up the white tablecloth from the trophy table. Beneath the cloth were enormous boxes stashed with children's toys. The children ran forward to grab as much as they could carry.

'It looks like toy shop,' Polina said.

'This is Mrs Mafia,' Leyla whispered.

As the valet brought their car around, Erdem inspected his filled party bag.

'That was so cool!' he cried. 'Mama: for my birthday, could I have a rugby party?'

•

THE GIRLS CALLED IN AT LEYLA'S APARTMENT TO DROP OFF Erdem and pick up Leyla's teenage daughter Aylin, who was waiting nervously for the birthday party at Jimmy'z. Polina was surprised by the nightclub venue for a 13-year-old's birthday party.

'Jimmy'z is nightclub for adults, no?' said Polina.

'I know, and is Saturday night too,' Leyla agreed. 'Exclusive use tonight for party until midnight.'

'More mafia?' asked Polina.

'No, but money is from oil in Libya. Birthday boy wears gold Rolex watch at school and has bodyguards on school trip.'

Aylin looked nervous as they arrived at Jimmy'z to see the other children looking very grown up in nightclub attire and designer accessories.

'Darling, you look beautiful,' Leyla said, encouragingly.

'Come, we all go in together,' Polina added. 'We rock this party!'

The wild-animal-themed evening kicked off with a magic show and animal demonstrations involving snakes and wild cats on the stage. These were matched by displays of exaggerated hysteria from some of the girls. Leyla and Polina retreated to the bar as the top London DJ — flown in especially for the evening — got the party going on the dance floor. They were saved from conversation by the loud music. Polina took in the scene as kids flirted with each other and six waiters arrived bearing a long board topped by a 20-foot-long crocodile cake.

For the second time that day, they drove home with a happy child inspecting the contents of their party bag.

'Oh no!' said Aylin. 'There's a €100 FNAC voucher in here.'

'But this is good, no?' Polina asked.

'No, is not good,' Leyla said. 'Aylin's gift to the birthday boy was a €50 FNAC voucher.'

16

Barbara

BARBARA HID BEHIND HER SAUCER-SIZED CHANEL sunglasses as she slunk into Gerhard's Café, a casual nautical-themed bar in Fontvieille, on a quiet midweek afternoon. She was unlikely to bump into any acquaintances in this blue-collar joint, frequented mostly by yachties. Barbara also wanted to talk to Polina out of Abigail's earshot. The precocious upstart had morphed into the book club's de-facto moral arbiter, and she didn't want a disapproving Abigail to torpedo her audacious plan. She ordered a *demi panaché* and slid to the back of the bar. She'd already drained her drink by the time Polina arrived. Polina had interpreted Barbara's message to 'be discreet' with a Pucci mini dress in sheer silk-chiffon.

'You're almost late,' said Barbara, gesturing Polina to the red-leather banquette opposite.

'I am on time.'

An unsmiling Polina sat down.

Barbara caught the attention of the barman and ordered two *panachés*. Polina couldn't hide her revulsion at the beer-and-lemonade concoction placed in front of her.

'There's no Cristal on the menu here, Olina,' said Barbara, before she took an unhurried sip from her ice-cold schooner.

Kukushkin was a desperate seller of prime real estate. She was a cash-rich bargain hunter who could buy his property portfolio on the cheap and evict *WeFork*. Making a handsome profit while plunging Marcus into bankruptcy was a deliciously enticing prospect. There was one small problem: the last person to approach Kukushkin in relation to *WeFork* ended up as fish food. She needed a go-between.

'I want you to deliver this to Kukushkin,' said Barbara, fishing an A4 manila envelope out of her handbag and sliding it across the table.

'No, no, no. I not work for Marcus now. Not my business.'

Barbara sighed. 'It's a very simple task.'

'It is dangerous task,' said Polina. 'He wants Marcus. I not get in way.'

'What he wants is someone to buy his properties and my offer is in this envelope. You'll be representing me, not bloody Marcus.'

Barbara took another long drink from her frosted glass. Barbara couldn't overlook the fact that Polina had been close enough to Marcus for him to share his murderous desires with her.

'Thousands of top graduates would leap at the chance to be my dogsbody, let alone this gold digger,' Barbara thought.

'It is good offer? Sergei not be angry?' asked Polina.

'It's the best offer he's going to get,' said Barbara. 'You have nothing to fear.'

'If nothing to fear, why you not deliver?' said Polina. 'Why I trust you?'

Barbara smiled. She almost respected Polina's bold impudence. Almost.

'Look, find Kukushkin and give him this damn envelope or get arrested for being an accessory to attempted murder.'

Polina's eyes widened in horror.

'Arrested? Me? I not understand!' she whispered, leaning forward.

'I could still go to the police about Marcus' attempt to kill me. Something that you knew about in advance,' Barbara said.

'I not help Marcus! I tell Abigail!'

'But who would the police believe?' Barbara paused. 'You or me?'

'You wouldn't want to waste your prime years in the slammer, would you?' she continued. 'Your assets would depreciate rather quickly.'

Barbara sat back to enjoy the shell-shocked expression on Polina's face. Conniving business rivals, incompetent underlings and her ex-husband often had the same look. Polina slowly picked up the envelope, handling it delicately as if it were laced with poison.

'But I not know when Sergei in Monaco.'

Satisfied, Barbara crossed her arms. As Polina marched out, Barbara heard her utter 'Bitch' under her breath. Barbara found that amusing. She picked up Polina's untouched drink and toasted her newest, and most unconventional, flunkey.

'Takes one to know one,' thought Barbara.

•

DAYS TICKED BY WITHOUT A WORD FROM POLINA. BARBARA'S mood was not helped by Marcus' unexpected high-profile PR fightback in London. Barbara lolled on the soft-leather sofa in her darkened home cinema room and flicked aimlessly through the TV channels, washing down Xanax with whisky, and snapping at Nora. The floor was strewn with Tunnock's caramel wafer wrappers and an empty whisky bottle. Without so much as a knock, the door opened suddenly, and Barbara squinted as light flooded the room. A silhouetted hourglass figure stood in the doorway.

'Barbara? Bodyguard let me in.'

It was Polina. At last.

Barbara sat up quickly, then sheepishly gathered up the chocolate wrappers and adjusted her crumpled silk pyjamas. She had no idea how long she'd been festering in the cinema room.

'You can't just barge in here unannounced,' Barbara said croakily. 'Go to the sitting room.'

Ashamed of her dishevelled appearance, Barbara headed to her dressing room, bouncing off the corridor wall along the way. After a bracing cold shower and quick application of makeup to camouflage the bruises and dark circles, she was ready to face Polina. She held her chin up as she walked into the sitting room straight to the drinks tray to pour a large vodka on the rocks.

'I take same,' Polina piped up.

Barbara filled another tumbler almost to the brim. She studied Polina as she walked over with the drinks. She sat down next to Polina as the two clinked glasses awkwardly.

'*Za nashu druzjbu,*' said Polina, taking a hearty slug of vodka, before grinning archly with the translation. 'To our friendship.'

'Have you spoken to Kukushkin?' said Barbara, curling her upper lip.

'*Da, da,*' Polina said, then flicked her hair.

'*And?*'

Polina got up and walked over to the drinks tray. She

picked up the tongs and after inspecting the contents of the ice bucket, carefully selected an ice cube to add to her already-chilled vodka. She swirled the glass before strolling back to the sofa.

'Spit it out then!' said Barbara.

'I wait in the American Bar for days,' Polina said finally. 'Then I see Sergei's bodyguard in hotel and ask for meeting. I go back at midnight and bodyguard take me in car to see Sergei.'

'You went alone in a car? At midnight?'

'What choice I have? Car or jail.'

'Go on.'

'We drive one hour. I meet Sergei at big villa. He not happy. He think I have message from Marcus, but I say I work with you.'

'Work *for* not *with*,' Barbara corrected.

'I say I have proposal from Barbara Esson, number 83 on *Sunday Times* Rich List, number two in Scotland and first chairwoman of FTSE 100 company.'

'Did you tell him my bra size as well?'

'So, Sergei interested,' continued Polina, unabashed. 'He put down gun.'

'Jesus.'

'Car take me home. I wait, I wait. Sergei call today.'

Barbara held her breath.

'Sergei read proposal and accept. Lawyer make papers and meet at bank like you ask.'

'Really? Thank God. That is music to my ears.' Barbara nodded approvingly at Polina. 'Thanks for your help. Good job.'

'Job?' asked Polina. 'People get money for job, no?'

'Well, let's wait until the ink is dry, shall we? Top up?'

Barbara rose unsteadily and reached for the glasses. But Polina put her hands over the tumblers.

'Stop. Too much vodka, too much pills. Not good, not good. Sit.'

'I'll open a bottle of Dom once she's buggered off,' thought Barbara, sitting down as ordered.

'You must have good head for meeting,' continued Polina. 'Is difficult time, but alcohol not answer. I say use bodyguard.'

'Excuse me?'

'Why pay young man only to stand at door? Old men in Monaco use money for sex. Sexy woman get money. Everyone happy,' Polina shrugged her shoulders, 'You do same.'

'I am not bloody old,' retorted Barbara.

•

WHILE THE BODYGUARD SHOWERED, BARBARA HASTILY donned a pair of weightless Loro Piana joggers and a white Joseph T-shirt. She smiled at herself in the mirror. She hated to admit that Polina had been right. She hadn't left the apartment for days and the blue sky looked so inviting. After leaving a hastily scribbled note on a pillow for the bodyguard, Barbara grabbed her car keys and snuck out. She felt like driving up to the Col d'Eze, a twisty mountain pass with a glorious 360° vista of the snow-capped Alpes Maritimes to the North and the glistening Mediterranean Sea to the South.

The aria, *Vesti la guibba*, blasted out of the speakers as Barbara zipped up the warren-like streets in her Aston Martin towards the Monaco-France border. Suddenly, a car appeared from an obscure side street and drove out into the main road right in front of Barbara. She reacted first with the horn, then with the brakes a split second later. The cars avoided a collision by millimetres. Near misses were quite common on Monaco's winding streets.

'You can't just pull out on a blind bend, idiot!' Barbara

shouted, before tapping the side of her head. '*Ça va pas la tête?*'

The other driver, in his 60s judging by his lined face and thatch of wiry, grey hair, yelled furiously at Barbara.

'*Vous êtes fou, connard!*' shouted Barbara in reply to his volley of abuse.

'*Vous devriez faire attention à qui vous parlez!*' he bellowed.

Barbara snorted. Barbara inspected the man's middle-of-the-range BMW and replied, 'Um, someone who can't afford a decent car?'

The female passenger tried to calm the driver, '*Bruno, arrête, calme-toi! Marche arrière.*'

Sulkily, Bruno reversed back no more than 10 inches, giving Barbara enough room to drive past.

'At least one of you knows the traffic laws!' shouted Barbara to the female passenger as she eased her car past.

'Muppet,' she growled, flipping her middle finger before slamming on the pedal and rocketing off.

•

BARBARA ANSWERED HER PHONE. HER MUSCULAR bodyguard whose name she didn't know (he never volunteered it, she never thought to ask) continued his sweaty, gymnastic foreplay.

'Judith?' She asked a little breathlessly.

She presumed the caller to be her private secretary as her contact details weren't in any public directory. All calls made to the number on her business card were automatically relayed to Judith, her loyal gatekeeper.

'Hi Barbara, I know you said you didn't want to be disturbed for a few days, but it's about the altercation you had with the Monaco police yesterday.'

Barbara sat up straight. 'The *what*?'

The bodyguard stuck his head out from under the sheets to see what the interruption was.

'The office of the, let me get this right, *Le Commandant Supérieur de la Force Publique* just called. They were very diplomatic but said that even someone of your stature shouldn't have insulted the Colonel-in-chief.'

'Oh God, you're kidding!' An impish grin appeared on her face. 'Imagine being head of the Monaco army... That's like being the tallest hobbit.'

'Who told you to stop?' Barbara looked down at the bodyguard, who slunk dutifully beneath the sheets.

'Excuse me?' asked Judith.

'Nothing,' Barbara's attention returned, with difficulty, to the phone conversation.

'What am I expected to do?' She was finding it harder to maintain her composure, 'And make it quick.'

'Quick?' said the swarthy, bearded chop.

'Not you.'

'I don't follow,' Judith said, sounding baffled.

'Look, presumably they aren't going to arrest me?' although the thought of handcuffs at that moment was rather appealing.

'The colonel's aide said you need to familiarise yourself with the traffic laws in the country, specifically, *priorité à droite.*'

'Give way to the right? I thought that stupid rule went out with the horse and cart.'

'He also kindly requested that you visit the *Force Publique* headquarters to apologise in person and perhaps bring a gift. Such as a bottle of vintage champagne.'

'Fine. Send me the details.' Barbara managed to say before throwing the mobile onto the floor and grabbing the bodyguard's wavy, dark locks.

•

AS SHE PUFFED ON A POST-COITAL CIGARETTE, BARBARA reflected that it was rather ironic being summoned to police headquarters given she made the contentious decision not to involve the police after Marcus' botched murder attempt. Lord knows, since there was one policeman for every 70 Monaco residents, they needed *something* to do. Barbara wouldn't normally kowtow to such a jumped-up bully, but she thought it was wise not to draw any more attention to herself and the book club's avenging antics.

'Hello? Hello? Barbara?' Barbara heard Abigail's anxious voice coming from the vestibule.

'Just a minute!' Barbara stubbed out her cigarette, got out of bed and went to splash water on her face. She looked in the mirror above the sink; the bruising on her face was barely discernible.

Barbara registered the disappointed looks on Lucinda and Abigail's faces as she wafted into the sitting room wearing a dressing gown.

'Barbara darling, you can't spend all day mooching in bed,' said Lucinda. 'It's not healthy.'

'Never mind that,' said Abigail. 'Barbara, I thought you had 24-hour security? Anyone could have walked in here.'

Barbara moseyed over to an armchair and gestured to her concerned visitors to sit down on the sofa.

'Relax, girls. Everything is under control.'

Moments later the po-faced bodyguard walked out of Barbara's bedroom, suited and booted, but with damp hair. He avoided eye contact with the three leering women as he walked through the apartment and resumed his official position outside the front door.

Abigail and Lucinda looked at each other and then stared

quizzically at Barbara. She casually picked up a magazine and started slowly flicking through the pages while smirking.

'No… Barbara! Aren't you the cat that got the cream?' said Abigail. 'Well, I guess he's hot.'

'Well done you. At least somebody is getting something,' added Lucinda.

'How did you wangle him into bed?' Abigail asked.

'Simple: I invited him in for a drink and took it from there. A little celebratory treat for myself.'

Abigail cocked her head. 'What are you celebrating?'

'Kukushkin has agreed to my proposal,' Barbara threw the magazine down on the coffee table. '*WeFork* will soon disappear off the face of the earth.'

'What proposal?' asked Abigail, frowning.

'I'm going to buy Kukushkin's property portfolio. Our lawyers are drawing up the paperwork. As soon as it's ready, we'll meet at the bank and sign the contracts.'

'When did all this happen?' said Abigail. 'Very risky to approach Kukushkin.'

'Obviously, there was no way *I* was going to meet him,' said Barbara. 'Olina proved useful for something.'

Lucinda joined the interrogation. 'You sent *Pol*-ina to find a mobster? Wasn't that rather dangerous?'

'Let's be realistic, who's more expendable? There's hardly a shortage of Russian blondes in Monaco, is there?'

'But there's only one Barbara Esson…' Lucinda ventured. 'Couldn't you have at least got one of your bodyguards to go with her?'

'That would only tie her back to me.'

'And does Polina get anything in return for doing your dirty work?' said Abigail. 'I think you should cover her legal expenses.'

Barbara pulled a face. 'I don't really want to get involved in her tawdry affairs.'

'Come on Barbara, we agreed to help each other out,' said Abigail. 'Your foundation gives away millions each year. Or are your charitable acts just for good publicity?'

'Fine. I will if it means we reach our goals sooner rather than later,' agreed Barbara, before adding a jibe. 'I mean I've pretty much stitched up Marcus already. The rest of you need to pick up the pace.'

'It's not a competition,' Abigail bristled. 'It's easy to score a quick financial win when you have deep pockets already. Anyway, we just wanted to update you on the Amsterdam trip since you're not coming.'

'Spare me the details,' Barbara said. 'I'm chairman of a multinational. I do strategy, not operations.'

'Fair enough, but I suggest you don't celebrate prematurely,' said Abigail. 'Marcus is a free man and still with Sophie.'

'I agree with Abigail. Don't be too cavalier,' urged Lucinda. 'You've landed the first blow, but don't underestimate Marcus. We might not know what he'll do next, but we do know what he's capable of.'

Barbara felt her still-sore face throb as she tried to block out the horrible memory of Marcus' assault. She shuddered involuntarily.

'Point taken. God, you've killed my buzz.'

'Sorry, we're only looking out for you,' said Lucinda.

'No need to apologise.' Barbara stood up. 'Just send the bodyguard in on your way out.'

17

Abigail

'DATING SERENA WAS A LITTLE LIKE BUYING A DRESS,' SAID Hank, draining the cafetière into his cup, and slurping it back in one shot.

'I saw the dress in the shop window and wanted to try it on. It looked great in the changing room, so I bought it. When I got it home, I didn't like it, so I returned it.'

Abigail avoided his glance as Hank looked towards her for affirmation. Hank's grotesque description of his ex-girlfriend Serena rendered Abigail speechless. Over the past few weeks, Abigail had noted Hank's increasingly erratic behaviour at work; his constant tirades. Her front-page exposé of another dodgy Monaco billionaire hadn't helped his mood. No doubt his restless fury was fuelled by losing Serena: though perhaps more by losing her to his former copy editor Rob than by losing her per se.

Hank jabbed the intercom and shouted at his assistant to bring another coffee tray. He then made a show of checking his emails, while Abigail waited and observed the dark circles under his eyes. His assistant broke the awkward silence as she arrived with a fresh tray of coffee. Hank helped himself and turned the conversation back to *Monaco Mail*.

'How are we doing on subscriptions?'

'There has been a 10% increase over the last month,' said Abigail. 'The dog event brought thousands of new subscribers. We're thinking of following up with a plastic-surgery symposium to generate more subscriptions next month.'

'Okay, but I want young, natural beauties for the photo coverage. None of those fucking duck-lipped, skin-stretched, mutton-dressed-as-lamb types.'

'Spoken like a true mysogynist,' thought Abigail.

'Plus, I'd like to do a double-page spread on that artist Lothko next week too.'

A telephone call brought their meeting to an abrupt end. Abigail retreated to her desk and opened up her computer. She continued editing her latest interview with celebrity chef Jean-Paul Roquefort. It seemed apt that he should be named after a famous French cheese. Indeed, this big cheese of the French culinary world boasted dozens of Michelin stars and a *Gault Millau* 'chef of the century' award. Despite turning 70, Roquefort showed no signs of retiring. During their interview, he talked excitedly about his restaurant group expanding into Asia.

'This is my first foray into continental China. I expected everyone to be dressed in Communist blue overalls, but the first thing I saw upon leaving the airport was a Rolls Royce. China is the clientele of tomorrow.'

Roquefort had long ties to Asia ever since Bocuse sent him to hotel school in Tokyo. He brought his love of the Far East back to Monte Carlo with the recent, glittering opening of his Michelin-starred Asian restaurant. It joined the gastronomic ranks of Roquefort's Monegasque mini empire. As Abigail delved into a quinoa ball from his new vegetarian menu, she wondered where the secret to his success lay.

'The golden word is kindness,' Roquefort replied. 'I know it's not a very French concept.'

He berated the cold academic formality of fine French dining where the focus was 'less on treating diners kindly and more on whether the silver fork is to the right or left of the plate'. For the record, Roquefort didn't use silverware at all as his cutlery was stainless steel. Abigail smiled in her realization that behind his gentle, grandfatherly façade lay a revolutionary.

As Abigail wrote up the interview, a message popped up on her phone from Serena wondering if she were free for lunch. An hour later, she rushed out the office across the casino gardens and straight into Mada One. This cafe was her new go-to meeting place. Serena and Rob greeted her. It was the first time she'd seen them since the casino debacle. Rob was living now at Serena's villa in rue Saint Roman. In a curious denouement, it turned out that Serena was an heiress in her own right and that the villa was owned by her, not Hank as Abigail previously assumed.

Abigail was struck by how happy they both looked. No longer poker-straight hair and a designer-mini-dress uniform for Serena: nowadays she preferred jeans, a fitted shirt and hair flowing in natural waves. Most notably, she was thinking about her long-forgotten career. Apart from modelling, her only ever job had been as an au pair.

'Why don't you set up a nanny agency?' suggested Abigail. 'From what I've seen, most Monaco women are far too busy at the gym and the spa to look after their own babies.'

Meanwhile, Rob looked tanned and chilled. Serena and

unemployment suited him. He'd switched his ubiquitous t-shirt for a polo shirt and he'd taken up boxing. Abigail smiled to herself as Rob littered their conversation with references to Serena. Luckily, his dry sense of humour remained. After all, who else could she discuss her editorial frustration and quantum mechanics with?

'Can I consider Monaco's freedom of the press to be both dead and alive at the same time until I have tested the limitations of acceptability in print?' mused Abigail. 'Can I say this is the best burger in Monaco or not until I have eaten burgers at every other potential venue in town. At which point, I may turn into a Super Size Me?'

'Not sure I get your point,' said Serena, raising her eyebrow.

Rob explained gently Abigail's joke about the *Monaco Mail*'s questionable press freedom through the dilemma of Schrödinger's cat.

'Schrödinger's cat is a cat imagined as being enclosed in a box with a radioactive source and a poison that will be released when the source unpredictably emits radiation. The cat is considered to be simultaneously both dead and alive until the box is opened, and the cat observed.'

'Seriously obscure,' giggled Serena. 'I prefer the Super-Size-Me bit after the guy who ate McDonald's for 30 days.'

'Well, there's nothing Super Size about you two. In fact, you're both looking radiant,' observed Abigail. 'If I didn't like you both so much, I'd be quite nauseous.'

•

THE SMELL OF FRESHLY-GROUND COFFEE WELCOMED Abigail into the Millefiori flat. Lucinda ushered her into the living room where boxes were piled up. A light patina of dust marked the walls where paintings had hung and the sofa looked desolate without any cushions. Peanut lay in his dog basket like a deposed prince. They took their coffees to the outdoor terrace: it was flooded in sunshine, though crisp in temperature. As they chatted, Abigail looked out upon the rooftop vista that extended towards the Mediterranean Sea. Down below at street level, she spotted fruit-laden orange trees that characterised the principality in winter months.

'Leo's keeping the flat,' said Lucinda. 'So I'm moving into a smaller flat near the casino behind Zara.'

'If you need to store any of your stuff, I have plenty of room,' offered Abigail. 'My dressing room is shamefully empty.'

'Thanks.'

'How did your meeting with Hank go yesterday?'

'Good, though he seemed more hyper than ever. I could have sworn he was trying to flirt with me too.'

'Did he offer you a Lothko, by any chance?'

'Yes, how did you guess?'

Lucinda took Abigail through her meeting with Hank. He had met her in the lobby of the Hôtel Métropole with its dramatic floral installations and diffuse light. Over jasmine tea and *orangettes* (chocolate-covered, orange candied peel), Hank talked non-stop for an entire hour with Lucinda barely contributing a word. As Lucinda spoke at length about his complimenting her radiant skin and large green eyes, Abigail wondered if she protested a little too much about his unwanted attention. Apparently, Hank also spent half an hour extolling the unmatched talents of Lothko before showing her pictures of a Lothko entitled *Orange, pink, yellow*.

'The painting had an intense colour field that was slightly clashing, but it made me gaze for ages,' said Lucinda. 'Of course, I'm still shocked by his quotation of €40 million. He obviously has no clue that I'm bankrupt. Luckily, my aristocratic title stopped him delving too far into my finances.'

'I'm not surprised by his lack of due diligence,' said Abigail. 'He's been far too busy acting like a sociopath since he split with Serena.'

After coffee, Abigail and Lucinda took a bus down to Port Hercules. The Monaco bus system was the best municipal bus service that Abigail had ever witnessed. Unlike the exorbitant Monaco taxi racket, Monaco buses were sensibly priced and spotlessly clean. They exited at Port Hercules and walked to a non-descript 70s building along rue Suffren Reymond. They were ushered through to a scruffy meeting room. Police captain Stéphane Girardo greeted them with the same officious nod favoured by bureaucrats across the principality and then offered them coffee in Styrofoam cups.

'*Eh bien*?'

Abigail paused for Girardo to finish his sentence, but he left the phrase hanging in the air like a gesture of impatience. Undeterred, Abigail outlined their plan for a sting operation. After about 10 minutes, she noticed Girardo starting to thaw.

'Yes, we've been investigating Hank Vert for a while,' said Girardo. 'He was reported to us five years ago by an important art collector with suspicions about the amount of commission Monsieur Vert charges on his private art sales. We suspect that he uses over-inflated, fake valuations to cover his tracks. Unfortunately, it's impossible to prove unless you have a well-placed mole. So how much contact has been made already?'

'I introduced Camille to Hank at a *Monaco Mail* forum last week. Camille managed to drop in a hint about elastic valuations before giving Hank her card.'

'Madame Marceau was too busy to come today?' asked Girardo.

'I'm afraid there's an auction of Hermès handbags this afternoon at the Hôtel de Paris,' said Abigail hesitantly, before pressing on. 'Also, Lucinda made contact with Hank yesterday to express an interest in a Lothko,' said Abigail.

'*D'accord*,' said Girardo, smiling at Lucinda. 'How much backup is Hank likely to have?'

'None,' said Abigail. 'Hank's a lone wolf.'

Half an hour later, the game plan for *Operation Pygargue* was agreed. While Lucinda would continue to push her interest in the Lothko, Camille would wait a few days before following up with Hank about a collaboration on the valuation. Abigail would help to liaise behind the scenes.

On their way out, Lucinda turned to Girardo in her inimitably charming manner.

'Monsieur Girardo, I wanted to tell you about two women I saw in the Millefiori last month,' said Lucinda.

Girardo gave Lucinda his most ingratiating smile, as he encouraged her to continue.

'Very interesting, Madame la Comtesse,' said Girardo, after Lucinda had finished detailing her suspicions. 'There have been seven copycat burglaries with the same *modus operandi* of tampered locks around the principality in the last six months.'

Girardo drew closer to Lucinda with a raise of the eyebrows and his head tilted in her direction: 'Perhaps you could return tomorrow to meet our resident artist to draw up a photofit of the locksmith girls?'

'A photofit and perhaps a dinner invitation too,' teased Abigail as she and Lucinda made their way out of the police station.

•

WITH JULIA ON A MINI-BREAK WITH THEIR GRASSE neighbour Jean-Pierre and with Daisy on a sleepover with her friend Aurora, Abigail found herself footloose and fancy-free that weekend. She decided to accept Damian's invitation to dinner at the spit-and-sawdust steak restaurant, La Bionda, in La Condamine district. At last, she'd found a close friend whose idea of going out didn't involve a superyacht or Michelin-starred gastronomy. Over Picanha steak, they exchanged news and laughed about larger-than-life Monaco characters. Little by little, their conversation edged towards intimacy. Abigail told tales about growing up with her mother and her bad-tempered stepfather in a Victorian terraced house in Balham and about escaping to Belgium after falling pregnant unexpectedly at the age of 23. Damian opened up about moving from Ghana to Mile End as a toddler and about the trials of boarding school. Abigail took in his earnest expression. She wasn't used to honesty in Monaco. Especially from a private banker. But there he was: handsome and humble.

'So what's it like working for Barbara?' said Abigail, as coffee arrived.

'She's a megalomaniac,' said Damian. 'But aren't all billionaires? What's it like working for Hank?'

Abigail's phone rang. It was Camille.

'Sorry, Damian. I have to take this call,' said Abigail.

'Hank's in police custody,' said Camille.

'Already?' said Abigail, moving outside to the terrace to continue her conversation discreetly. 'I thought Hank wasn't meant to give you the cash until next week?'

'He changed the meeting to this evening,' said Camille. 'We'd never have pulled the switch off anywhere but Monaco.'

'Interesting,' said Abigail. 'It's as if Hank sniffed something was off.'

'In the end, he turned up 10 minutes early, with a suitcase of cash to pay for the fake Lothko valuation,' said Camille. 'Luckily Girardo and his team were fully prepped and following the scene in the next-door office via a hidden camera. Just as

Hank opened up the combination key on the suitcase, Girardo and his officers stormed in with guns.'

'Like clockwork,' said Abigail.

'It was straight out of *American Hustle*,' said Camille. 'He seemed extremely wired. He kept touching his neck dimple as he spoke.'

'Another thing,' added Camille 'As the police were cuffing him, Hank started ranting about how the art sale was the only thing keeping *Monaco Mail* from bankruptcy. Girardo is going to the *Monaco Mail* office tomorrow morning with a warrant. It turns out that Hank's also wanted for art fraud in France too, so the French police will be collaborating for his criminal trial.'

As Abigail finally hung up, Damian joined her outside.

'I've sorted the bill. Let's go,' he said. He took her hand and arched his eyebrow flirtatiously like Regé-Jean Page.

'I think you'd better come back to mine. There's a lot to explain to you,' said Abigail in a higher-pitched tone than normal.

And then Damian kissed her. Five minutes suspended in time outside the dog-eat-dog Monaco circuit. Five minutes of believing in fairy-tale endings. Abigail felt giddy as they walked back to Fontvieille hand in hand under the moonlight.

•

THE NEXT MORNING, ABIGAIL AWOKE EARLY. DAMIAN WAS sleeping beside her. She breathed in his scent and smiled.

By 8.30 a.m., she arrived at avenue de la Costa ready to open up the *Monaco Mail* office for the police search. While she opened up all the window shutters for Girardo and his team, she developed an abdominal cramp. To take her mind off the police search and off her stomach ache, she went off to buy a coffee for everyone at Casa del Caffè. With its tables spilling onto the pavement, this neighbourhood cafe was the antidote to Monaco's high-life living and one of the few places where you'd ever see construction workers and Lululemon-clad millionairesses sitting cheek-by-jowl.

Half an hour later and armed with coffees, she arrived back at the office. A police officer was sawing off the padlock to a filing cabinet. Out flooded hundreds of unpaid *Monaco Mail* bills. Like a house of cards. Vert had been right about his insolvency. The horrible truth dawned upon Abigail: it wasn't just Vert's career that was finished, her own job was finished too.

18

Lucinda

LUCINDA'S REQUEST TO HAVE MORE TIME TO WORK ON A future with Leo had been rejected. She had a few weeks before she would go back to court. A few weeks to request *attestations* demonstrating she was a good person with a fine character, in order to defend herself. A few weeks to get together these witness statements and present them to Madame Morales, while trying to work on her marriage. She was on the defensive, yet still clinging to the mirage of her fading wedlock.

She was home, or what had been her home for several years. Her packed boxes filled the living room. Leo was in the office.

'Shall we go for a drive?' she suggested to Leo, hoping that his love of speeding on narrow lanes, and a change of scenery might make a difference. 'How about Auberge de la Croix du Pape?'

'Actually, why not?'

Lucinda tried to repress her usual fear as he overtook several cars on the narrow Beausoleil roads towards the Grande Corniche, a rock-clinging route designed to facilitate Napoleon's Italy campaign of 1796. No one with a Monegasque license plate received speeding tickets, except in Monaco. It was one of the many perks of Monaco life. Leo enjoyed that advantage to the fullest.

In right-hand-drive Southern France, their left-hand-drive car meant that Lucinda was on the receiving end of angry drivers' insults and middle fingers meant for Leo. He aggressively overtook other drivers: driving less than a metre behind them at top speed, flashing his lights and then overtaking on blind corners. Today she tried her best to ignore the cursing and furious faces, as well as the oncoming traffic.

They arrived at the simple auberge, greeted the owner, who they had met several times, ordered two coffees, and sat down to enjoy the steep view over Eze village.

'I honestly do not understand why you want to prolong this whole ordeal,' said Leo.

'You don't understand why I want to give us another chance, or to give us some time?'

'No.'

She didn't wholly understand herself at this point. She felt it was pretty irreparable. She also didn't understand why he was in such a hurry.

Her phone rang. 'Hi Abigail.'

'Hi there. You okay?'

'Just having a coffee with Leo…,' said Lucinda as if the occasion was normal.

'Oh. Okay. Just a quick one: would you like to join me and Barbara for dinner later tonight at Buddha Bar? Say 8:30?'

'Sounds perfect.'

'Fantastic. See you there.'

She put the phone down.

'Can I ask you something?' said Lucinda. 'What's that book you're reading — *Journey to Healing* — about?

'It's about taking care of yourself and doing what is good for you. There is no room for guilt,' he said.

How predictable! Leo's synopsis of this bestselling survivor narrative intended for people trying to heal past wounds that continue to sabotage their future had been moulded into a get-out-of-jail-free card with no guilt attached. There was no point in arguing with him.

'Fancy a game of backgammon?' she asked.

He took out their old travel backgammon board. They were both relieved to play a game together with straightforward rules, as the sun started to set.

•

of the dimly lit Buddha Bar restaurant about to raise a toast over champagne.

'Wait for me!' she said, as she placed her mother's vintage Yves Saint Laurent purse on the table. 'What are we celebrating?'

'Eternal youth,' said Barbara.

'Dedicated staff,' said Abigail.

Confused, Lucinda picked up a glass the waiter had just poured. Barbara had insisted on getting Dom Pérignon.

'Updike said it best, *Sex is like money. Only too much is enough*,' said Barbara.

'Ha!' Abigail giggled.

'Cheers to that, Barbara. You're an example to us all,' said Lucinda, taking a big gulp.

'I hate to admit it, but Polina is pretty observant,' Barbara continued. 'It's thanks to her I decided to re-evaluate the responsibilities of my staff,' she winked.

With its crimson lamps, dark-wood chairs and fabrics that ranged from berry to gold, Buddha Bar felt like a nightclub. At the neighbouring table sat a couple with a child. The couple barely spoke while eating: to each other or to their child who equally did not utter a word. He must have been about six years old.

'I can't believe they brought their child here to Buddha Bar,' said Lucinda. 'How very inappropriate!'

'Children should be banned from the premises,' added Barbara.

'So, the great news is that Hank is in police custody,' announced Abigail. 'The bad news is I have no clue if I have a job or a desk to go to. *Monaco Mail* has folded.'

'Ah, never mind,' sighed Barbara. 'Drink up. Nothing like a good Dom Pérignon to take my mind off my blasted son-in-law.'

The child at the neighbouring table was eating tomato pasta and playing with a cherry tomato on his fork.

'Have you written my *attestation* for me to sign, Lucinda?' asked Barbara, speaking to Lucinda as she would speak to anyone on her payroll.

'No, not yet,' said Lucinda. 'I'm going to write about the time when you first met Leo. Do you remember when he lost his temper with me for shortening little Peanut's lead? He was just a pup and that terrifying Staffordshire bull terrier nearly bit his head off.'

At that moment, the small red tomato landed in Barbara's champagne glass. The parents looked embarrassed, but they did not say a word to the boy.

'Yes, he was berating you and explaining that dogs have to work things out for themselves,' Barbara continued, as she moved the glass to the side without looking at it, before a waiter promptly picked it up. 'If it had been Leo's prick on the end of that lead, I can tell you he would have shortened that lead.'

'I've written my statement,' said Abigail. 'I will send it later. I just have to scan a copy of my passport for your lawyer.'

'Thank you both so much,' said Lucinda. 'I can't tell you how much I appreciate you being there for me.'

•

LUCINDA REACHED THE GATES TO BETH'S ST-JEAN-CAP-Ferrat villa, *Le Grand Bleu*, and pressed the bell.

'There you are,' said Beth over the intercom. 'The rosé is chilled and waiting for you by the pool.'

She parked the car. Peanut cried with excitement and licked Lucinda's ears, while she kissed him.

'Help yourself to wine and snacks," Beth shouted from the kitchen. 'I'll be out in a second.'

Lucinda walked to the inviting pool and sat down on a sunbed. A bottle of Miraval rosé chilled in a clear cooler, next to a bowl of ice and some glasses. Olive trees dotted around the green immaculate lawn, with a bronze Sacha Sosno torso statue framing the sea in the distance.

'How are *you*?' Beth appeared at the kitchen doorway, looking straight into Lucinda's eyes. She walked over to another sunbed, phone in hand.

Lucinda took a deep breath and exhaled. Peanut filled in the awkward silence with barks of delight as he rolled his back and shoulders on the lush lawn.

'I'm not doing well at all.'

Lucinda wanted to say more. She wanted to have a candid chat with Beth, her oldest Monaco friend. To ask why she'd been avoiding her and spending so much time with Leo. But Beth's cold stare didn't invite a heart-to-heart.

At that moment, a roaring helicopter approached and started flying quite low. It was hovering above the pool. Lucinda welcomed the deafening sound to alleviate the awkwardness.

'What the hell?' shouted Lucinda.

'Oh, ignore it,' Beth shouted back. 'It's just our neighbour, Viktor Rodrovic. He wants to buy the house and I don't want to sell. This is his Plan B. It should stop soon. The longest so far has been 15 minutes. I'll wait until he comes back with Plan C and a better price.'

Putting her hurt feelings to one side, Lucinda tried an easier tack.

'I have to ask you a favour,' she shouted. 'Could you write me an *attestation*, a witness statement, like the one I wrote for you when you were getting divorced? Not a statement against Leo, just a sort of character statement in support of me.'

She smiled to appear positive. It would be a no-brainer for Beth to empathise. She'd suffered so much herself during her own divorce, when she'd been betrayed by a close girlfriend attacking her in a damning witness statement, and then suffered chronic haemorrhoids straight afterwards.

'I can't.'

'What? Why?'

'I would strongly suggest,' Beth continued, 'that you try to come to an amicable financial agreement with Leo without all this mud-slinging.' She used her thumb and index finger to flick off a stray hair of Peanut's that had landed on her Hermès beach towel.

'Mud-slinging? I've been forced into a position where I have to defend myself against the man who is still my husband who, until a few weeks ago, I thought was my life, my love.'

That last word 'love' felt empty. Leo did not want her. He did not want to work on it. It was over.

'I can't because James has written one of the *attestations*,' Beth replied, taking a sip of her rosé.

The helicopter flew off and the noise of the rotor blades subsided.

'James?' Lucinda repeated incredulously.

'Yes. I told him not to, but I think Leo managed to convince him. Anyway, I can't do anything.'

'I don't understand why you can't — or won't — help me.'

'Because of James.'

'What do you mean *because of James*?'

'Well…'

'Well, what?'

'I need James.'

'You have got to be kidding me.'

Lucinda felt betrayed. She had always defended Beth. She had never listened to the rumours about her outrageous flirtations, about her unspoken financial relationship with her boyfriend James. Beth was a wealthy divorcée in her own right: she'd acquired a Monaco flat in her kids' names from her ex-mother-in-law, and a house in St-Jean-Cap-Ferrat from her divorce. But without James, she couldn't maintain her lifestyle. He provided all of the extra essentials from holidays abroad to designer jewellery.

'It's a form of long-term prostitution,' thought Lucinda, in her fury.

'I can't risk losing James, Lu. And I simply don't want to get involved in your acrimonious divorce.'

She had a point about not wanting to get involved. But this was not London or New York, where women were on a level playing field. This was Monaco. It seemed she'd already taken sides: Leo's.

'What could James possibly have said that would be negative, anyway?' asked Lucinda.

'He said that you left Leo in his time of need, after that dinner at yours.'

'His time of need?'

'Yes, when Leo had cancer. That night we all had dinner and we all had too much to drink, and you came to mine afterwards?' Beth lay on her back, with her eyes closed, while Lucinda was sitting straight up, looking at her.

'That night I left in tears after he had been putting me down the entire time and I went back to yours for support?'

'Yes.'

'First of all, Leo had had his operation and no longer had cancer and you know as well as I do that nobody cared more about Leo's health than I did. I went with him to each and every consultation. I was the one who made sure he saw a doctor in the first place.'

'I'm sorry if you think I'm letting you down,' Beth continued. 'What difference does it make anyway? If it was after Leo's operation, you can easily prove that with hospital records.'

Lucinda was not giving up easily.

'If James won't retract his witness statement, then won't you just write your own statement explaining what really happened that night: that I was upset by Leo constantly putting me down, and went to yours around the corner and had a cry while James stayed with Leo? You are not discrediting Leo. You are merely defending your close friend. You know very well that what James is writing is complete bullshit. I get that you feel uncomfortable, but why won't you help me?'

'Quite frankly, Lu, I find you are being very confrontational and rude, and I have done nothing but support you. Bear in mind: I still have to live here with my children and have had enough problems to last a lifetime.'

'Wow... Okay.' She put out her cigarette, picked up

Peanut, who by now was lying just beneath the sunbed, and walked towards her car.

'Lu, I am still here for you,' said Beth, looking relieved as Lucinda got into her car.

•

LUCINDA ARRIVED BACK AT THE FLAT TO FIND MORE ART from Leo's family gone from the walls. She could smell a cigarette. Leo was on the terrace smoking, looking at his phone.

'How *could* you ask James to write an *attestation*?' she asked him.

He appeared surprised she had discovered the truth.

'I had no choice.'

'What do you mean you had no choice? Of course, you had a choice.'

'This is the only way to protect myself during the divorce process.'

'So you agree it is not amicable, as you assured me it would be.'

'No. I mean, yes, it is amicable as long as you do what I ask you to do.'

Lucinda walked out and into the bedroom where she sat, taking everything in.

•

LUCINDA HAD JUST ARRIVED AT THE ADDRESS OF A SMALL flat on avenue Princesse Alice in the Palais Saint James apartment block, which Emily reserved for guests and said she could use for the time being. It was early morning. She parked just in front of the Jolie Thing boutique, where she had helped Victoria buy a €6,000 gold, sequinned dress for a 50th birthday party in Dublin last summer. Lucinda recalled how the sequins drew attention to her trim waist and her big bust. In the window, there was a portrait of Prince Albert. All businesses and shops were required by law to prominently display his portrait.

Lucinda made her way up with Peanut. There was a tiny lift with an old door that had to be pulled shut in order to work. The hallway was dark and narrow. She entered the flat and turned on the light. Peanut scurried around, smelling all around the flat. On the kitchen counter, she found a paper with Emily's witness statement, which she had promised.

I, *the undersigned, Emily Rochester, do hereby solemnly affirm…*

I have known Lucinda Kiddington for five years. She has always been a warm person and sensitive to the feelings of others. On many occasions, Leo was unduly rude and insulting to her, calling her an idiot, stupid, dumb, etc. In the kitchen, he could be especially dictatorial, ordering her around, and demanding she come when he call her, telling her to get out of his way at other times. She was bullied by him and treated as a stupid child. This was unfair and humiliating for her. His disagreeable conduct was often over trivial matters which then became more heated.

While in the relationship with Leo, I saw Lucinda change from a confident and independent woman to an insecure one, always fearful of being further reproached.

The undersigned accepts to have this statement adduced in Court and acknowledges being aware of the criminal penalties set forth in Article 103 of the Criminal Code in case of misrepresentation.

Emily had never mentioned this to her face. But it was all true.

The flat was on the third floor. The open-plan kitchen and living room was filled with her boxes. She opened the closed shutters. There was no view, no light. She could hear construction workers working on the building next door.

'It will do fine,' she told herself. 'I just need a place to sleep.'

It was in the *Carré d'Or* (Golden Square district), not too far from the Millefiori, but far enough that she felt she had some space. She would just have to avoid avenue de la Costa where Leo hung out with Victoria at Casa del Caffè.

Her phone beeped with a text from Leo.

I just want to warn you that I would like custody of Peanut.

Lucinda sat on the sofa and lit a cigarette. Now she was angry.

19

Barbara

AFTER A DEMON-BANISHING SESSION WITH HER PERSONAL trainer, Barbara endured three minutes at -85°C in the cryotherapy chamber. She dressed back into an effortlessly chic, Brunello Cucinelli outfit that cost more than the average monthly salary on the Côte d'Azur. Then she decamped to the Thermes Marins' alfresco restaurant for a healthy lunch. Over a vanilla-protein shake with a shot of rum, Barbara savoured the iconic view of the Port Hercules and cast a critical eye over the assorted body sizes lounging around on the adjacent sun terrace.

Her mobile phone buzzed on the table. It was Damian checking in before the Kukushkin meeting. His bank had arranged attractive financing for Barbara to acquire the *WeFork* properties.

'Is the paperwork all in order?' he asked.

'Yes. Both legal teams are satisfied,' Barbara replied. 'I

asked for one extra clause to be inserted, but it shouldn't stop Kukushkin from signing tomorrow as planned.'

'Good, good. So, we'll finally meet the man himself.'

'Saves us a trip to the zoo,' said Barbara, recalling the CCTV image of a bearish man with caterpillar eyebrows. 'Of course, it's not strictly necessary that we meet, but my father always insisted on doing business face to face. By the way, change of location: Kukushkin wants to meet at his bank.'

'Banque Mercure, ugh,' Damian groaned. 'No dollar, dirham or ruble too suspect for their coffers. I hope no one spots us going in.'

'Just a little power play,' Barbara said. 'He's still on the back foot though.'

A tanned, trim young waiter placed a surprisingly appetising quinoa salad in front of Barbara. From behind her dark sunglasses, she threw an appreciative glance at his pert *derrière,* as he sauntered off, before her mind snapped back to the phone call.

'Right, my lunch has arrived. Meet us in the lobby at the Roccabella at 10:45,' Barbara instructed.

'Us?'

'Olina from Marcus' office will be there for any ad hoc translating. Also handy to have one of *WeFork*'s insiders, for lack of a better word, on my side of the table don't you think?'

'I guess so,' said Damian. 'Do you find Polina trustworthy?'

'Hard to tell,' said Barbara. 'But she's in my pocket.'

'Unlikely bedfellows, I must say!'

'Well, she does what she's told and is pretty gutsy.'

'High praise coming from you.'

'Well, there isn't exactly a deep talent pool in Monaco is there? Anyway, I can't wait to see an end to this bloody *WeFork* palaver and I can go back to dealing with oil megalomaniacs.'

Damian chuckled. 'Amen to that.'

•

BARBARA ALMOST DIDN'T RECOGNISE POLINA IN A CHIC, YET sober black trouser suit and hair tied up in a smart low bun.

'Going to a funeral?' Barbara quipped, as their heels clacked in unison across the marble foyer towards the purring Bentley waiting outside.

Damian appeared by the car. Insisting chivalrously that Polina sit in the back, Damian travelled up front with the driver. It was a five-minute drive to Banque Mercure, the black sheep of the buccaneering Monaco private banking sector. The modern concrete and glass two storey building on Place des Moulins was a far cry from Damian's sumptuous Belle-Epoque office near the casino. Damian held the door for them as they walked in.

'I feel like we should be carrying suitcases of cash going in here,' whispered Damian.

Kukushkin's banker greeted Barbara deferentially in the reception area and ushered them into a cramped and windowless, meeting room.

'So this is how the other half bank?' said Barbara, eyeing up the spartan surroundings.

Damian flicked through the pre-approved contract as they waited for Kukushkin.

'Nice suit,' said Barbara.

'Gucci,' said Polina.

'Really? Their cut doesn't usually flatter the shorter physique,' said Barbara.

'Every cut good on young woman,' retorted Polina.

Barbara took out her phone and looked at a flight-radar app tracking the plane transporting Sophie and Marcus back from the UK. It was scheduled to touch down in Nice in just over an hour.

Fifteen minutes and two espressos later, the meeting room door opened. Kukushkin clomped in, flanked by his entourage. The meeting room felt even more claustrophobic. Kukushkin was squeezed into a camouflage T-shirt with Valentino's 'V' logo emblazoned across the front. It was figure-hugging, but not in a good way. He gruffly introduced himself in pidgin English and held out an enormous hand to shake. Barbara was surprised at the softness of the great hulk's manicured hand.

'Pity the beautician who has to chisel those 50p-sized nails,' she thought.

As Kukushkin squeezed into a leather office chair opposite Barbara, he gave a grunt of recognition on seeing a po-faced Polina at the table.

'Right,' said Barbara. 'So there's one extra clause at the end of the contract.'

The Russian team turned to the back of the document to see what Barbara had added at the eleventh hour.

'Sergei Kukushkin and Marcus Staples or their affiliates will never enter into any business arrangement.'

After this was translated for Kukushkin, he looked across at Barbara and chuckled.

'Good with me.'

'Excellent.'

With a casual air, Barbara extended her arm and held out a pen. But Kukushkin didn't reach for it. He turned to one of his associates and they started whispering intensely.

'Classic stalling tactics,' Barbara whispered, with her hand concealing her lips, to Damian. 'I wonder what he's got up his sleeve.'

Concluding his discussion with his lawyer, Kukushkin reclined in his chair rocking gently. The lawyer cleared his throat.

'Mr. Kukushkin has decided number is too low. We increase 30% or no deal. Still very good price.'

Barbara took an unhurried sip of coffee. She stared at Kukushkin, who held her gaze, but fidgeted awkwardly. As she pondered what to do, she noticed Polina trying to suppress a smile. She leant over to Polina.

'What is it?' Barbara whispered.

'Sergei bluff. He always touch chain on neck when have bad cards at casino.'

'Well, Miss Esson, do we have a deal?' asked the lawyer.

Barbara's phone started ringing loudly in her handbag.

'Excuse me. I thought I had put it on silent,' She said as she reached into her bag for her mobile. 'Oh, I should take this, it's my daughter. Marcus' wife.'

At the mention of Marcus, Kukushkin shifted uncomfortably in his chair. Barbara spun her chair around, with her back to Kukushkin. But she didn't lower her voice as she answered the phone.

'Hello, darling. Is everything okay? […]I see, and what did his lawyer say? […] Look, I'll have to call you back, but I think he should wait 24 hours before turning himself in for questioning. […] Okay, bye.'

Barbara spun around slowly.

'Well, Mr. Kukushkin, it appears Marcus is ready to squeal to the authorities. For your sake, I suggest we stick to the original price and sign without delay.'

The lawyer spoke rapidly to Kukushkin. Kukushkin slammed his slab of a hand down on the table. Then he rose, sighing slowly, and nodded his head. Barbara slid her pen coolly across the table.

'After you.'

•

sunshine with broad grins on their faces. There was a fleeting moment of triumphant camaraderie.

'Well, that went swimmingly,' said Barbara. 'Quite the dream team aren't we, Polina?'

'I see phone screen,' said Polina. 'Abigail, not Sophie call.'

'That's right. It may surprise you to know I didn't get this far on looks alone.'

'You cunning fox,' said Damian. 'And there was me thinking it was divine intervention. Well, I think this calls for a glass of champagne if you have no other plans?'

'Absolutely. Give my driver the contracts to take back to Roccabella and we can walk somewhere. Oh, don't look so horrified, Polina, a two-minute walk won't kill you.'

'I'll ask a couple of friends to join us,' Barbara fished her phone out of her bag and began typing a message in the book-club group chat.

As she typed, Barbara said, 'You know Polina, if you're looking for a new job, send me your CV.'

Polina looked away from her towards Damian, who let out a half snort, half cough.

'I wait for court case,' said Polina. 'I win, I not need job. Thank you.'

'Suit yourself. Right, let's go.'

Barbara strutted off in the direction of the rue du Portier. As they walked down the narrow alleyways and small staircases that wove their way through the concrete jungle, Damian and Barbara chatted. A few metres behind, Polina took up the rear.

'So, you think there's a place for young Polina in your business empire?' Damian asked.

Barbara glanced behind her to make sure Polina wasn't eavesdropping.

'Perhaps. At the very least, I thought her CV might give me a good laugh. A local recruitment agency used to send me some real peaches. I mean one girl graduated from an Académie des Mannequins, whatever that is. And, of course, an honourable mention must go to Monaco uni's beloved Masters in Luxury Management.'

Barbara stopped outside Trinity, Monaco's rowdy Irish pub. 'Ah, here we are.'

Polina made no effort to hide her disappointment. 'Next we eat at MacDonald's?'

Just then Lucinda and Peanut appeared. 'Gosh, you're all looking very slick today.'

'I think it's best if the book club doesn't meet in our regular haunts,' Barbara explained to Polina. 'I know it must be hard for you to slum it, but do try, dear.'

The women took a table under the awning, while Damian went inside to order drinks at the bar. Barbara was relieved to have someone else to speak to other than Polina, who looked uncomfortably at the sea of Celtic memorabilia. Damian plonked a tray laden with three luscious pints of Guinness and a bottle of Cristal champagne on the table.

'Sláinte!' Lucinda said, raising an inky glass of Guinness. 'Got to have a pint of the black stuff in an Irish pub, don't you? Are you sure you don't want to try it, Polina? It's great for your hair.'

'I take Cristal,' Polina said, holding up a flute in Damian's direction as he removed the foil from the top of the bottle.

With his thumb primed, Damian turned away from the table and popped the cork. At that moment, Abigail arrived at the table. The cork struck Abigail's windpipe at maximum velocity.

Damian rushed over to Abigail and put his hand on her shoulder. Barbara, Lucinda and Polina burst out laughing before guiltily asking Abigail if she was okay. Abigail's cheeks flushed as she rubbed her throat delicately.

'Good aim,' said Abigail as she sat down.

Damian sat down in the empty chair beside Abigail. He poured five glasses of champagne and dished them out. After a cursory clinking of glasses, the women chugged down the Cristal as if it were water.

'Polina, shove up,' said Barbara. 'Damian: come and sit here.'

Damian glanced at Abigail as he rose from his seat to sit beside Barbara. Abigail turned the conversation to book-club business. 'So, I assume it went well at the bank then?'

'Exactly as planned,' Barbara confirmed. 'Eviction notices are being drawn up as we speak. Since I bought the portfolio for peanuts, I can offer rent at a slight discount to the market rates so there'll be no trouble getting new tenants. I think it'll bring in just under €20 million a year. Not bad for a morning's work, don't you think?'

Abigail rolled her eyes at Damian, while Lucinda remarked, 'Impressive, Barbara. As always.'

•

BARBARA WALKED ALONG THE AISLES OF CARREFOUR IN Fontvieille at a leisurely pace. She wanted to get out of the house and knew she would never bump into Marcus at a supermarket. Marcus' violent attack haunted her. But even more so his suggestion that her daughter Sophie had known about it.

After the novel experience of pushing a shopping trolley for the first time in years, she paused for a coffee at Le Kiosque – an outdoor pitstop at the *Centre Commercial* – before going into Decathlon, the sporting goods emporium. Barbara emerged a short time later with a fishing rod, cycling helmet and two-man tent, which was odd considering she found angling tedious, didn't own a bicycle and hated camping. Barbara deposited her shopping in the car and headed to the Fontvieille waterfront for lunch at La Salière, where the waiters worshipped her. She ordered the seafood linguine with a glass of white wine and scrolled through the latest media coverage on *WeFork*'s spectacular collapse. She growled when she read Marcus' self-pitying soundbite in *The Daily Telegraph*: 'We built a great brand, but the rug was pulled from under our feet.' Aside from damning autopsies in the financial press, photos of Marcus lounging around on his luxurious boat seemingly without a care in the world provoked further opprobrium.

Barbara was enjoying her pasta when she caught sight of Marcus swaggering towards the restaurant with a male friend. Her heart started pounding; he would see her in a matter of seconds.

'You idiot,' she thought. 'He always comes here on Thursdays for the ossobuco.'

Barbara cursed her absent-mindedness and contemplated making a cowardly dash to the ladies. But it was too late. Marcus had spotted her. Motioning his friend to their table, Marcus stalked over to Barbara with an ear-to-ear smile. Barbara felt nauseous.

'Long time, no see! Keeping well?' he asked, as he sat down opposite.

'Very well. How are *you* holding up, more importantly?' said Barbara. 'Being crucified by the media can't be much fun. It's kind of ironic, your reputation is already in the toilet. But they don't even know the half of it.'

'Water off a duck's back, Barbara. Just makes the comeback more interesting,' retorted Marcus. 'Anyway, I just wanted to thank you.'

'Thank me?'

'Rubislaw Holdings?' said Marcus knowingly. It was the name of her trust for her non-oil related investments.

'It's great! You got Sergei off my back and owning a restaurant chain was all so last century, a bit like the oil industry, eh? I'm now unshackled and free to invest in tech start-ups.' Marcus reached over and took a slurp of her wine. 'You've taken a weight off my mind.'

Barbara snatched her wine glass back and had to stop herself throwing the contents in his face.

'Your pasta will get cold, so I won't keep you but, um, I assume you don't want me to tell Sophie that you stuck a knife in my back?'

'What?'

'She always complains about you interfering. So, I doubt she'd be very happy to find out you killed my business.'

'Killed your business?' Barbara gripped her fork tightly. 'You've got some nerve.'

'Take it easy, Britannia,' said Marcus. 'Look, why don't we just say we're even? We'll probably look back on this petty spat one day and laugh.'

'Un-bloody likely!'

Marcus stood up. 'Well, I'm glad we had this little chat and cleared the air. In the interest of family harmony, it would be good if you could send a bit more cash our way to tide us over until my next venture takes off.'

Marcus winked at Barbara. As he walked away, Marcus caught the attention of a passing waitress. 'A magnum of Whispering Angel to my table over there please.'

Barbara had lost her appetite. She quickly settled the bill and scurried out of the restaurant with Marcus' rambunctious laugh reverberating in her ears.

•

AFTER ANOTHER FITFUL NIGHT'S SLEEP, BARBARA MADE A beeline for the study. Her zest for deal-making had been reignited by the successful property transaction and it was high time she refocused on her day job. She called the Esson Group head of strategy and grilled him on potential acquisition targets. After a two-hour phone call criticising her competitors, she hung up and flexed her shoulders. She turned over her mobile and saw a message from Sophie.

Hi, we'll come over tonight if you've nothing on? So much to catch up on! Poor Marcus, he's really cut up about WeFork. A nice quiet family dinner would be great. I've asked Nora to make spag bol ;-) xx.

'Puke,' Barbara snarled.

She knew she couldn't fob off Sophie forever, but a cosy dinner for three was just too explosive a scenario. The bodyguard would be on duty so she wasn't worried about her physical safety. What Barbara needed was emotional support. Polina and Marcus were too incendiary a combo, so she decided to invite Abigail and Lucinda over to help maintain the peace.

Barbara walked through to the kitchen and was making a coffee when her mobile buzzed.

'Hi Judith. How are you?'

'Hello Barbara, is, er, now a good time?'

'Yes, I'm just making a cup of coffee. What's up?'

'Oh good, right.' There was audible relief in Judith's voice. 'You've received an invoice from Sass Café.'

'What for? I haven't been there recently,' She took the espresso and sat down at the breakfast counter.

'I called them to get to the bottom of it and I'm afraid you're not going to like it.'

'Go on.'

216

She raised the dainty espresso cup to her mouth.

'Marcus ordered 100 bottles of Krug last night, then said you'd foot the bill.'

Barbara spat out her coffee. 'One-hundred bottles of Krug? What's that, €50,000?'

'Yes, in that ballpark. What do you want to do?'

'Pay it,' Barbara said, before adding bitterly, 'I'll deal with that toerag later.'

•

AFTER A HASTILY ARRANGED TENNIS LESSON TO WORK OUT some of her aggression before the family get-together, Barbara got ready for dinner. She was determined to put on a bold front and, more importantly, look her radiant best.

With her diamonds sparkling, Barbara picked at her food at the head of the table with her daughter and son-in-law to her left and the book clubbers to her right. It was a restrained affair with the guests deliberately side-stepping inflammatory topics such as deceit, fraud, and attempted murder. Marcus pawed Sophie with overt affection. Barbara was convinced these cloying PDAs were purely to goad her into losing her cool.

After Nora cleared away the dinner plates, Sophie dabbed her mouth with her napkin and spoke to her mother.

'I was wondering if you could spare Nora a couple of times a week?' said Sophie. 'I let my cleaner go. We're tightening our belts until Marcus starts a new business and I won't get the commission on the Poons sculpture for at least another six months.'

Barbara was sure that this token sacking of their cleaner wouldn't make much of a dent in their huge monthly overheads, but she decided to rise above it. 'Sure, no problem.'

'That's very kind of you, Barbara,' Marcus grinned. He

placed his arm around Sophie's shoulders and moved his fingertips gently up and down her arm.

'I know you understand the highs and lows of running your own business. I mean your old man almost went bust a few times, didn't he?'

'Operating in a highly cyclical industry, not by mismanaging his company, you fool,' said Barbara.

Abigail and Lucinda exchanged alarmed looks.

'Mum, there's no need to…,' Sophie placed a reassuring hand on her husband's thigh. 'Marcus tried his best. Sadly, the new landlord promised to renegotiate the rent, but went back on his word.'

'No darling, *she* did not.'

'Oh boy,' Lucinda whispered with her eyes fixated on her placemat.

'She? How would you know?' Sophie looked at her husband. 'Marcus?'

'Anyone got any nice plans for Christmas?' Abigail asked in a futile attempt to steer the conversation away from *WeFork*.

Marcus gave the briefest of smirks at Barbara, before turning to Sophie. 'Oh poppet, I didn't want to upset you, but it turns out that your mother's talents aren't only confined to the oil industry.'

Sophie's expression darkened. 'What do you mean?'

'There's no nice way of saying this. Barbara refused to help me, then bought the properties behind my back. She's the one who evicted me.'

'What?' Sophie shrieked. 'That's outrageous!'

'I know, shocking,' Marcus said, with a resigned shrug of his shoulders.

Sophie glared at her mother. 'Is this true?'

Barbara struggled to find the right words. 'You've got to understand the context. I…'

'Oh, shove your context,' shouted Sophie. 'You've always

resented the fact that Marcus built his business from scratch and didn't inherit a company like you did.'

'What garbage! Don't be ridiculous.'

'Now, now girls, let's just dial down the emotion, shall we?' Marcus said, though he was clearly enjoying the spectacle.

'I agree with Marcus, for once,' Abigail said.

Sophie shook her head in bewilderment. 'How could you be so vindictive? You evil witch.'

'Evil?'

Barbara cracked. 'That bastard tried to kill me!'

All eyes honed in on Sophie to see her reaction to this monstrous revelation.

'What? Are you insane?' Sophie grabbed Marcus' hand and stood up. 'Come on, we're not listening to this crap.'

'Barbara, seriously, that's a horrible slur,' Marcus reproached, as he was led away by his furious wife.

Sophie picked up Laird as he scampered towards her.

'You're coming with us. I'm not leaving you with that unhinged cow.'

•

BARBARA SAT IN A SHELL-SHOCKED SILENCE.

'That could have gone better,' Lucinda said.

'To put it mildly,' Abigail said. 'You wanted to split up Marcus and Sophie, but you've only succeeded in pushing them closer together.'

'And they've taken your dog,' wailed Lucinda.

'Thanks for the synopsis. Very handy,' Barbara threw her napkin on the table. 'I think we should call it a night.'

As Lucinda and Abigail slunk off, Barbara rehashed Marcus' taunts in her mind: '… why don't we just say we're even?'

'Even?' Barbara fumed. 'I'll show him even.'

20

Polina

POLINA SAT AT HER DESK LOOKING AT THE PIECE OF PAPER IN front of her. Under two columns headed 'In' and 'Out', she had painstakingly listed her income and outgoings. The totals at the bottom of each column confirmed her position. She needed to earn more or spend less.

'God forbid Barbara should find out that I'm following her bossy budgeting advice,' she thought.

Until now, Polina's overriding mantra of 'more is more' had motivated her prolific work ethic, which resulted in an impressive income. But the easy indulgent life Dimitri offered had robbed her of that edge, causing her to wind down her escort income in the lead-up to their wedding. Her energies had been directed happily into the blog collaboration, which was steadily growing in earnings and popularity. But it would be a while before that alone could support her penthouse-dwelling Monaco lifestyle.

Barbara's job offer was another possibility to consider, but Polina seriously doubted that the two of them could co-exist; especially when Madame B held such a significant upper hand. As for reducing spending, well, Polina simply could not go there.

Reaching for her calculator she tapped out some numbers and arrived at a final calculation, then wrote a big number six on the paper. She would need to see six clients per month to make ends meet. With a weary sigh, she dropped her pen on the paper and admired the brilliant sparkle from her engagement ring as it caught the sun through the window. As she twisted her hand this way and that, something about the blinding dazzle gave her pause for thought.

Of course! Why had she not thought of it sooner? She could sell her engagement ring and the Christobelle Jensen wedding dress. Reaching for her calculator she did a new set of sums, this time scribbling out the number six on her paper and replacing it with a large zero. It got her thinking. It was well known among ladies of the night and over-indulged mistresses that a certain shop on boulevard des Moulins was the place to turn unwanted designer handbag gifts into cash. Polina was generally savvy enough to direct her generous gentlemen friends toward the specific item she wanted, but occasionally, alas, they went off-piste and made their own selection. She thought of one such item in her wardrobe; a Dior saddle bag in a putrid shade of lime green, still nestled in its dust bag and box because she'd never been in the least tempted to wear it.

Now she felt much happier. She'd take the saddle bag to boulevard des Moulins today and perhaps permit herself to reinvest the proceeds over at Dior to celebrate.

·

conservatively when you go to court tomorrow.'

Abigail's concerned voice reverberated from the speaker phone on Polina's bedside table, as Polina flicked through her wardrobe.

'Is not problem. I have serious clothes,' Polina replied.

'Yes, I know. But I think there could be some, um, cultural differences about what we each view as conservative. I think it would be best if you explain to me what you plan to wear.'

'Abigail I am, as you say, in many steps ahead.'

'Okay, great. Would you mind describing your outfit to me?'

'I will wear bow of the pussies.'

'The what?'

'The bow of the pussies covers everything at front. Is in *Tatler* so you will like.'

Abigail was silent for a moment.

'Oh, you mean a pussy-bow blouse! Thank heavens for that. You had me rather concerned there. Yes, that's perfect.'

'Exactly, and I wear with Chanel tweed suit.'

'Goodness, Chanel. Amazing. You really are a step ahead of me, aren't you?' Abigail said. 'I must learn not to underestimate you.'

'Not only you,' Polina murmured to herself, and then louder, '*Thank you* for helping me,' to show Abigail that she had taken her sage advice about British manners onboard.

•

WALKING INTO THE COURTROOM THE NEXT MORNING WITH Madame Chamet was an unnerving experience. Taking her lawyer's advice, Polina avoided eye contact with Dimitri. But she could feel his steely gaze upon her, and his bulky frame was continually in her periphery vision.

The proceedings seemed straightforward, with the lawyers

doing most of the talking. Relevant documents were exchanged between the parties and a date was set for the full hearing. Madame Chamet argued successfully for a gag order on Polina's identity (against fierce opposition from the other side) due to the unnecessary attention Dimitri's salacious accusations would attract, and the lack of relevance those allegations had to the central case being pleaded; that a properly executed cheque cannot be given conditionally. Polina would be known only as 'Rebecca', and the inevitable press coverage would not contain any recognisable details as to her identity.

'Well 'Rebecca', I think that went as well as could be expected,' Madame Chamet said afterwards as they walked down the steps of the Palais de Justice before pausing at the bottom. 'Next we shall prepare for the hearing, where you will be required to give evidence.'

Madame Chamet turned to leave and then paused. 'Beautiful outfit, by the way. Perhaps you might consider this type of clothing more often?'

•

POLINA ARRIVED HOME FROM AN EARLY MORNING photoshoot with beautifully styled hair, courtesy of a new shampoo brand they were advertising on the blog.

We wish to match the indulgent luxury of our science-based hair products with the aspirational Monaco lifestyle, their pitch to the *Monaco Mail* had read.

'There's imagination,' Abigail said, rolling her eyes when she read the description. 'Let me guess: big, blonde bouncy hair, long legs, high heels, statement jewellery, and a small fluffy pampered pooch.'

Polina added to the description. 'On steps of Hôtel de Paris, with casino in background.'

Abigail groaned.

'They want, we give,' Polina said happily. Quite frankly, she liked working to a formula she understood so well.

A clever rebranding of the blog to *Powder Puff* + had effectively squeezed Leyla out of the picture, enabling the new collaboration to flourish without interference. The combination of Polina's physical appeal and Abigail's clever way with words was beginning to gain momentum.

Today Polina's freshly styled hair wouldn't go to waste. She had a very important lunchtime date and an evening party.

•

THIERRY HELD THE CHAIR OUT FOR POLINA AND THEN TOOK his own seat opposite her.

'Is nice change to come to Italy for lunch,' Polina said as she looked around at the rustic surroundings from the restaurant terrace. 'Sometimes in Monaco, too many eyes.'

'Precisely, which is why I chose Dolceaqua, although you can run into people from Monaco at any of the Italian border towns,' Thierry said with man-speak authority.

Polina wriggled slightly in her chair so that her cross-over silk top fell open a little lower. Thierry's eyes followed obediently.

Lifting his gaze to her face, he took back control by asking, 'Tell me Polina, do you prefer that we continue speaking in English? What other languages do you speak?'

'Not so many. Belarusian of course, and Russian, which is mother tongue. I have French of beginners, everybody does, but now I trying hard to get better with the English.'

'No Dutch then. Well, we shall continue to speak in English so you can improve.'

Polina responded with a sweet smile.

'Thomas' had popped up on hopeandwisdom.com in an unremarkable way, except that Polina's eagle eye saw something she recognised in his profile photo. In the blurry background, she saw a Monaco apartment building, and closer in she could make out a garden and Belle-Epoque shuttered window. 'Thomas' was standing in the grounds of a Monaco villa.

Using Google word and map searches, it didn't take long to ascertain that it was the Villa d'Or, owned by one Thierry Abreo, third generation heir to a Swiss chocolate empire. Their fortune was based on the success of the *Chocolat d'Or* brand which according to the website, '*can be found in its distinctive gold wrapper in 120 countries worldwide.*'Also known as Lord Esden (he purchased the crumbling wreck of Esden Castle for the title, but never visited), Thierry was 74 years old, currently divorcing wife number two, and had no children. Living between homes in Monaco, Switzerland, New York, and the United Kingdom, he led a carefree existence as a *bon vivant* supported by an income stream that continued to grow year upon year. Less golden was Thierry's sense of entitlement, which had a tendency to erupt in less than gracious ways, such as a drunken temper tantrum in a British court room and another reported incident of him loudly interjecting when a Duke was addressing a high-society audience.

By the time dessert arrived, Polina was recognising the tell-tales signs of a man smitten, ably assisted by the quantity of alcohol he'd imbibed.

'Polina, you are a beautiful woman and I like your candour,' he said as he poured them each another glass of wine.

Polina hoped that 'candour', whatever it meant, was a good thing and smiled encouragingly.

'Okay, I know you said you were Dutch and I called myself 'Thomas', but that's just what we do to weed out the weirdos on these sites.'

'This is true, Thierry.'

'The premise of the hopeandwisdom.com site allows for honesty about what a man and woman want from each other,' he continued. 'A wealthy man is willing to provide financial security to a beautiful young woman in return for her adoration and companionship.'

'I like your honesty too,' Polina said.

'It removes the tiresome game playing,' continued Thierry. 'The women who try to catch you by pretending they don't care about money and the insecure ones who become overly demanding to try and redress the power imbalance.'

Polina swallowed hard.

'I do not like the game playing also,' she said.

'Good. Well, let's arrange our next date at my home where we can have some privacy and talk more about our arrangement.'

•

SEVERAL HOURS LATER POLINA ENTERED BARBARA'S apartment, wearing a bright red dress to match her high spirits. Styled as a strapless fitted sheath sitting low across the bust, it featured large cut outs at the side and a very low back, with the tiniest of halter neck straps attached under each arm to keep it in place. Sky-high heels and a red, patent-leather clutch completed the red theme.

'Hello Polina,' Barbara welcomed her guest, 'I see you've interpreted the dress code in your inimitable way.'

With no idea what that meant, Polina decided to ignore it.

'I bring you gift Barbara; I hope I guess size correct. Is for open later in private,' Polina said as she held out an Agent Provocateur bag.

'I assume you included a gift receipt,' Barbara laughed, as she accepted the package.

'Yes, but you must try on. Is beautiful sexy lingerie and salesgirl tell me is good style for mature figure to look the best.'

'Did she now?' Barbara bristled. 'How very thoughtful of you to discuss my body with a saleswoman in a shop. Now go on through, you'll recognise a few people I dare say.'

'Hello, my friend!' Polina heard a familiar voice that deflated her buoyant mood.

'Leyla, what are you doing here?' she said as she swung around to face her.

'I am invited by Barbara.'

Polina was perplexed momentarily until she remembered that Leyla would be pivotal in Barbara's impending revenge plot. How typical of Barbara to be getting her ducks in a row.

'How are your kids?' Polina asked, steering the conversation on to neutral territory.

'Children are good, but International School is not good. The more rich the father, the less discipline by teachers. Rich kids do what they want.'

Leyla warmed to her topic. 'Teachers come for Monaco good life, and don't care about job. They go to Rascasse and Slammers and hope to find rich husband.'

At this, they passed a knowing look and smirked. Maybe a teacher's version of a rich husband could be found in the affordable bars of Monaco. But it would never do for them.

'Erdem has gold-digger teacher from UK,' Leyla continued. 'Parent-teacher interview night was cocktail party at the Yacht Club. No organisation, no name badge, just get drunk and find teachers for interview. Gold-digger teacher Miss Black was wearing long, silky slip dress without bra.'

'She wants to steal a rich father,' Polina said.

'Yes, exactly. After I fight off fathers and finally talk with teacher, she only tell me joke Erdem tell her at school last week.'

'What joke?'

'Erdem say, "Miss Black I have new sneakers," and she say, "wow you have big feet."'

'Okaaay,' said Polina.

'Erdem say to teacher "you know what they say about big feet..."'

'Oh my God, he says this?' Polina was shocked.

'Then Erdem say, "big socks!" and teacher thinks this is very funny.'

Polina was saved from further kiddie talk by Leyla's phone beeping. After a brief check of the message, she announced her departure.

'I go now. Sergei wants I come to client dinner.'

'Good luck for that,' Polina said as they kissed farewell and Leyla dashed off.

Polina spent the next hour trying to reach Abigail and Lucinda who were at the other end of the room. Every time she took a few steps in their direction, another man would appear and hold her up with inane conversation until she could shake him off.

With relief, Polina finally reached her friends who by that stage were talking to a tall, slim and attractive woman in a short fitted Pucci dress. Polina assessed the woman in her customary manner, quickly tallying the cost of her outfit and arriving at a total figure of €6,000 — jewellery included — save for the bumper diamond ring on her hand, which was too difficult to assess at distance.

'Polina, this is Jeanne,' Lucinda said in a depressed-sounding voice, 'and, by a rather bizarre coincidence, Jeanne has been at my place tonight. No, let me correct that, she's been at *Leo's place* tonight, attending a birthday party he threw for Victoria.'

'I'm so sorry you had to hear about it like this,' Jeanne said to Lucinda in an apologetic way. 'I don't even know Leo and Victoria. My friend invited me to accompany her.'

Seeing Lucinda's obvious misery, Jeanne appeared to consider for a moment and then said, 'Shall I tell you something funny that happened there?'

'Please do,' said Abigail.

'Well,' Jeanne spoke in a lowered conspiratorial tone, 'Victoria has a sister who flew from the UK for the party. It was the sister who greeted us as we arrived and told us that she is Victoria's *identical* twin.'

'Identical?' Lucinda was perplexed. 'She's never mentioned that before.'

'I think I know why,' Jeanne continued as a little smirk formed at the corner of her mouth. 'Imagine my shock when Victoria joined us and I saw them next to each other. They looked like before and after photos for cosmetic surgery.'

Polina failed to see why this was amusing, while Lucinda laughed uproariously. 'Oh how funny! You must tell me all the details, Jeanne!'

'Hmm, let's just say Victoria's twin sister is flat chested, has an unfortunate honk of a nose, and looks rather drawn in the face.'

That set Lucinda off afresh. The rest of the group had a good giggle too, while Polina feigned amusement and marvelled — not for the first time — at the anglophone sense of humour.

'Victoria always told me she'd had nothing done,' Lucinda said, as she wiped tears of laughter from her face, 'even though the puffy cheeks and massive boobs were so obvious.'

'There won't be any hiding it from Leo now,' Abigail giggled, much to Lucinda's further delight.

'Please don't repeat what I told you,' Jeanne said, 'but I am pleased that I cheered you up.'

'Hellooo, who or what are we laughing about?' asked Barbara in an exaggerated Scottish accent as she joined the group, lifting her whisky glass up high in a greeting that resembled a wobbly quasi salute before lowering it again.

'I'm pleased you've all met Jeanne,' she said, hooking her free arm through Jeanne's and pulling her close. 'Don't be fooled by the package. This is an accomplished businesswoman and a good friend of mine.'

'Thanks Barbara,' Jeanne said awkwardly, but playing along.

'She's also a saint,' Barbara paused for dramatic effect. 'To put up with that husband of hers.'

A second awkward silence fell, before Barbara continued: 'Rod McWilliam was certainly punching above his weight when he convinced Jeanne to marry him.'

•

'BARBARA IS CHEAP!' POLINA FUMED AS THE AIRPORT TAXI dropped the three women off at their Amsterdam hotel. 'Cattle-class flight and four-star hotel!'

'It's because we mustn't draw attention to ourselves,' Abigail ventured.

'Hmm, if you say so,' Lucinda replied, clearly not convinced.

Polina ordered the doorman to bring her bags from the car and stormed into reception to check in, bumping against her two travel companions and knocking over their cases as she went. At least she'd be sure to have her first choice of the three rooms Barbara's secretary had booked. She was the one doing the dirty work after all.

Two hours later, she entered the beautiful five-star hotel where Leo had booked a room for the night. Nervously at the door of his suite, she rechecked her handbag for the replica gun. Next she removed her coat to reveal her Marilyn Monroe outfit, and sent a thumbs up message to Abigail and Lucinda with the room number, before ringing the bell.

Leo swung the door wide open.

'Perfect! Just as I expected,' he said appreciatively. 'Come in.'

An almost empty bottle of whisky sat open on the oversized coffee table alongside a magnum of champagne in an ice bucket. Specs of white powder were scattered on the table surface.

'Let's have a drink,' he said, 'I'd like to look at you for a while.'

Polina obediently sat down and accepted his offer of champagne, reminding herself of her strategy; to put him at his ease, not talk too much, and ask him questions that allowed him to man-speak and show off.

Between copious quantities of champagne, whisky and cocaine, Leo proved to be an ideal candidate for her tactics: rambling on with his self-important stories, while Polina smiled and feigned interest, tipping each glass of champagne he gave her into a pot plant and wiping her lines of coke from the table when his back was turned.

'...and in Monaco there's always a banker chasing me to get my business...'

'Leo, I like to prepare myself for you,' Polina cut through his self-congratulatory reverie. 'Bedroom is that way?'

'Yes, oh yes. Tell me when I should come in,' he said, as he bent over the coffee table and inhaled another line of coke.

In the bedroom, Polina locked the door and surveyed the room quickly. The bureau opposite the end of the bed would be perfect to film from.

Opening her case on the bed, she took out her tools of trade and placed them strategically. Then she changed into a black lace lingerie set comprising a bra, panties and suspender belt, which interconnected via tiny satin straps that wound around her neck and down her cleavage. Very sexy but complicated to remove, which would slow things down to the pace Polina required. Rolling on the stockings, she clipped them to the suspender and stepped into soaring, spike-heel shoes.

With one last glance around the room, she sent Abigail another message, *bedroom starts* and turned the video on, then opened the door to the sitting room and posed sexily against the door frame.

'Where is naughty boy?' Polina asked.

Leo turned around and gasped. With a look of pure desire on his face, he got up and walked over to her, his eyes transfixed by her body. Leading him further into the bedroom, Polina whispered in his ear, 'You want we play?'

'Yes,' Leo whispered back in a voice hoarse with lust.

'Take off your clothes and lie on the bed,' she said in a slightly bossier voice, testing him out to see what style he preferred.

Leo obediently did as he was told, walking into the camera field of vision and laying on his back on the bed. Facing away from the camera, Polina straddled him and reached beneath the pillow to take some handcuffs, which she dangled in front of him with a little smile.

'Mmmm,' he murmured, telling her everything she needed to know.

Clipping the handcuffs on him, she lifted his arms above his head. 'I think you like tickle,' she whispered, taking a feather duster from beside the bed and running it lightly over his body, moving to the side of him as she did so that everything would be caught on camera.

As she continued, Leo's moans increased. She went on teasing him, leaning in close with her breasts by his face and then pulling further away, brushing him with the feathers and taking them away. His desire became more and more urgent as he begged her to stop it and let him take her.

'Come here, get on top of me, please, let me have you,

232

come on, oh God,' he yelled out, lost to desire and completely at her mercy. 'Fuck me!' he screamed.

At that moment, something went horribly wrong. Leo's passion turned to moans of pain and confusion as he twisted and turned on the bed, gasping for breath and crying out, his words garbled and slurred. Polina quickly undid the handcuffs and watched in horror, not sure what was happening or what to do about it. One side of his face had dropped, and he looked grotesque.

In a panic, Polina phoned Abigail, breathlessly telling her what had happened.

'Oh my God, it sounds like he's had a stroke,' Abigail said in a shaky voice that barely disguised her distress. 'He needs an ambulance right away.'

'Yes,' Polina replied robotically, still stunned at what she'd witnessed.

'Polina, listen to me. I'm going to stay on the phone, while you do everything I say.'

'Yes.'

'First get dressed. I'm here waiting.'

After a few minutes, Polina returned to the phone.

'Am dressed.'

'Okay good. Now I want you to find everything you took into that hotel room and put it in your bag.'

'Is already done,' Polina said, and then, 'Abigail?'

'Yes?'

'Now he makes no noise.'

'Oh my God, is he breathing Polina? Is he breathing?'

A moment passed.

'Yes, he breathes.'

Abigail spoke now in a clear, calm and measured voice.

'That's good, Polina. Very good. Now I'm going to call an ambulance. Then I'm going to call the hotel.'

'Yes.'

'Polina, take all your things and get out of that room right now!'

21

Lucinda

SHE ARRIVED AT THE ACADEMIC MEDICAL CENTER IN
Amsterdam bearing flowers. A mass of tubes and needles
surrounded sleeping Leo. The left side of his face drooped. He
was on a liquid diet as he'd developed dysphagia, an inability to
swallow foods with ease.

Lucinda placed the bamboo straws she'd brought on a
bedside table. She was so tired she could have fallen asleep in
the hospital chair. Waiting for him to wake up, she remembered
the last time she'd seen Leo in hospital, when he had bladder
cancer. When he'd escaped from Princess Grace Hospital in
the middle of the night and sent them all on a wild goose
chase around Monte Carlo searching for him. Only to turn
up back in his hospital bed the next morning as if nothing had
happened.

He opened his eyes slowly, looked up and saw Lucinda.

'Oh, it's you,' he said, lisping. He sat up, straightening his arms to prop himself up. 'What is this playth? The nurthes aren't even good looking.'

Lucinda had hoped for an apology or even a hint of remorse. Instead, he looked disappointed. Not just by the unattractive nurses, but by her visit. No doubt he'd been hoping that Victoria would pay him a visit — which of course she hadn't.

That was it. Lucinda finally cracked. All her frustrated desire to please Leo came to an end. All the blame that she'd heaped upon Victoria — now she blamed Leo. All her shame at a second failed marriage became unimportant. Even when she'd seen the divorce papers, Lucinda refused to accept reality. She was so desperate to make things work that she ignored all the tell-tale signs of their crumbling marriage. Perhaps she believed she could steal him back from Victoria's grasp. That with Victoria out the picture, they'd have a future together. That he'd mature at last and try to make his fourth marriage work. He was too old to remain a cad forever, wasn't he? He'd eventually love her back. But no. It was all her own make-believe. He was incapable of love.

'Leo, I have arranged for you to have 24-hour nursing care. I'm afraid the sultriness of the staff was not part of the job description,' said Lucinda, enjoying his frustration. 'You can watch the snooker, the slalom skiing, the golf, the racing, and the tennis any time you want. You have TV and sport on demand.'

And with that, Lucinda left and headed straight to the airport.

•

THAT AFTERNOON, LUCINDA HAD JUST ARRIVED BACK IN Monaco when the phone rang.

'Sorry? What did you say?' said Lucinda down the line to Dr Buenaventura.

'I am so very sorry,' said the doctor. 'Your husband passed away. We did everything we could.'

Peanut nuzzled her gently.

'He collapsed while he was drinking his lunch.'

'Just like that? How?' said Lucinda.

'It was an accident. He was just starting to get used to his liquid diet. He was drinking through a straw when he had a fall.'

'My husband had a fall from his hospital bed?'

'Yes. He was cursing at the slalom skiing on TV when he started coughing. The coughing became a fit, which led to a cardiac arrest. We thought he was just cursing at the TV as usual, but the cardiac arrest led to his collapse. The stainless-steel straw entered his left eye socket and pierced his brain.'

'Stainless steel?' said Lucinda. 'I bought him bamboo straws. He said the bamboo reminded him of his childhood family trip to the Angkor Wat jungle in the 1960s.'

'His sister sent him a stainless-steel straw.'

Lucinda was silent.

'I'm so sorry for your loss,' said the doctor. 'Please let us know your family's burial wishes.'

'Yes of course, doctor. I'll ring his brother. He'll take care of the paperwork and repatriation. Thank you so much for letting me know. You did everything you could.'

Lucinda sat on a small foldable chair on the terrace facing the courtyard, smoking her yellow American Spirit cigarettes. She felt calm, as if the worst was over. Her life might be in ruins like the building site opposite. But the sun still shone on her face. Peanut kept her company, picking up each fresh scent travelling on the breeze.

•

Monaco Yacht Club. The club had moved from one side of Port Hercules to the other, into a new building designed by Norman Foster. With its deck-like terraces and glass throughout, it resembled a superyacht. The perfect place for parties, they had never thought to consider the problem of accommodating women when they need to use the restroom. A lot of the evening was spent queueing to go to the ladies. No doubt the space got in the way of the rentable area. Here as elsewhere, women's needs were low on the priority list.

Still, she had enjoyed champagne and laughs — it was a temporary distraction from all the stress. Afterwards, she walked along the avenue Princesse Grace, on the south side of the road, overlooking Larvotto Beach. She saw families and couples enjoying themselves at the beach clubs: some light jazz from the Note Bleue competed discreetly with the samba of Miami Plage. The breeze in the air blew into her hair, as well as Peanut's, as they walked in the direction of the Roccabella. She planned to pop into Barbara's to give her the news about Leo.

She was just approaching Maya Bay Restaurant, next to the Roccabella, when Peanut growled. She noticed Victoria speaking with the restaurant manager. Victoria smiled, holding onto the lead of her new dog: a beautiful Tibetan Mastiff, wearing a Swiss dog collar with brass cows from Alpen Schatz. There was no way she could avoid her ex-friend at this point.

Finishing her laugh, Victoria looked in the direction of Peanut, growling and narrowing his eyes.

Her breasts were still facing the restaurant manager, who remained attentive to them, while she turned her face to Lucinda.

'Hi, Lucinda. How are you?' Victoria said, matter-of-factly, staring her directly in the eye. Victoria was even more toned and muscular than the last time she saw her. She was wearing a tight leopard-print top with a low-scoop neck allowing her breasts to get some air; her lilac lace bra showed beneath the top. Her black high-heeled sandals made her appear even taller than usual.

'Fine,' she answered, forcing a smile, and trying to sound as unemotional as Victoria. If only she could switch off her sizzling anger. She continued walking straight ahead towards the entrance to the Roccabella, counting the seconds until she was out of view. Why did she answer 'fine'? She was furious with herself. She was not fine. She was miserable and had nightmares every night.

As she turned into the building, she could feel Victoria still staring at her. Peanut continued to glare at the Tibetan Mastiff until he was out of view. As Peanut let out a little sigh, Lucinda realised she was hardly breathing herself. She'd held her breath during those few seconds, which seemed to last an eternity; Lucinda took a deep breath.

•

GETTING INTO THE LIFT, SHE IMMEDIATELY RECOGNISED THE two attractive young girls from the Millefiori. There was no mistaking them, even though they were wearing sunglasses, and one was wearing a strawberry-blonde, bobbed wig. They joined her in the lift. Peanut walked over to them and smelled their feet, at which point he sneezed. The girls did not flinch and remained silent. They got off on the eighth floor. She counted the seconds until she reached Barbara's flat, so that she could call the police.

Barbara opened the door, looking nonplussed. An excited Peanut ran directly to his favourite room, the kitchen, to check out any tasty morsels in the dog bowl. Lucinda rushed through the door into the living room and started dialling on her phone.

'Uh, hello?' said Barbara in her dressing gown

'I just saw the two burglar girls,' Lucinda whispered. 'I'm calling the police.'

'What are you on, Lucinda?'

'Emergency services?' said Lucinda. 'I need the police to come immediately to the Roccabella. Two burglars are here about to break into one of the flats.'

'And here was I looking forward to a quiet night in,' Barbara rolled her eyes, before walking to the bespoke walnut drinks cabinet to pour herself a whisky.

'It's Lucinda Kiddington speaking,' Lucinda said.

'Madame la Comtesse. It's me, Stephane Girardo. Hold on, I'll send someone along immediately […] *D'accord*, they're on their way. Tell me the details.'

'Remember, I told you about those two young women in the Millefiori, that time I saw you with my friend Abigail? That I gave you the photofit for? I spotted them right here just now in the lift at the Roccabella.'

'What floor are they on? What do they look like?'

'They were going up to the eighth floor. One of them was wearing a strawberry-blonde wig. They were both wearing stiletto heels, skinny jeans, Gucci tops and oversized sunglasses. I'm 100% sure it's the same girls that burgled a flat in the Millefiori.'

'Thank you,' said Stephane. 'I'll call you back later if we need any more details.'

'The police here don't get much practice with urgent police matters, do they?' she said to Barbara as she hung up and grabbed a cigarette from her bag.

'Would you like a glass of champagne to go with that?' Barbara offered, as she walked to the wine fridge.

Seconds later, they heard a siren. Sirens were not unusual in Monaco. Police cars and fire trucks put on their sirens all the time. Indeed, there were more sirens in Monaco than in New York and London. It was such a regular occurrence that it wouldn't even disturb the thieves.

The police waited in the reception for the girls matching Lucinda's photofit and description. Confronting them discreetly, the police discovered a gold-and-diamond Rolex, along with an Alhambra pendant, Van Cleef & Arpels earrings and a small red Cartier ring box. With all the old-fashioned locks around Monaco, they'd managed to carry out a dozen burglaries in Monaco before Lucinda detected them.

•

THE NEXT MORNING, LUCINDA WAS TAKING A SHOWER WHEN the phone rang. What more information did the police require from her? She grabbed a towel and picked up the phone. It wasn't the police. It was a man with a strong Belgian accent, who introduced himself as Leo's lawyer. Not his divorce lawyer, but his family lawyer.

'Madame la Comtesse?'

'Yes?'

'My name is Paul Toutmemoire. I'm your late husband's lawyer. I'm calling about his will.'

Lucinda sat down on the bed, rubbing her wet hair with a hand towel.

'I realise you were in the process of getting a divorce, but you were still married when he died. According to his will, everything goes to you.'

'Everything?'

'It appears that way. I am certain you're aware he has some very fine works of art, as well as furniture, and some very valuable jewellery.'

She thought about the exquisite Fabergé clock he kept in

a safe in Hanover, and the Giacometti sculptures he had in storage. She wouldn't have to worry about paying the rent now. Falling back onto the bed, she daydreamed about her change of fortune as the lawyer droned on about meeting to go through the paperwork.

22

Polina

POLINA WAS INDULGING IN HER FAVOURITE PASTIME: FINDING the perfect outfit. A flawless ensemble of clothes, accessories, hair, and makeup required far more thought than simply dressing appropriately for the occasion and the weather. Polina's philosophy for optimum dressing considered two key elements:

1. Will the outfit make me feel fabulous; a master of the activity at hand?
2. How will the outfit make others feel; will they be jaw-drop impressed?

Tomorrow was the judge's final verdict for her court case. Location: Monaco's fairy-tale *Palais de Justice* (Supreme Court), with its sweeping staircases and yellow-stone facade. With points one and two of her dress code firmly in mind, she shortlisted three outfits and laid them out on the bed for further consideration.

To her relief, the lead-up to tomorrow's verdict had shown Dimitri in his true light. Any sympathy he might have gleaned from the judge was surely lost by his egotistical antics: from angry outbursts to under-his-breath mutterings and fuming facial expressions.

Comments leaked to the media by Dimitri telling his side of the story backfired when the resulting articles gave full identifying details such as his name, his business history, and photos of his yacht, yet only referred to Polina as 'Rebecca'. As Madame Chamet pointed out, 'that type of salacious online coverage never goes away.'

Her decision was made; a close-fitting baby-pink Dior dress with a double-ended front zipper. Depending on zip positions, it made her feel powerfully business-like or brazenly sexy. Tomorrow she would zip it demurely all the way to the top: keeping within the bounds of propriety for the court, while reminding Dimitri what he was missing out on: easy-access dresses drove him wild with desire. She snapped a selfie and posted it to her Instagram with the caption: *Nothing beautiful asks for attention.*

Lucinda's name flashed up on her phone.

'Hello,' Polina said.

'You sound happy,' Lucinda replied, 'Aren't you even a little bit nervous about tomorrow?'

'More excited. Court battle finishes and I put bastard out of life forever.'

'Well, I know how that feels.' After a brief pause Lucinda continued. 'Actually, I'm having mixed reactions about Leo.'

Empathy wasn't Polina's forte, but she made a stab at it.

'Am sorry you feel this Lucinda.'

'Thanks, I appreciate that. The reason I'm calling is that I heard something about Dimitri which might interest you.'

'Oh, tell me.'

'My gallery friend was just chatting with me about Hank's arrest. And she let it slip that Dimitri's art collection is only worth half of what it used to be.'

'Half. Is millions, no?'

'Oh, yes. Many millions, I suspect.'

'This will make him angry. He does not like to lose the money or the face.'

'I'm sure. He is an alpha male with a capital A, after all.'

Polina's phone beeped again.

'Is Abigail on phone. I go now,' she said, abruptly cutting the call with Lucinda.

'Hello Abigail,' said Polina. 'I was talk with Lucinda.'

'Oh, that's nice. How is she?'

'She say me Dimitri loses millions for fraud art.'

'Of course, yes, he would have. The Lothko wasn't the only painting he purchased from Hank.'

'Dimitri has many paintings in house, on boat, every room, everywhere.'

'I don't think that's the only problem he has right now,' Abigail said somewhat mysteriously.

'He has more problems?'

'Yes, that's why I'm calling you,' Abigail paused briefly, then continued. 'Don't repeat the source because it was rather indiscreet of Damian to tell me this. It seems that Dimitri's application to renew his Monaco residency has been turned down. Something to do with online gambling being his main income, apparently.'

'This is two very bad things in one day.'

'Indeed. If he loses the case tomorrow, it will be a trifecta.'

'Trifecta?'

'When you bet on three horses, and then they come first, second and third,' said Abigail. 'Here's hoping for a strong finish tomorrow. Sorry, I must run. But good luck, and call me as soon as it's over,' she said, ending the call.

•

POLINA AND MADAME CHAMET SAT TOGETHER IN THE courtroom as the judge gave his verdict. While he spoke, Polina watched the deep scowl on Dimitri's sleep-deprived face deepen with each word.

'Monsieur Nalimov, you gave Mademoiselle Petrova a cheque for €1 million of your own volition, without pressure from her or anyone else to so do. You gave the cheque as a surprise, alongside the gift of a six-carat, diamond engagement ring. With these two gifts, you implied both verbally and by the nature of the gifts themselves, that Mademoiselle Petrova could expect significant financial security from you, and a future life together. It was your choice alone to set the value of the cheque at €1 million. One can surmise that you wanted to impress the young woman with this gesture, and I have no doubt that you did. Notwithstanding your subsequent change of heart, no conditions were set upon gifting this cheque. What is more, the legal position is clear; a cheque cannot be given conditionally. In layman's terms, Monsieur Nalimov, you cannot dishonour a cheque just because the person you wished to impress with it is no longer to your liking. Therefore, my decision is made. I find in favour of the claimant, and order the defendant to pay €1 million, plus damages of €50,000.'

It was a moment before Polina's elation kicked in.

'Madame Chamet, we win! Thank you,' she said, turning to her lawyer who responded with a wide smile.

'It's always satisfying to win these interesting cases,' said Madame Chamet. 'Thank *you*. You have been a good client, Polina.'

As the two women left the courtroom, they passed Dimitri, clenching his fists in frustration.

'Congratulations for trifecta!' Polina said happily.

'What the fuck?' Dimitri responded, turning his ravaged face to look at her.

'Art collection is a horse, *carte de séjour* is a horse, €1 million cheque is a horse,' Polina said.

Dimitri took a moment to process her comment. As it dawned on him what she meant, his expression turned to pure fury.

'*Allez. On y va*,' Madame Chamet said, taking Polina by the elbow and leading her outside.

'I have absolutely no idea what you were talking about back there,' she said. 'But you certainly hit him where it hurts.'

•

THREE PHONES RANG AT ONCE AS POLINA DIALLED THE WhatsApp book club group.

'Hello. What do you want?' said Barbara, picking up on the first ring, closely followed by a cheerful 'hi everyone,' from Abigail and a simple 'hello Polina,' from Lucinda.

'I win case for €1 million from Dimitri,' Polina said.

'Fantastic!' Abigail said. 'It was a trifecta for Dimitri after all, and a wonderful result for you.'

'Congratulations, Polina! That's great news,' said Lucinda.

'I'm pleased my investment in your legal fees paid off, Polina,' said Barbara. 'You must be thrilled.'

'Yes, very happy.'

Polina paused before addressing the main reason for her call.

'I like to bring you for special surprise in two weeks. Saturday all day. You all come?'

Everyone agreed they could make it, although Barbara wanted more info.

'I'd like to know the *what, where, why,* and *how.* Thank you, Polina,' said Barbara. 'How do we know what to wear for a start?'

'Is called 'surprise', Barbara. Dress like you go to best restaurant in world for lunch and bring passport. Car comes to your house at 11a.m.'

'I'm not getting in a car or on a plane or any other transport if I don't know where I'm going,' Barbara said. 'Especially if it requires a passport.'

'Is not kidnap, Barbara,' Polina teased.

'How wonderful, I love surprises,' Abigail said.

'Me too,' Lucinda added. 'It's lovely to have an intriguing occasion to look forward to.'

'Right. Well, if we're done with the cloak-and-dagger arrangements, I need to go,' Barbara said, bringing the group discussion to a close.

'Abigail, you stay online?' Polina asked, double checking that the other two had left the call before broaching the topic on her mind.

'How can I help, Polina?'

'You tell me funny story about gynaecologist who gives vibrator.'

'Ah, Dr. Pimpant. It's not a story and it's not a vibrator. But that's okay, I know what you mean.'

'Can you get me appointment? Bypass five years waiting list? You say he is best, and I want best.'

'As a matter of fact, I think I can. But it might require a donation to his new charity.'

'Is no problem, I give €50,000. Is enough? Where do I send?'

'I think that may well do the trick,' Abigail said, laughing. 'Leave it with me and I'll get back to you.'

•

POLINA'S HEELS ECHOED LOUDLY ON THE MARBLE FLOOR as she walked through her apartment. Now devoid of all furniture and fittings, the buzzing of her phone sounded twice as loud in the large, empty rooms. It was Rod, again. Perhaps she owed him one last conversation before cutting him off for good.

'Hello Rod.'

'Hi Polina. Thanks for picking up. I've been trying to call you for days. But then you know that, don't you? Why don't you take my calls?'

'What you want, Rod?'

'I just wanted to have a chat really. How are you? Are you okay?'

'Am good.'

'I'm not very good, my sweet. In fact, I'm very upset.'

'What happens?'

'My wife has left me, that's what has happened. Twelve years of marriage and she's ended it. Just like that.'

'Maybe she comes back.'

'I don't think so. She's got another man, a toy boy. Can you believe it? He's years younger. It's disgusting.'

'Your wife is Jeanne, yes? I meet her at party. Very attractive, nice woman.'

'Don't rub it in. She's on cloud nine. All happy and glowing like she's on a never-ending spa treatment. She says she's in love with him. Oh God, I can't bear to think what they're getting up to.'

'You want I explain?'

'Oh, stop it! I expected some sympathy from you, Polina. Jeanne says they got together recently, but I've got my suspicions that it's been going on for a while. I reckon she lost interest in

249

me a couple of years ago. I bet she's been up to no good every time I've been away.'

Suddenly Polina felt rather angry.

'Rod! You have sex with many women, in places everywhere — Caribbean sex island, girls at wax salon, ladies you pay, always being naughty boy. You lie to wife with big, stupid stories. Why you blame Jeanne? What you expect, Rod?'

'All men do it, Polina. Especially in Monaco. I'm just like my mates, no different.'

'And now comes the karma. Jeanne has hot sex with toy boy and doesn't care.'

'I'm beginning to wish I hadn't called you. You're really not helping,' said Rod. After a pause, his voice became pensive.

'We always got on well, didn't we?' he asked. 'It wasn't just about the money was it? I felt we had a genuine connection.'

Polina sighed.

'Now you know how good I am at job.'

•

IN MONACO-VILLE ATOP LE ROCHER, THREE BLACK chauffeur-driven cars pulled up simultaneously. The drivers climbed out and opened the rear doors for Barbara, Lucinda and Abigail. Each stepped out, looking their best, in ladies-who-lunch dresses.

Polina watched her three friends taking in the scene. She and Thierry were standing hand in hand on the steps of the Mairie, where all marriages in the principality take place. Polina had chosen a modest Zimmerman midi dress: all floaty, white lace with asymmetrical hem and delicate edging. Her gently waved, long blonde hair set off the outfit, while a delicate Chopard diamond-ball necklace glistened in the nape of her neck. She felt glowing.

Thierry's immaculate suit, tailormade on Saville Row, made the most of his well-maintained physique, and his professionally-coloured hair took a few years off. But no amount of expensive grooming could take away from the fact that he looked more like Polina's grandfather, than her husband-to-be.

With Thierry squeezing her hand, Polina made the introductions. 'Ladies, meet fiancé, Thierry. Thierry; meet Abigail, Lucinda, and Barbara. We get married in five minutes, and I ask you here to be witnesses.'

The three women looked at each other, speechless. Barbara broke the silence.

'So that's what the passports are for,' she said, referencing the ID requirement for witnesses to a marriage.

'Goodness, look at us, standing here gaping like goldfish!' said Lucinda. 'Congratulations Polina and... Thierry.'

'Thank you,' Thierry said. 'I'm sorry if this is all a bit of a shock. But Polina has been *so* modest about what she wanted for her wedding day, and very clear that we tell the world after our private celebration. I hope you're okay to be our witnesses. We've told no one at all. You're the first to know.'

'Of course, we'll be honoured to be your witnesses,' Abigail said in a faux-bright voice.

'We'll be delighted to,' Lucinda added, stifling a small choke.

Following the short marriage ceremony at La Mairie, the cars drove in convoy down to the Port, and up the hill on the other side, coming to a stop outside the Hôtel de Paris, where they were welcomed by the maître d' of the Louis XV restaurant.

The sumptuous Bordello-chic dining room and the masterful Alain Ducasse cuisine set the scene for the small but grand wedding party.

As the drinks went down — some very special bottles

from the famous Hôtel de Paris wine cellar — and the level of merriment went up, the book club girls became more openly inquisitive about how this 'romance' had slipped beneath their radar. But still, no one mentioned Thierry's age.

Polina knew they would titter afterwards about the age gap and Thierry's wealth. But that was because they would never understand the world she came from. How could they? The grim circumstances of her early years in Gomel and her resolve to make a better life had taken her to some strange and unpleasant places. But she was a survivor; able to compartmentalise difficult times and move on, self-reliant and equipped with a steely determination to achieve her goals.

After the main course, a somewhat tipsy Thierry rose to speak.

'I think an official toast is called for, to seal our marriage.'

Turning to Polina, the septuagenarian spoke in an emotional voice:

'I couldn't be a happier man to have found you, Polina. It goes without saying that you are beautiful, and I consider myself a very lucky man indeed.'

'I know I'm a little older,' he continued to awkward laughs from the inebriated book clubbers. 'But we're going to make the most of the years we have together. Please raise your glasses and join me in a toast to my beautiful wife, Polina, Lady Esden.'

•

POLINA'S PHONE BUZZED WITH A BOOK CLUB WHATSAPP call.

'Hi everyone,' she said, breezily.

Three voices tried to talk to her at once, but Barbara pushed through and took the floor.

'Quiet everyone, I've got the conche,' she yelled down the line. 'Good grief, Lady Polina! That was a surprise. You've managed to nab the errant grandson of the famous founder of *Chocolat d'Or* and made him utterly besotted with you. Do you realise the extent of his wealth?' Barbara didn't require or wait for an answer as she continued incredulously.

'We're talking bottomless-pit billionaire. Monaco high-society status. No kids to inherit and nothing else for him to do, but swan around the world partying with movie stars and high-net-worth individuals.'

Abigail and Lucinda spoke over the top of each other, trying to ask Polina how she met him.

'On *Hope and Wisdom* site when making Leo want me. Is always good to find benefit when given dirty job.'

The three women fell silent as Polina paused for her comment to sink in.

'So, are you going to knock out a little insurance policy now?' Barbara asked. 'I hear that Viagra is very helpful for seniors.'

'What insurance I need?' Polina asked.

'I think she means: 'Are you going to have a baby?'' Abigail explained.

'Ah,' Polina paused. 'Very funny, baby for insurance, I now understand joke,' she said, pushing Barbara's barbed comment and her hurt feelings aside. 'Now one job left for book club. Set up Marcus and Leyla. Is very important we keep marriage to Thierry secret until after.'

'Totally understood, Polina,' said Abigail. 'The last thing you need is Leyla ruining your future for a second time.'

'Yes,' said Polina. 'Tomorrow we ruin her instead.'

•

POLINA OPTED FOR AN UNUSUALLY LOW-KEY OUTFIT AS SHE stepped into Sass. For possibly the first time ever, she was early.

This was business, not social. She'd reserved a table inside the main restaurant, alongside the music room and within sight of the bar and entrance.

As she sat down, Polina motioned to the waiter for the drinks order: champagne, vodka and mixers. For the umpteenth time, she felt inside her handbag for the bottle of medicinal alcohol in the zipped pocket. The inhibition-releasing formula was going to make for an interesting evening.

Leyla arrived first.

'I am drinking since lunchtime, I need food,' she said in a vaguely slurring voice.

'No problem, I have big dinner all arranged, coming soon,' Polina lied.

'Champagne?' she said, as she held forth a glass of champagne spiked with medicinal alcohol.

Leyla necked half the glass of champagne and set her glass down, looking at Polina with a wide smile. 'I'm so happy we be friends again,' Leyla said, somewhat incoherently. Polina gave an inward sigh. For the next hour, Polina continued to pour drinks as they gossiped and laughed; Polina calling upon all her acting skills, Leyla blissfully ignorant.

'Marcus comes for drinks tonight too. I tell you secret before he arrives,' Polina moved closer to Leyla in a conspiratorial manner, and lowered her voice. 'He say me, Leyla is perfect woman. He wants he could put shoes under your bed.'

'Hello beautiful girls,' Marcus said as if on cue, appearing at the table and seating himself next to Leyla. 'You both look as gorgeous as ever.'

'I go freshen up,' Leyla said, excusing herself in a slightly flustered fashion to go to the ladies.

'Marcus, your favourite,' Polina said as she poured a heavy dose of his favourite vodka and an energy drink into an already spiked glass.

A lengthy one-way conversation ensued with Marcus piling one insult after another about Barbara. Polina feigned interest as she continued to pour drinks.

'Where is Leyla?' she wondered. 'She's taking far too long.'

As she listened to Marcus, Polina thought about how every conversation with a man in Monaco was like this: a one-way diatribe of chest thumping and mansplaining.

'Marcus, did you know Leyla has hots for you?' Polina cut across his monologue. 'She say me you are best-looking man in Monaco.'

'Really? Well, she's a very attractive woman,' he slurred. 'I always thought that.'

When Leyla returned to the table, Marcus jumped up.

'Let's go dance,' he said, taking her by the arm and guiding her into the music room.

Polina watched as their dancing turned intimate when *Beggin'* by Madcon came on; Marcus rubbed his hands up and down the side of her body and Leyla lifted her arms in the air and thrust her breasts into his chest. In full view of everyone, they continued their dirty dancing, oblivious to all but each other. Polina watched with satisfaction as she paid the bill and quietly slipped out of the restaurant.

•

'AH, THERE YOU ARE,' THIERRY SAID AS POLINA ENTERED THE majestic sitting room of the villa she now called home. 'I'm pleased you're back early. I don't like you being out without me.'

Polina smiled in reply.

'Did you enjoy your book club dinner?' he asked. 'What book are you reading?'

Polina paused for a moment, trying to remember the title

of their alibi book; the massive tome that was sitting on the side when they met at Abigail's.

'*Count of Monte Cristo*,' she said as it came to her.

'Ah, a tale of revenge,' Thierry said. 'Did you enjoy it?'

'Yes, I enjoy very much. But now is finished.'

23

Barbara

BARBARA SAT IN HER CAR OUTSIDE THE PRINCESSE GRACE Hospital and scoffed the prescribed pills: weapons-grade painkillers, anti-inflammatory tablets, and finally anti-nausea pills in case the first two caused queasiness.

She cursed her decision to dress up to the nines for a casual lunch date. Those Louboutin heels were asking for trouble. Luckily a prompt X-ray showed no break, but a sprained ankle.

'Treated in one hour flat,' thought Barbara. 'All thanks to the greatest nation of hypochondriacs on earth.'

As the nonchalant doctor had bandaged her bruised and swollen foot, he asked Barbara if she worked.

'Yes…' Barbara answered tentatively, as though it might have been a trick question.

The doctor reached for his headed notepaper. 'Okay, I'll write a letter for your boss. Is two weeks off enough?'

It took Barbara a few seconds to realise that the doctor wasn't being facetious.

'Better make it three,' she replied, making a mental note to check the Esson Group's absence policy for sick leave.

Would you like us to arrange for a wheelchair and ambulance to take you home?' asked the doctor.

'Absolutely not,' replied Barbara.

'A walking stick, at least?'

With great reluctance, Barbara accepted the aluminium walking stick. Hobbling along with an ergonomic cane wasn't in her DNA. While waiting for the painkillers to kick in, she dialled Sophie's number. She wasn't picking up again. Barbara left another grovelling voicemail apology for her 'misjudgement' and proposed a conciliatory mother-daughter dinner.

Finally, Sophie made contact a few days later. Barbara was on her way to Yoshi for a rescheduled lunch with Jeanne. She was dying to hear how the laddish Rod had his comeuppance. Though sensational, Jeanne's toy boy was eclipsed in the gossip stakes by Polina's unexpected elevation to titled billionairess, leapfrogging Barbara in wealth and respectability. Sophie's phone call pushed Barbara's jealousy to one side.

'Darling. Good of you to call me back,' said Barbara. 'Does this mean I'm forgiven?'

'Hmph. I'm only calling because Marcus told me to,' said Sophie, sounding prickly. 'He might have forgiven you, but I'm not sure I do. He said all's fair in love and business.'

'How gracious.'

Barbara scolded herself for her sarcasm. She needed to be nice.

'Yes well, you're lucky he's being the bigger man and focusing on new opportunities,' Sophie lectured.

Barbara tapped her fingers on the smooth leather armrest.

'I'll meet you for dinner,' continued Sophie. 'If you promise

258

to apologise to Marcus for saying he attacked you. He's deeply hurt.'

'I can do that,' Barbara lied.

'Good. You really put me in an awkward position, you know. I didn't know how to explain your outburst,' said Sophie. 'Luckily for you, Marcus put it down to the menopause.'

'Did he now?' Barbara said flatly. She despised Marcus with every ounce of her being.

'Anyway, what about dinner tomorrow?'

'Perfect. How about Cantinetta Antinori? But not too early. I don't know what time I'll get back from St. Moritz.'

'St. Moritz? Is that a new restaurant?' Sophie asked.

'No. St. Moritz the ski resort in Switzerland. Randy Hamilton is testing out his new PJ and we're flying there for lunch. He's taken friends there and back every day this week. Not sure why I'm so far down the pecking order. Saving the best company 'til last I suppose.'

'No prob, I'll book a table for 9:30,' replied Sophie, airily unsurprised at Randy's use of his private jet as transport for lunch.

Barbara hung up and immediately fired off a message to the book club.

Finally heard from ingrate daughter. Going out for dinner tomorrow. Polina, you know what to do.

•

BARBARA EASED OUT OF THE BENTLEY WITH A HELPING hand from her driver. Since heels were out of the question, she had paired her failsafe YSL tux with a roomy pair of black Prada trainers. To round off Barbara's invalid-chic look, the ever-resourceful Nora had procured an ebony walking stick inlaid with Swarovski crystal threads. Barbara paused outside the restaurant, taking a moment to steel herself for the evening ahead.

'It's for her own good,' Barbara reasoned firmly before heading inside.

The Tuscan trattoria was buzzing and Barbara was shown to a prime corner banquette table. Though she preferred the old-school charm of Pulcinella, Cantinetta Antinori was a short hop (literally in her case) to Sass Café. She recognised the rotund scion of a German ball-bearing fortune sitting at the next table. He was accompanied by four fawning blondes with identikit lips, noses and breasts. The collagen collective was grazing on a savoury antipasti platter, while the chubby man-child golloped a large helping of chocolate ice cream.

Barbara sipped champagne as she waited. She hadn't suggested their usual weekly catch-up over aperitifs on her roof terrace. She figured mother and daughter were less likely to erupt into a heated quarrel in public. All she had to do was eat humble pie and steer Sophie into Sass after dinner. Half of Monaco gravitated there on a Friday night so it wasn't exactly a complicated plan to execute. After the Amsterdam sting, she was confident in Polina's ability to pull off the seduction trap. What could possibly go wrong?

'Be nice. Be nice. Be nice.'

Barbara repeated her temporary mantra as she casually surveyed the restaurant. It was a glittering microcosm of Monaco — ageing lotharios, vampish gold diggers, bored heiresses and wonderstruck tourists. Barbara never grew tired of people watching.

She spotted Sophie waving from the restaurant entrance. Barbara smiled at her daughter's sequin-embellished pink Pucci cocktail dress and killer heels. It wasn't an outfit that suggested after-dinner Horlicks curled up on the sofa. She was dressed for Friday-night Sass: akin to Mass on Sundays for the faithful.

As Barbara pecked Sophie on each cheek, she noticed the flower-shaped diamond earrings: her last Christmas gift. Obviously, Sophie intended to curry favour.

'How's the gammy foot?'

'Throbbing but I'll live.'

Sophie leant in and winced slightly as she asked, 'And how's Lucinda? I knew about her split with Leo. But still, what a shocker!'

'Wasn't it just?'

Barbara didn't have much of an appetite, but she picked up the menu as a prop.

'What do you fancy?'

'God, it seems the wider Ludwig gets, the more girls he's surrounded by,' interjected Sophie. 'Maybe he should just get a gastric band.'

Barbara and Sophie exchanged a conspiratorial smirk over the top of their menus. Sophie wasn't entirely dissimilar to her mother.

Two hours followed without mention of the infamous dinner party. Barbara ordered a double espresso and requested the bill. She stifled a yawn, while her daughter checked the time.

'It's almost midnight. Up for a cleansing glass of champagne at Sass?' Sophie proposed as she shimmied along to the background music.

Barbara paused for effect. 'Oh, go on then. Just the one.'

Mother and daughter linked arms as they headed next door to their favourite late-night fleshpot. They waltzed past the gaggle of hopefuls lingering by the front door.

On their way in, Sophie turned to Barbara: 'No dancing on tables for you tonight.'

She took her mother's hand and led the way. They were inching forward through the bottleneck in the entrance area when Jono, a preachy ageing Irish rock star, squeezed past on his way towards the exit.

'Babs! How are ya?' he yelled cheerfully, above the pumping Euro beats.

Barbara hated being called 'Babs'. But her mind was elsewhere. She watched Sophie glance into the music room and turn rigid. A boisterous influx of revellers blocked Barbara's view. A split second later, she saw Sophie hurtling past her towards the kerbside melee. Somewhat unexpectedly, Barbara's heart sank. She smacked her cane across the ankles of people hovering in the doorway as she tried to hobble out onto the road to get a better view. Finally, she spotted Sophie storming off in the direction of the Roccabella, not towards her marital abode.

•

BY THE TIME BARBARA POSTED AN UPDATE INTO THE BOOK club WhatsApp chat the next morning, word of Marcus' indiscreet leching had already spread throughout Monaco.

Lucinda replied first: *I've had messages from five different people today including words such as 'paralytic', 'tonsil hockey' and 'dry humping'. It was enough to put me off my cornflakes.*

Abigail followed up a few minutes later: *Marcus is toast! Couldn't happen to a nicer bloke. Hope Sophie is okay though.*

Last but not least, Polina: *He is bastard.*

Barbara had spent an hour holding back Sophie's hair as she vomited up the bottle of vodka used to drown her sorrows. Eventually, they had passed out fully-clothed: Barbara in Sophie's childhood bedroom, Sophie beside the toilet in the ensuite bathroom. A 'thunk' and a loud groan from the bathroom woke Barbara sometime later. Sophie had come to and hit her head on the underside of the toilet. Barbara tucked up her daughter into bed, and then retreated to her own bedroom and collapsed in a heap.

After a deep sleep and a Berocca, Barbara felt human again. She peeked her head into the guest bedroom to check on Sophie. She was curled up in a ball and snoring softly, so Barbara retreated silently into her study. She turned on her computer and pulled up the contact details of Samantha Vladescu, the most feared divorce lawyer in the UK.

'I'll call Vlad the Impaler first thing Monday morning,' Barbara thought with grim satisfaction.

She walked over to the bookcase, picked up a framed wedding photo of Sophie and Marcus, and dumped it into the wastepaper bin.

'Can't wait to see you try and worm your way out of this one, you weasel,' thought Barbara.

•

FOUR DAYS PASSED. STILL NOTHING FROM MARCUS. HAVING forked out £5,000 to engage the divorce lawyer, Barbara wasn't in the mood for a game of hide-and-seek. She dispatched Nora to the Mirabeau ostensibly to retrieve Laird, but mainly to check up on Marcus. Nora returned with Laird: scraggy and dehydrated. But no Marcus. Judging by Laird's state, it seemed that the dog had been neglected for days. Sophie's fury ebbed to concern.

•

VOICEMAILS, EMAILS, EVEN POST-ITS ON THE FRIDGE DOOR. Marcus hadn't responded to any of his wife's messages.

Barbara urged Sophie to be patient: 'I'm sure he's just mortified and can't face the music.'

Barbara and Sophie sat on the terrace playing backgammon half-heartedly. After a week holed up in her reclaimed bedroom weeping to 1980s ballads, Sophie was outside for the first time. Under the table, Laird glowed phosphorous white after a trip to the groomers.

'If anything, this chickenshit behaviour is further proof you're better off without him,' ventured Barbara.

Sophie closed her eyes. 'Give it a rest, will you?'

'Sorry darling, I'm only trying to help. I know what you're going through. I should never have tolerated your father's cheating for as long as I did.'

The comment roused Sophie from her torpor.

'Oh, *Dad's* cheating…'

'What's that supposed to mean?'

'I was ten, not deaf,' Sophie retorted. 'You were always on the phone plotting some dirty stop-out.'

'Uff, well, I…'

'You couldn't ship me off to boarding school fast enough.'

Sophie lurched over to a sun lounger for a siesta.

•

THE FOLLOWING MORNING, BARBARA WAS BUSY AT WORK IN her study, when Nora knocked at the door.

'Excuse me Miss Esson, the police are here to see Miss Sophie.'

'The police?'

Barbara stood open-mouthed for a moment.

'Um, right. I'll go and talk to the police. Get Sophie out of bed. And make sure she doesn't come through in a skimpy nightie.'

Barbara introduced herself to the two plain-clothes police officers as they flashed their ID.

'My daughter is just coming. Please have a seat.'

Sophie rushed into the sitting room still tying a knot in her dressing-gown cord.

'Come sit next to me, darling.'

Sophie sat next to her mother as instructed.

'You could have combed your hair,' Barbara whispered.

The elder detective cleared his throat and looked directly at Sophie.

'Unfortunately, I have bad news about your husband, Monsieur Staples. His body has been found under the Pont Sainte-Dévote.'

'What?'

'He had a tragic accident. We're waiting on the coroner to confirm the time and cause of his death. It seems that he fell from the Sainte-Dévote bridge on his way to the train station.'

Barbara and Sophie shrieked simultaneously, 'The train station?'

Sophie shook her head.

'There must be some mistake. Marcus doesn't use public transport.'

•

BARBARA CREPT INTO SOPHIE'S ROOM AND PLACED A MUG of sweet, milky tea on the bedside table. She picked up a remote control and pointed it at the curtains.

'Keep them closed,' Sophie grumbled with one eye half open.

'Ah, you're awake. I've brought you a cup of tea. Builder's, two sugars.'

Even in the semi-darkness, Barbara could see Sophie's ashen pallor. She sat down on the bed and stroked Sophie's tear-tracked cheeks.

'Don't worry, we'll get through this together. Come to the terrace and get some sunshine. It'll do you good.'

Sophie squirmed under the duvet. 'No, I'm staying in bed. My boobs are sore.'

'Okay, darling, just call if there's anything you need. Nora's here.'

It had just gone midday. Barbara's stomach growled as she walked to the kitchen. She hadn't eaten anything since the police visited the day before.

'Is it too early for a glass of bubbly?' thought Barbara.

Just then, Abigail stuck her head around the kitchen door.

'Hi, the bodyguard let me in.'

She walked to the other side of the breakfast counter.

'I guess you don't need his services any longer,' added Abigail.

'Oh, I don't suppose I do,' said Barbara. 'Damn.'

'Are you free to talk?'

'Yes, you hungry? There's plenty of salad.'

'I'm good, thanks. Don't have much of an appetite to be honest. How's Sophie?'

Barbara puffed out her cheeks. 'How d'you think? There's a bottle of champagne in the fridge behind you and glasses in the cupboard on the right.'

'Champagne? Really?' Abigail said with a pained expression.

'Do you expect me to be mourning that arsehole? The goal was to separate them.'

'Yes, but not by six feet of earth,' said Abigail. 'God, first Leo and now Marcus. Our book club has a body count.'

Barbara sniggered and went to retrieve the chilled champagne herself.

'In retrospect, it probably wasn't one of your better ideas, was it?'

Barbara returned to her stool and started opening the champagne.

'So, was your police source able to shed any light on this implausible fell-on-his-way-to-the-train-station story?' asked Barbara.

'I met him for a walk just now. He was far more candid than usual since the *Mail's* collapse,' Abigail said, accepting a glass of champagne. 'You're not going to believe this. The police suspect Russian mafia involvement in Marcus' death.'

'So much for Monaco, the crime-free paradise,' said Barbara, putting her glass back down on the counter without taking a sip. 'What makes them think that?'

'Well, his body wasn't found on the rocks at the bottom of the ravine. It was buried *under* the rocks.'

Barbara looked down at her glass. 'I think I need something a bit stronger than champagne. What else did he say?'

'He wouldn't go into any detail, but he said CCTV footage strongly suggests Marcus was killed the Friday before last.'

'The night we set him up at Sass. But where does the mafia come in? I mean, I saw Kukushkin getting out of a car as I was leaving, but I didn't pay him any attention. Did Marcus have other shady Russian contacts?'

Barbara reached down for a conveniently stashed bottle and tumblers from a shelf under the breakfast countertop. 'Whisky?'

Abigail clasped her hand over her mouth. 'Wait, did you just say Kukushkin went to Sass that night?'

'I assume that's where he was headed. What of it? He wouldn't have an axe to grind with Marcus after I paid him off.'

The colour had drained from Abigail's cheeks.

'Leyla is Kukushkin's girlfriend.'

'Of all the whores in Monaco you could have chosen to do the job,' snarled Barbara.

'How were we supposed to know he'd show up?' Abigail said.

Looking beyond her, Abigail took a sudden intake of breath: 'Sophie!'

Barbara spun around in horror.

Sophie stood in the kitchen doorway with an empty mug dangling on her fingers.

'What did you two do to my husband?'

Barbara took a step towards her daughter, 'Darling, I...'

'Don't come near me!'

Sophie screamed, hurling the mug at Barbara. It narrowly missed her head and smashed on a wall.

'I hate you!'

She disappeared down the hallway. Abigail cowered in a corner of the kitchen. Barbara turned away from Abigail to hide the tears welling up in her eyes.

Her favourite *Queen Bee* mug lay shattered into pieces.

24

Abigail

ON THE OLIVE FARM, ABIGAIL AND DAMIAN SOAKED IN THE summertime dusk on the terrace. Only birdsong broke the quiet of this countryside idyll on the outskirts of France's perfume capital, Grasse. Cradling mugs of builder's tea, they chatted through the first draft of Abigail's novel. The working title was *The Monte Carlo Book Club*, but she was considering a title with a gambling theme. After all, Monaco revolved around the casino and her own story revolved around chance. They scanned a list of gambling terms: *Ladies, Fourth Street, Key Hand, All in*.

'That seems rather apt,' said Damian, fixing on the last term, and its accompanying description: 'betting your entire stack on a single hand'.

At that moment, they were disturbed by a whirring noise above. They looked up to see a helicopter heading towards the crest of the hill where Grasse prison was located. As they followed its trajectory, they were surprised to see the helicopter land on the prison roof.

'Why would a helicopter be arriving there on a Saturday evening?' wondered Abigail out loud.

The doorbell rang announcing the arrival of Abigail's book club guests. She closed her computer quickly. Since the denouement of their revenge plot and the folding of *Monaco Mail*, the book clubbers hadn't gathered all together in many months. Abigail had no regrets for bringing Dimitri down a peg or avenging Vert's victims. But she felt queasy every time she thought about Leo and Marcus. Whenever she thought about the Monte Carlo book club revenge, she pictured the Rodigliani: the naked woman with lustrous blonde curls, and weird blank eyes. Beautiful or ugly? Just like Monaco. It made her shudder. Everything was a fraud.

The memories of her penultimate encounter with Barbara haunted her. As she played that conversation over in her head again and again, she rationalised that Barbara's blame game was unfair. After all, they held equal agency in the book club denouement. Ever the peacemaker, Abigail had met up with Barbara eventually to broker a fragile armistice. Writing the novel had been a form of therapy. As her pain ebbed, curiosity grew. She decided to organise a reunion and invited them all to her olive farm where their collaboration began.

Her fellow book clubbers arrived together, as Barbara had passed by Nice airport to pick up Lucinda — who had flown in from London — on their way through from Monaco. First to step out the car was Polina, her figure and face more implausibly perfect than ever. Next Lucinda bustled out with an enormous suitcase that looked as if she intended to stay for a week. Last out was Barbara, immaculate and foreboding.

Damian helped them in with their bags before disappearing

for a ride on his Triumph Tiger 1200 motorbike. After somewhat formal greetings, Abigail broke the awkwardness with glasses of chilled rosé. They sat down on the terrace exchanging niceties about the weather and the olive farm.

'Where are these wine glasses from?' asked Lucinda, eyeing up the bubble glass.

'They're from the Biot glass-blowing factory,' said Abigail. 'They're the *Dad's Army* of glassmaking, but the bubble-strewn glass is surprisingly beautiful. I can take you tomorrow if you like. It's funny to watch the guys in shorts and sandals blowing on molten glass down the end of long metal pipes.'

Polina reached to pick up her wine glass with one hand and flashed a knuckle-dusting diamond ring on the other. She had an inimitable way of pushing her assets to the fore. With her glowing skin and slender shape tightly packaged into an expensive-looking cream suit, it was hard to believe that Polina had pulled off motherhood, marriage, and the acquisition of the bankrupt *Monaco Mail* all in less than a year. This doe-eyed blonde had turned the tables on the misogynistic Monaco crowd.

'Well, Lady Esden, you're an advert for second marriages,' said Abigail.

'That's quite a rock,' added Lucinda, impressed by her wedding ring. 'Do you have any photos of your baby boy?'

Lucinda cooed as Polina showed a shot of her blonde-locked cherub.

'What a cute insurance policy!' said Barbara.

Ignoring Barbara's sardonic humour, Polina chatted about marital bliss. Abigail went off to the kitchen to check on dinner. She had prepared a *boeuf bourguignon* with the help of Julia. Julia had moved in with their *Pétanque*-playing neighbour Jean-Pierre a couple of months ago, but still came over most days. The beef stew was unashamedly old-fashioned, like many of Abigail's choices. There were side dishes of mashed potatoes and green beans fresh from the garden. As she waited for the beans to cook, Abigail thought about Polina's change of fortune. Polina had planned everything and kept it all to herself.

By chance, Abigail found out about Polina's pregnancy a few months back. She was visiting her friend Serena, who had just set up her nanny agency. As they sat on her terrace chatting, Serena's work phone rang.

'Hello, *Monaco Nannies* speaking. How can I help you?'

'Hello,' said a woman with a strong Russian accent. 'I want to recruit a nanny for my employer who's due to give birth in six weeks.'

'Of course,' said Serena. 'Can I take some details? Does your employer live in Monaco?'

'Yes, my employer has just moved to the Tour Odéon,' said the woman.

The sumptuous Tour Odéon was one of Monaco's newest and most expensive buildings where flats sold for hundreds of millions, and even a parking space went for €250,000.

'Perfect,' continued Serena. 'And your employer's name?'

'Lady Esden.'

'And you are?'

'I'm her housekeeper.'

Abigail reeled in surprise at Polina's pregnancy. She had hidden her growing bump not only through the final months of her court case, but even on her wedding day. It explained her unusual choice of a floaty wedding dress. It also dawned upon Abigail that Serena had no idea about Polina's secret wedding to Lord Esden. She gestured wildly at Serena who — no doubt used to her friend's eccentric behaviour — continued her phone conversation unabated:

'I think you mean a carer. I don't think Lady Esden needs a nanny at her age,' said Serena in an attempt at well-meaning humour. 'Is she suffering from dementia?'

'Not the old Lady Esden, I mean the new Lady Esden,' retorted the housekeeper. 'She's 28 years old so I don't think she has dementia.'

Abigail stifled a giggle as she watched Serena wince. The housekeeper reeled off a list of job requirements from bottle-feeding at nights to accompanying Lord and Lady Esden on holidays abroad. Serena recovered her composure enough to explain that maternity nurses would cover all aspects of baby care from feeding to laundering baby clothes, and that their working hours were flexible up to a maximum of six days per week with a couple of hours per day off.

'No, Lady Esden needs 24/7,' insisted the housekeeper.

'Then Lady Esden will need two nannies on a rotational basis,' said Serena.

•

THE KITCHEN TIMER RANG. THE VEGETABLES WERE READY. Abigail put everything onto a trolley, rolled it out to the terrace, and served the food as Polina held the floor.

'Abigail,' said Polina. 'Everyone miss you at *Monaco Mail*. Rob say you not recognise the office now editorial 'moles' moved. I never understand his jokes.'

Abigail smiled. 'I think he's referring to your moving of the editorial office from that dark, windowless basement to the light-filled ground and first floors.'

'Ah,' said Polina. 'Basement only good for stock and office kitchen.'

Polina's reign at *Monaco Mail* had brought many positive changes. After retrieving the paper from bankruptcy, she had proven all her naysayers wrong in embracing her new role as publisher of *Monaco Mail*.

'Thierry say: "Whatever is good for your soul, do that." He

proud of me, he say I too modest. He so romantic: he buy me Chanel suit yesterday.'

Abigail pretended not to notice Barbara rolling her eyes at Polina's Instagram caption-speak.

'How is Rob doing with his baby boy?' asked Abigail.

'Luke is beautiful baby,' said Polina. 'Serena bring him to office last week.'

'Serena was looking remarkably glowing for a new Mum when I saw her,' said Abigail.

'Well, she won't be short of maternity help after setting up a nannying agency,' interjected Barbara. 'I mean, she needs time for all those Botox injections.'

'How have we all coped without your caustic observations?' said Abigail moving the conversation away from her close friend Serena. 'How's Jeanne these days?'

'Her divorce with Rod was finalised a few months ago. He went back home to Queensland's Gold Coast. Last week he married a woman who's a less attractive, plumper version of Jeanne. And she has three kids too.'

'Funny: Rod hate kids,' said Polina. 'He call them little brats.'

'The best bit,' continued Barbara. 'Jeanne said that Rod has renamed their yacht from *Wet Dream* to *Dream On.*'

'Dream on… that Jeanne would ever take him back,' laughed Abigail.

'Exactly,' said Barbara. 'Jeanne is now happily dating a younger man with a full head of hair and without an Olympic-sized ego.'

Lucinda interrupted.

'I have a new boyfriend too,' said Lucinda. 'Well, actually I've had quite a few, but this one is serious. We've been dating for three months.'

'What does he do?' asked Barbara.

Lucinda replied vaguely about Hugo not having to work in an office, which Abigail took to mean a large trust fund.

'When he inherits the family farm, Hugo plans to invest in hydroponics,' said Lucinda. 'He says this intensive farming will allow for other sections of their land to be 'rewilded'.'

'Rewilded?' asked Polina.

'Oh, it's a trendy term for restoring land to its natural uncultivated state,' explained Lucinda.

As she listened to Lucinda's excitement about her boyfriend's life, Abigail worried that Lucinda might be raising her hopes too fast about Hugo's commitment and side-lining her own career plans to fit in with his.

'And what about your plans to work in an art gallery?' asked Abigail.

'Gosh, I haven't had time to think about that,' said Lucinda. 'We're really too busy with everything.'

'Where you live now?' asked Polina.

'We have a house on Glebe Place, just off the King's Road. It's around the corner from my favourite Italian restaurant, Alfredo's: Alexander met me there once after London Fashion Week. We have takeaways from there at least three times a week,' Lucinda hardly paused for breath. 'We've also adopted a puppy, Butter. Peanut is happy to have a four-legged companion at last.'

'Well, life has certainly turned around for you,' said Barbara. 'A new puppy and a new trust-funder, no less. What breed is Butter?' asked Barbara.

'She's a golden-furred cockapoo. Quite stunning. In fact, she and Peanut starred together in last month's TV advert for *Extralux* coffee.'

'Peanut-butter bliss,' mused Abigail.

'Has anyone heard anything about Victoria or Beth?' asked Lucinda. Her continuing interest in her two former friends suggested that she had not fully moved on from Leo.

'Last I heard, they had fallen out,' said Abigail. 'Serena told me about a recent ladies' night where Beth spurted out her woes.'

'Do tell,' implored Lucinda.

Abigail settled into Serena's tale. 'It was one of those classic Monaco ladies' nights that start elegantly at Buddha Bar and end in an inebriated stupor around 4 a.m. at that dodgy nightclub that closed down recently.

'Beth looked tired. She'd just had permanent eye-liner tattoos that apparently made the dark circles under her eyes more prominent. After more than a few drinks, Beth told everyone about James dumping her for an 'identikit new girlfriend, only a decade younger'. And then she told everyone about falling out with Victoria over a foursome.'

'Sounds too good to be true,' giggled Lucinda. 'Tell me more about the foursome.'

Abigail indulged the book clubbers with more lurid details about the foursome evening, which had ended in a drunken row with Victoria accusing Beth of stealing all the attention and the two men mumbling under their breath about "mad tarts, especially that one with the crocodile face" as they departed.'

'One word: Karma,' said Lucinda, looking victorious.

Abigail noticed the loquacious Barbara appeared rather tight-lipped. In an effort to bring her into the conversation, Abigail turned to her.

'And how's business, Barbara?'

'I pop loo,' said Polina.

As soon as the word 'business' had passed Abigail's lips, Barbara went into auto pilot. She reeled out an array of business deals, share options and hostile takeovers. She was so passionate about fossil fuel demand, decommissioning costs, industry-consolidation prospects and other mind-bogglingly boring topics — it was no wonder that she had reached billionaire status. Listening to her corporate eloquence, Abigail mused upon her perfection as a businesswoman compared to the wreck of her personal and private life. Ten minutes later, Barbara was still in full flow, when Polina came back from the toilet. Abigail whispered to her:

'How's it going with Dr Pimpant?'

'We just friends,' said Polina defensively.

'I meant the perineal re-education,' said Abigail, while wondering whether Polina might be enjoying more than the official vaginal stimulation from Dr Pimpant.

'Oh, yes, fine,' said Polina, smiling sheepishly.

'Gosh, you're a dark horse,' said Abigail.

'What is with you and horse talk?' said Polina.

Just then, Barbara's monologue rose to a crescendo as she recounted her tribulations with an incompetent cleaner that she'd sacked the week before:

'She didn't know one end of a mop from the other.'

'What about Sophie?' interjected Polina. 'I hear she has daughter. What's it like being grandmother?'

'Sophie had a baby?' said Abigail. 'Gosh, I'm out of the loop. You certainly kept that quiet, Barbara. Who's the father?'

'Marcus is the father. It turns out that Marcus knocked her up, while I was waiting for dinner with Sophie at Cantinetta Antinori on the evening he died,' said Barbara with a stony face. 'Anyway, I haven't met Ella, or even seen Sophie for that matter. She blames me for the *WeFork* collapse, and even ludicrously for Marcus' death.'

There was a moment of silence. None of the other book club members wanted to speak about Marcus. His demise had become their collective Chernobyl: a happening so awful that it could not be discussed. Finally, Abigail rose to her feet.

'I think that calls for another bottle of rosé,' said Abigail, walking to the kitchen.

'I see Leyla last week,' said Polina. 'She look tired.'

'I heard that Kukushkin dumped her,' said Barbara.

Her words hung in the air with all the implications that went with them. Abigail watched each of them reflecting silently upon the Sass Café night when Kukushkin had no doubt witnessed his girlfriend Leyla making out with Marcus.

'She live in Jardin Exotique studio,' said Polina, moving towards safer territory.

This idyllic-sounding suburb of Monaco was on the ugly outskirts of the principality. To residents, a studio in Jardin Exotique meant social suicide.

Four hours and several bottles of rosé later, the four book clubbers were bleary-eyed and ready for bed. Damian came downstairs to make himself a hot toddy, while Abigail busied herself making sure that each guest had a towel to take to their rooms.

'Wait, before we say goodnight. We've heard about news from everyone, but not you,' said Lucinda, turning to Abigail. 'What have you been up to since *Monaco Mail?*'

'Oh, I've been catching up on sleep, spending time with Daisy and making olive oil,' said Abigail vaguely.

•

THE NEXT MORNING, ABIGAIL COOKED AN ENGLISH breakfast replete with bacon, sausages, fried bread, and baked beans. Lucinda and Barbara scoffed their plates, while Polina played with hers. They exchanged light chatter about their plans for the day, each emphasising their busy agenda as if to avoid the possibility for further group activity. Afterwards, Abigail gave them each a can of olive oil to take home as they air-kissed one another with empty promises about future reunions.

'How did it go?' asked Damian, scooping Abigail up to kiss her, as the chauffeur-driven car rolled out of the drive.

'Weird,' said Abigail, 'but nice weird, I think.'

Damian and Abigail sat in companionable silence. Damian caught up with the news by flicking through *The Week*, while Abigail tuned into *Riviera Radio*. The news update was drawing to a close.

'And finally, to prove that truth is often stranger than fiction [...],' said the newsreader in his mellifluous Irish lilt.

The newsreader elaborated upon an inmate who had escaped from the high-security Grasse prison by helicopter the night before with the help of four masked gunmen. The gunmen landed the single-engine Squirrel on the roof before forcing their way into the prison and threatening the guards with sawn-off shotguns and machine pistols. Minutes later, they reappeared on the roof with a prisoner who they bundled into the helicopter. Later, they touched down at a heliport next to the hospital in Brignoles. Then all the men disappeared except for the hijacked pilot who was left unharmed. The escaped prisoner was named as Hank Vert who was serving 30 years for offences including money laundering, corporate fraud, financial record keeping, bribery and extortion.

'I guess Monsieur Vert has had a rub of the green,' finished the newsreader before his voice drifted out to the tune of Adam Ant's *Stand and Deliver*.

Abigail's phone rang. It was Camille.

This book is printed on paper from sustainable sources managed under the Forest Stewardship Council (FSC) scheme.

It has been printed in the UK to reduce transportation miles and their impact upon the environment.

For every new title that Matador publishes, we plant a tree to offset CO_2, partnering with the More Trees scheme.

For more about how Matador offsets its environmental impact, see www.troubador.co.uk/about/